THE ALPHA'S CURSE

†

FATED DESTINIES SERIES
BOOK THREE

Heather K. Carson

Table of Contents

To the readers who see the heart beyond the furs and claws, the ones that preferred the beast over the prince, and the ones that believe in a "happy ever after" even for monsters:

We should form a support group.

"Do I really need to do this?"

"We talked about it." Coral rolls her eyes. "It's important to make sure everyone is on the same page."

"Fine," I grumble. "In case you've forgotten how we ended up here, let me give you a quick breakdown. One day, almost a year ago, this witch and her sister show up in Cerberus pack territory. They came from the purist city where humans think magic doesn't exist, wolf shifters are mutant freaks, and the world is in ruins outside of their walls. You should see the witch's ridiculous little car."

"Don't talk crap about my sister's car."

"Do you want me to do this or not?"

"Continue, Alpha." Coral waves her hand.

Ugh. I hate when she calls me that. "Anyway, the witch, Sage, mated with my Uncle Maddock and he finally relaxed enough to let me lead. I challenged my father for Alpha and won, taking over the Cerberus pack. Then started rebuilding everything that was destroyed during my father's tyrannical reign. Oh, and I made Coral my Beta. But she decided to hide the fact that she scented her fated mate on the Fenrir pack border which is where my dead mother's family is from and we had to–"

"This story isn't about me." Coral growls.

"The last one was." I deadpan. "And for the record, you're lucky it worked out like it did with Fenrir deciding to accept us back into the region. Or I would–"

"Yeah. We know you'd kill everything."

Maybe not everything. "So now we are here at my grandparent's house with this stupid ceremony to properly introduce us to other packs."

"This is where it gets good." She smiles.

I shake my head, knowing good things are rare and hard to find. "No. This is just where it starts."

5

1
† Kera †

Once upon a time, there was a young wolf trapped in a tower. Or maybe she was locked in a cage.

That seems more realistic.

In her world, everyone knew there was one person on the planet who was destined to be their fated mate. They set out on the hunt shortly after coming of age and didn't rest until they found them. But the wolf girl we were talking about?

She'd long since grown past the hope that someone was coming to save her. Fairy tales were for little girls who didn't have a pack to claim. So, she learned to fight and ripped off her chains. If she wanted to survive the nightmare she was living, she had to save herself.

Which was what I did.

And that was why I couldn't move from this chair despite the demanding call of my beast.

Dark blue eyes stared into my soul. Unruly black curls topped his head. I know he saw me. Could feel the vibrations of a raging tempest through the connection across the room. The essence of his powerful Alpha wolf was drawing and teasing mine.

Go to him. My wolf whined in my head, trying to force the shift and claim the Alpha who stood still, watching. He made no move to close the distance and neither did I. A smirk turned the corner of his full lips. This was a challenge. One I couldn't turn down. Alphas didn't bend.

Did they bend to each other though?

I swallowed hard, still not believing this was real. Why now? After all this time?

How was this supposed to work?

Mate, she demanded.

My wolf was a simple beast. The thrill of the hunt and basic instinct drove her. She was a good Alpha wolf who still believed in the force of nature.

I, on the other hand, knew there were some things nature could get wrong. *Let him come to us.*

I dug my heels into the satin slipper flats I was wearing, pressing them hard against the marble floors of the grand hall as I reached for the beer on the table. The music started. A string orchestra played in the corner as shifters mingled around the tables.

It wasn't loud enough to drown out my wolf.

Mine. She growled, fed up with the delay.

I ignored her, breaking eye contact with the Alpha to look into my empty beer. Damn it. I needed another drink to cool the burning sensation in my throat and dry itch of my skin.

"Did you say mate?" Coral whispered as she leaned against my side.

I grabbed her glass of white wine and downed it, grimacing at the too sweet taste as I nodded.

"Where?" Her voice rose to a shriek.

I didn't want to look again, but I didn't need to. I could still feel his eyes on me. Instead, I looked to my grandparents and the other shifters discussing the happy reunion of Cerberus pack being accepted back into the region. This was supposed to be our party, but I hadn't wanted to come. There was no real reason to make some sort of pompous impression on these people. Cerberus pack was mine and no one was going to take it.

But I'm going to take him.

Not in public, I snarled back at her, shunning tradition. Shifters wouldn't care if we mated on the dance floor. They probably would have expected it. But if he wasn't moving, I wouldn't be the one to bow to the challenge.

"Who is he?" Coral's painted fingernails dug into my arm, pulling my attention back to her. I blinked. The lights from the chandelier were blurring as my wolf tried to force her way out through my skin. I held her back with a growl which Coral misinterpreted.

"What's wrong? Do we need to go?" Her panic broke through my haze and spoke to my wolf.

The best way to make an Alpha forget about their own problems was to rile up the protective instinct. "He's over there." I pointed my chin in the general direction, trying to calm her down.

"Which one?" Coral asked.

Then I looked again.

I shouldn't have looked again.

He ran his hand through his disheveled hair and I clenched my thighs together as my wolf howled. My heart beat hard, fur sprouting on my arms as his fangs extended. He was fighting his beast too. And we both were losing. The knowledge emboldened my wolf. She didn't care which challenge she won. And right now, she was winning the fight against me.

I stood, gaining control of my beast.

The Alpha smirked again, this time taking a step forward through the crowd as if me standing was a sign of submission. Great. He was an asshole.

And no. He didn't win.

I stood steady despite the strength of his power pulsing through the room and clashing with mine as the noise faded to a steady drumbeat in my ears. Shifters growled as they glanced over their shoulders, sensing the moment that called to their primitive nature.

I raised my chin, standing tall under the scrutiny, and letting him know this wasn't me backing down. He took another step and my resolve faltered.

But I still refused to move.

What is wrong with me?

I was fighting submission to a perceived challenge and denying my wolf, for what? It wasn't like me. I didn't let emotions control my actions like this and I trusted my instincts. I trusted my wolf.

If I was strong enough to defeat my father and take control of my pack, I was strong enough to face my mate and whatever the future would bring. This was it. The moment every shifter dreamed of.

And I was terrified of floating away.

I'm not, my wolf purred as the Alpha sniffed the air. He caught scent of his hunt. His eyes widened as the thrill coursed through him and my own blood burned with need in response.

It didn't hurt that he was easily the hottest man I'd ever seen.

But he's an Alpha!

Yes. He is. My wolf was salivating, chomping at the bits, as he took another step forward. The dark and mysterious shifter raised his hand, curling a long finger in my direction.

Oh hell no.

He was beckoning me.

Even my wolf paused, confused at the action. There was no way he could really expect me to come at a call like that. Pride and lust warred, making my fists clench at my side and my breath hitch in my chest.

"No freaking way!" Coral screeched as she jumped to her heels and shoved me behind her. I bared my teeth at her sudden impulsive anger. The glasses on the table rattled. Shifters stopped talking, shooting her a worried glance as she pointed a finger across the room. "I don't know what's going on, but you better fix your shit before you come sniffing around my friend."

"What?" I growled, looking past her. A cold rush of air dampened the heat on my skin, the place where the Alpha stood was empty. He'd disappeared in the blink of an eye.

And everyone was staring at us.

"Coral, stop." I hissed through our pack link. She was the one who was adamant on not causing a scene. Yet here we were at the center of the commotion.

"It's not what you think." Skoll stood, reaching an arm out as he tried to soothe her.

In a murderous rage, Coral's wolf pressed close to the surface and she spun to her mate. "We'll discuss this outside."

Outside. That was a good plan. I nodded as I felt the weight of all the eyes and ears directed our way. My brain was muddy and my heart still beating too fast. Fresh air would help me think while I figured out what was going on.

My mate was here.

Coral was pissed.

This dress itched like you wouldn't believe.

And I really wanted to go home.

*

Coral was pacing in the hall outside the ballroom, watching the door with a protective fury like an army would break through any minute. It was riling my wolf who was howling in my head, begging to be set free to claim her mate and also wondering who we should kill.

"You need to explain what is happening," I commanded. My Beta and her sister had weird habits that I figured came from their time living in the purist city. Normally, I'd brush them off. But my patience was wearing thin.

"In a minute." She pulled open the door, yanking Skoll into the hall and slamming the door closed behind him. The big shifter stumbled forward and she pushed him back against the wall. "I don't know what game he is playing, but you need to fix it."

I rubbed my head which was splitting in two with my wolf trying to force the shift. "Fix what?"

Skoll raised his hands. "This isn't any game."

"Enough." I growled, letting just enough Alpha power out with my voice to make my pack members freeze. I hated using it on them, but if there was some sort of threat then I had to get Coral to calm down so I could protect her. "Explain."

Tears misted her big brown eyes as my Beta turned to me. "This has to be some sort of mistake. He can't be your mate."

My mate? What did he have to do with this?

He's mine. I breathed deeply, calming my angry wolf who was clawing at my spine. "What is wrong with my mate?"

Besides his cocky arrogance in the ballroom. But that was something I could deal with later once I calmed Coral down.

"Is there something wrong with me?" The deep voice danced along my skin, sending shivers down my arms. I caught the scent. Dusty sage with the hint of pepper.

My wolf purred in delight as I turned to look over my shoulder. Dim amber lights lit the hall.

13

Shadows seemed to move around him. The gleam of the hunt was in those dark blue eyes, so deep they almost shone black as he walked down the hall with a predator's grace.

All rational thought fled for a moment and I swallowed down my urge to howl. The bond flared, drawing my beast to his beast.

I sucked in a deep breath.

Every glorious inch of his body stretched the black silk shirt and pants he wore. The material fit him flawlessly, cut to his muscles and shining like midnight as he continued to stalk forward.

My senses heightened, feeling the dangerous power that swirled around him like a storm. Every inch of him screamed Alpha and my power surged in response.

Coral growled as her fangs extended. It was my job to pick up on disturbances within my pack and act accordingly. But in this moment, I was torn between wanting to fight alongside her and wondering if she'd really gone mad.

"Stop." I held her back as she lunged forward, issuing an Alpha command. She froze like a pup caught on the neck from its mother's jaw as a frustrated growl slipped from her lips. "What is going on with you?"

"It's not me, it's him." She spit.

"There are many things wrong with me. You'll have to be more specific." That deep voice drawled again, made more inviting with a teasing lilt. It was rich and dark and I wanted to roll in it.

I released my Beta, putting her behind my back as the Alpha continued his hunt. Maybe I should have been more embarrassed to be introduced to another Alpha when I clearly had no control of my pack, but Coral was my friend, not just my Beta. Besides, I wasn't like other Alphas and had no intentions to be.

"What have you done to my Beta to make her act this way?" I eyed him warily, torn between an aching primal need and utter confusion.

He stepped into my space. His scent filled the air, encasing me in the warmth of it, and roused the desire of my howling wolf. I forgot how to breathe as he smiled and lowered his strong jaw to my bare neck. *Damn this dress for leaving me so exposed.*

Nostrils flaring, he inhaled deeply. "Offered her a job."

"Huh?" I shook my head, trying to dispel the swirling cloud of emotions that tugged through our bond.

"Where is your Luna?" Coral sidestepped me, glaring daggers at his back. "Or does Ophelia know you aren't her mate, Alpha Jareth."

"That's what's got you so riled up." He chuckled as he leaned away, winking at Coral. "I can assure you Ophelia doesn't care who I share my bed with."

It'd been a long time since I felt a punch to the gut. Growing up with a father like mine, I learned to protect my vulnerable parts. But that was the only way I could describe the instant pain and sickness. I stepped back. My whole body tensed as my wolf roared, ready to fight.

"Luna?" I hated how choked the word sounded. "Alpha Jareth?"

I pieced it together then, the parts that I was missing. Coral had been to Anubis pack with Skoll and met the Alpha. Progressive is what she'd called him. But if it was sharing bedmates, I wanted no part of this.

"Maybe there has been a misunderstanding." I took another step away, refusing to get sucked into the bond further.

"We're mates. It's not that hard to understand." His dark eyebrows shot up. The amusement on his face only served to further enrage my beast. This couldn't be happening. I thought of my mother and the stories they told. How she'd entered into marriage with my dad only to find her fated mate. The darkness that tainted my childhood.

I bit the inside of my cheek so hard I tasted blood. "We may be fated, but no mate of mine would promise himself to another and speak of sharing a bed with someone else."

"Are you rejecting me?" Jareth growled.

I stood steady in the pummel of his swirling emotions. The mysterious storm pushed against my soul and mixed with my own confused feelings. If we completed the bond, I could sort through these new sensations. But I couldn't stand here a second longer in this chaos without wanting to fight for control. I was barely hanging onto my wolf as it was.

Could I reject him?

I didn't know. Memories of my father came to me then. A life of rejection. The sickness that slowly ate his soul. His curse.

The walls started closing in as everyone held their breath, waiting for my answer. Would I reject a man I just met?

We can't.

We don't have to decide right now.

I bunched the fabric of the constricting green silk ballgown in my fists and took another step back. "I don't know."

My voice was hollow to my own ears and I shut my eyes, drawing on the strength of my wolf. There was nothing there but a howling pain. She couldn't understand the complexity of why we didn't claim our mate and complete the bond like nature wanted.

"Back off and give her a minute to figure this out." Ever the perceptive Beta, Coral was by my side and staring down the Alpha who could snap her like a twig. My protective instinct surpassed all other thought and I took a step forward, knowing Alphas didn't take kindly to a threat like hers.

But Jareth was already walking backwards. Disgust marred his face as he held up his hands. "Whatever you want, princess."

His made my cheeks flush, but I glared as I raised my chin. "Are you mocking me?"

He huffed out a laugh, shaking his head. "Maybe this is a mistake."

"Maybe," I whispered dryly, not prepared for the unease that tightened my chest. I was no stranger to disappointment, but I didn't think it could feel this strong anymore.

"Hang on a second." Skoll growled, marching to Jareth's side. The Anubis Alpha placed a hand on his shoulder, silencing him with a nod that spoke of secrets. The two male shifters shared a familiar ease that went deeper than pack links. Within that was something Jareth obviously didn't think I deserved to know.

But I wasn't his Luna.

I wasn't even truly his mate without completing the bond.

I was… Nothing.

No. I was Kera, Alpha of Cerberus pack.

And I didn't need a mate anyway.

"Excuse me." I kept my chin held high, intending to walk down this hall with my dignity intact while I held to my frantic and confused wolf.

The soft sent of jasmine drifted in as the door to the ballroom edged open. Out stepped the prettiest woman I'd ever seen with long raven black hair and a delicate face.

"Oh, there you are." Her voice was musical, birdlike and soft, as she smiled and waved. "It's so good to finally meet you, Alpha Kera. My name is Ophelia and I see you've found Jareth."

I couldn't hold onto her any longer. My wolf won, breaking from my skin as my claws extended and my bones rearranged. I sighed, giving into her

18

release and accepting the beast in me as the stupid silk dress ripped at the seams and she was finally set free.

2
† Jareth †

"She doesn't know who I am yet." Ophelia gasped and put her hands in the air.

The beautiful reddish gold wolf stalked closer, baring her teeth as she sniffed Ophelia's skirts.

"She didn't ask." I edged closer. My wolf was fighting to break free since the moment he'd locked eyes with Kera. I held him back, trying to stay in control of his primal urges. In this moment, it was because I was concerned with what the seemingly scorned female wolf would do.

And what my wolf would not do.

I'd protect Ophelia with my life. Yet natural law would prevent him from attacking his mate. At best, I could subdue her. Though I'd never sensed a female Alpha's power this raw and strong.

"This is all a misunderstanding," Skoll spoke behind me, still trying to soothe his fated. Trouble-maker was an apt name for the latent wolf. Then again, that was the way of the world. People made assumptions and didn't think past the surface of what they saw. I'd expected more from the spy's offspring.

But she wasn't my concern now.

There was anger coming through the weak bond that drew me to Kera. A mixture of confusing emotions, but the rage was apparent. Bloodlust fueled an Alpha. I recognized the feeling.

I kept moving closer, slowly so as not to anger her further, and anticipated the moment when she'd lunge. This was a hell of an introduction to a fated mate. I wondered if we'd end the night tangled on the floor with her jaw at my throat.

Kera's wolf huffed with a small sneeze and I hesitated, arching an eyebrow as I studied her further. She kept walking down the hall like this was nothing. Whatever rage I felt through the bond dissipated into something softer. A deep ache of disappointment maybe? I was used to that feeling too.

My wolf cried out to hers and she ignored it. She left without a backwards glance.

Interesting.

Crisis averted, I leaned back against the wall and rubbed my hands over my face. Gods, I needed a cigarette.

"You should probably fix this." Ophelia let out the breath she was holding and turned with a swish of her gypsy skirts. Unpractical apparel. A waste of money and excess fabric. But it made her happy and she did her job, so I didn't complain about them out loud.

"I'm going to run damage control in the ballroom. Shifters are already talking." Ophelia's charcoal lined eyes were wide as she nodded to the trouble maker. "It's good to see you again, Coral. Let me know about our chocolate and wine date."

"I don't… What's going on?" Coral stuttered as Ophelia slipped back into the ballroom.

I exhaled slowly, patting my pockets as I looked down the hall to where Kera's earthy scent still lingered. Redwood and moss. It was sweet and sharp. A scent I hadn't smelled in years. And her human form was just as beautiful as the wolf.

Ivory skin covered in that green formal dress with the tops of her firm breasts on display. Soft demure lips pouted and utterly kissable. Strong arms and shoulders. Layers of reddish gold hair that fell forward, half covering stormy blue eyes.

Every young male shifter could only dream to be paired with a woman like that. But beauty was only skin deep. Sure, it roused my interest as an Alpha when she didn't immediately come to me. Then she spoke, automatically assuming the worst, without taking a moment to ask questions.

It was best to protect my beast's heart. We'd never make a perfect match with someone like that.

She's perfect. My wolf snarled, trying to drown out my human thoughts. I hated fighting with myself. It was going to be a major headache trying to make the primal side of me see reason.

I turned to look at Skoll, the only shifter I called a real friend in this two-faced world. "It doesn't matter."

Skoll growled, holding Coral possessively at his side. "You're a damn fool, Jareth. At least tell her the truth."

"Yeah." Coral echoed her mate's growl. "Enlighten me too before I kill you."

Ah. That was the spark I was looking for when I'd dug up her mother's files. "About that job…"

"I'm done." Coral shrugged off Skoll's arm, pointing a dangerously sharp finger at my chest. "If you hurt my friend, you're dead."

The Beta had the nerve to shoulder check me as she marched down the hall. I chuckled as I stepped back, bowing with my arms spread to the side, and moved out of her way as she raced after her Alpha.

Kera. My mate. I had a mate. After all this time. Fate really liked to throw a wrench at me.

"What in Gods' names is wrong with you?" Skoll crossed his arms over his chest.

Everything. My wolf growled.

I grinned, rising back to my full height. "Does Nolan still hide the good liquor in his study?"

*

She's heading back upstairs. My wolf was frantic, pacing the confines of my mind.

I know.

The layout of Nolan's house was embedded in my internal eye as a rudimentary map. I never went anywhere without knowing exactly where I was. While my anxious beast was hyper fixated on her movements and tracking them through the bond, I barely had to think about where she'd gone. Kera made a quick run outside before sneaking back through the back entrance and heading up to one of the guest rooms.

That was fine. I wanted her somewhere safe and away from other shifters until I figured out how to solve this problem.

"You better talk quick." Skoll rummaged through Nolan's liquor cabinet. "I've got about ten minutes until I'm in the doghouse with my mate and I'm not sleeping there tonight because of whatever crazy stunt you're trying to pull."

He took a bottle of bourbon from the cabinet and pulled the cork out with his teeth before spitting it to the floor. The liquid glugged as he drank straight from the bottle. Sighing, I made my way around him to find us a couple of glasses.

"You're supposed to be domesticated now. Too bad she couldn't break your heathen ways." I set the glasses on the mahogany desk and snatched the bottle from his hand.

"You think I need help?" Skoll chuckled as he watched me pour us each two fingers' worth. "You're the one with a mate upstairs, but you're messing with fate because you can't get out of your own head."

"Says the wolf who never believed in fate." I savored the taste of the bourbon as it rolled across my tongue. Nolan was holding out on the guests. It'd been far too long since Skoll and I had raided this liquor cabinet.

"You'll understand soon." Skoll grabbed my shoulder and gave it a rough shake. "Once you stop whatever this is and embrace your destiny, you'll see what the fuss is about."

I downed the rest of my glass and poured another, smiling as I sat back in Nolan's chair. "Is that so?"

Skoll glared. "You're being a dumbass."

He was never one to hold back with me. That's why I trusted him more than most.

"I see you picked up some of your mate's vocabulary."

"Is that what this is about?" He sighed. "Is the great Alpha of Anubis pack worried he'll lose himself if he opens up to the mate bond?"

Not really.

At least, I didn't think so.

I swirled the amber liquid around in the glass, studying it like it held answers. "No. I'm worried about being mated to the wrong woman. One that doesn't understand the dangers coming our way."

"Not this again." Skoll groaned as he pinched the bridge of his nose. His annoyance was well noted. I often annoyed myself. But it was difficult for me to turn a blind eye when I was aware of the dark truths in this world.

He turned to look at the door, half focusing on our conversation and whatever else was going on inside that thick skull. "Listen, I may have my own issues with Kera, but she's a strong Alpha. If that's your hesitation in telling her the truth, then you are blinded by your own mistrust."

"She didn't ask for the truth." I shrugged. "Fate must have gotten this wrong. I wouldn't be mated with someone who doesn't question everything. It would drive her insane to be paired with me."

You have no problem driving me crazy. My wolf was anxious and pacing. The urge to hunt riling him up and the primitive need to rut overshadowing rational thought.

Would you wish this on the innocent female? I took another sip, trying to subdue my beast.

Skoll growled. "Brother, I respect you. But you are delusional. You won't know if you don't speak to her and learn to trust more than your inner circle. As for her questioning what she saw, did you not do your research on Cerberus pack? Her own mother killed herself because she'd entered into a chosen bond with the Alpha Apollo and then found her fated mate. Kera has no stomach for other woman or man drama. You should have explained everything and she would have understood."

The mention of her dark past had my wolf howling with a protective fury.

"You speak highly of her," I said softly, trying to calm my beast. He was often agitated. This was nothing new. But never had his focus been on a female shifter like this. The mate bond would be a problem we had to solve quick.

"Yes." Skoll nodded, already walking to the door. Apparently, our time was up. "She claimed her pack through a fair challenge and won. She fights for

26

them every day. She has different ideas on how to lead and is changing the way things were done. The two of you aren't so different. So pull your head out of your ass before you mess fate up."

I raised my glass to salute the door closing behind him.

*

There are too many unmated males here.

I know. I pushed open the window of Nolan's study and lit a cigarette.

I don't like this. She's not safe.

She'll be fine in her room. I blew out a cloud of smoke into the salty night air.

We belong with her.

I gritted my teeth against the onslaught of his emotions. We belonged in Anubis pack. She belonged with Cerberus. How would this even work?

Skoll's devotion piqued my interest, but I'd already done my research on that pack. The lone daughter of the mad Alpha had finally stuck it to her old man. Most of the region was surprised it took her so long. There were whispers about her eccentric ways which I was interested in learning more about. Not because of the mate bond, but just to ease my natural curiosity.

We have a mate.

I tipped the glass of bourbon to my lips, staring at the shoreline below while the whitecapped waves beat against the sand in the moonlight.

27

I'd searched for her once.

Like any normal teenage pup, my late father had bid me farewell when I set out on the hunt. It should have been an easy one. A primitive challenge that even the most basic of brains could accomplish.

It was the first time I ever failed.

I'd dragged myself home with my tail between my legs after searching the region. There was one border I couldn't cross and it didn't take a genius to figure out that was where she probably was. But as the Alpha heir, crossing those pack lines would have started a war. That was right before the Mohave battle and we were needed to fight the purists.

I returned home where I belonged.

Now here she was after all these years and the sacrifices I'd made as Alpha. I was no longer that doe-eyed pup looking for the other half of my soul—trying to find the love my parents had.

We need to go to her.

What would I even do with the graveyard princess? She was spoiled, probably. Surrounded by people who only saw her beauty and the novelty of a young female Alpha.

I closed my eyes, remembering her in perfect clarity in the ballroom. She hadn't wanted to bend to the call either and refused to show submission to fate.

Well, neither would I. It wasn't in my nature. I didn't need her anyway. She was just another pretty face. I'd done well enough so far without a mate.

What use did I have for one now?

We'll be sick.

I chuckled as I drank the last of my bourbon. *Are you questioning our tolerance?*

She'll get sick. He growled, knowing that was the one thing I couldn't ignore.

Damn the protective nature of the Alpha.

I pressed my fingers against my temples to stop his incessant demands. *Fine. I'll ease the moon-sickness tonight. But tomorrow, we go home.*

*

Moonlight bathed the bed Kera lay sprawled on. Her hair spread over the top of the mattress as she snored. The pillow was bunched beneath her arms and she gripped it vise-like as if it was going to escape her grasp. I inhaled her earthy smell again. The deep roots of a redwood forest filled my senses. It was so foreign to the crisp desert scents I was accustomed to.

Another reminder that we didn't belong together.

I resisted the urge to brush my fingers across her sharp cheekbones and soft lips that were relaxed now with the depth of sleep. She was beauty incarnate. Nature would have made it so. And I was drawn to the essence of her being because that's how the mate bond worked.

I could distance myself enough to fight through the haze of lust and recognize this pull for what it was. A biological reaction to a pretty face.

What I wasn't prepared for was the aching desire to keep her close. She was a princess for sure, drawing on the base and primal parts of me that demanded I protect and claim.

Except I wasn't some knight in shining armor.

I had a pack of nearly four-thousand to lead. My soul divided with each shifter that called me Alpha. True, I had a system in place to deal with the magnitude of my lands. But I didn't have time to ride off on some white horse into the sunset.

We'll make time.

I moved to the armchair near the window I left open when I'd crawled through it and took a seat where I could watch her quietly.

This wasn't going to work.

Maybe it was best that I let her believe whatever she wanted. Then she could reject the bond and be none the wiser. We'd go our separate ways…

No, my beast growled.

I sighed as I leaned back in the chair. This was a Gods forsaken mess. Was it even natural to have two Alphas mating? I bet the archives had some intelligence on this situation. It couldn't have been the first time in history two pack Alphas had a fated mate bond. But basic survival argued…

You think too much.

I closed my eyes, ignoring him as he basked in the scent of his mate and whined to be closer. My thoughts drifted through different scenarios, trying to find the logic and coming up short. Because no matter how I looked at it, I knew that some things couldn't be left up to fate.

3
† Kera †

Sometime in the middle of the night my body had finally relaxed and I fell into a dreamless sleep. It was a welcome relief from the usual nightmares that plagued both me and my wolf. Seagulls squawked outside the window and the morning rays of sun drifted into the room along with the fresh ocean breeze.

I sat up with a start, clutching the sheet to my chest. The window was open. I know I closed it last night. My nostrils flared as I looked around the room, catching the scent of *him*. Dusty sage and pepper drifting from the armchair in the corner near the window that overlooked the sea. The sharp masculine smell was strong and foreign and deliciously intoxicating. But it felt forbidden to think so.

He was here! My wolf barked excitedly.

Anger flushed my skin. That slimy, mocking, controlling asshole had been in my room last night without my consent.

He's our mate, she whined.

Hush. I kicked away the tangle of blankets from my legs and jumped off the bed. Even if he was a decent mate–ha, what a joke–no one sneaks into my private space and gets away with it.

What if it had been someone else? I couldn't afford to make mistakes like this. We were vulnerable off pack lands and I shouldn't have let my guard down. It was this stupid mating bond that was throwing me off my game. The sooner I got rid of it, the better.

We are not rejecting—

I growled at my wolf, cutting off her thoughts. Now was not the time to pretend we had a future with this Alpha. I glared at the chair and forced every bit of rage I felt through my eyes at the piece of furniture as I yanked my knotted hair into a tight braid.

I should have already cut my hair off. All it did was get in the way. If Coral and Sage hadn't arrived when they did and showed me how to style it, I would have gotten rid of at least a few inches. But the one time I'd done my own bangs hadn't gone so well.

My father's taunts still haunted me.

Apollo, the asshole. How fitting that I was fated to another Alpha like that.

Not for much longer though.

I want him.

You don't know what you want.

That wasn't true. Most of the time she did. We made a good team, me and my wolf, and with Sage and Coral here now, we didn't need anyone else.

Definitely not a cheating jerk of a mate who snuck into my room at night like some kind of stalker.

I wonder what his Luna would think if she knew.

My wolf growled in disgust.

We were back on the same page.

Because under no circumstances would I be the person who destroyed someone's home or relationship. And I would never be the other woman.

He could keep his Luna. I had a pack to lead anyway. As soon as I found my damn hair tie, I was going to give that Alpha a piece of my mind and get the hell out of here.

*

My hair tie was on my wrist. It took an embarrassingly long time to remember that. This mate bond thing was serious. It really messed with your mind. No wonder Coral had been such an idiot. I took a deep breath to steady myself as the grand house echoed my steps down the hall and tried to ignore the chill creeping along my skin.

This was the house where my mother had grown up. Despite the tragedy that was her life, I was hoping I'd find a piece of what had made her happy here. Then Alpha Jareth had to come ruin it all.

Stop thinking about him.

We were supposed to head back to Cerberus lands this afternoon. I wanted to speak with my grandparents more last night. Now I needed to sneak in a few minutes this morning after I dealt with this mate business.

Another deep breath in and out.

I was going to have to reject him. He wasn't mine anyway. The fates didn't always get things right. I was no stranger to mistakes.

But he came to us last night. My sweet wolf whined, confusion warring with her basic needs.

He doesn't deserve you. It was my job to protect my beast just like I protected everyone in my pack. She didn't have to understand that men could be pigs. I'd keep her safe behind the walls I built and never let her get hurt again.

Tentatively, I reached out through the pack link to Coral, sensing she was awake and not caught in the throes of passion. She hadn't yet learned how to fully mute her connection and this past month had been a little awkward when I called on her during more private times.

"I want to talk with Nolan and Gertrude before we leave today." I took the stairs two at a time, trying to ignore the lingering scent of the Alpha asshole who'd also been here.

"Oh good! You're up." Coral's tone was way too excited for the anger that I felt this morning. *"There's something I have to tell you."*

"I'm listening." I paused at the bottom of the stairs in front of the family portraits in the hall. My grandparents, Alpha Nolan and his Luna Gertrude, stood stoic in the first painting. Beyond them were life-like renditions of the young Alpha heir Aiden, Skoll with his hardened expression, and the largest painting was her. My mother Delilah.

The artists they had in Fenrir pack were better than I'd ever be.

The painting in the gilded frame was beautiful. They'd captured her in perfect detail. The way her eyes shone with a carefree happiness. A light green, so different from the bluish-gray that I'd gotten from my Cerberus blood. Her hair was perfectly plaited. The soft pink dress was fitting just so as it fell loose from her delicate shoulders. I reached up to touch mine.

She didn't have my muscle definition or the haunted look on her face I saw in the mirror. The world was hers and she was young, even though she couldn't have been much older in the painting than me. It was like staring at a distorted reflection of yourself in a lake where the current rippled across the image. It was me, but it wasn't me. A ghost of what I could have been.

"I'm really sorry," Coral was still talking.

I blinked back the burning sensation behind my eyes and popped the bones in my neck, turning my head side to side. *"Sorry about what?"*

Leaving the portraits behind, I followed my nose and growling stomach to the dining room. I'd deal with this mate bond situation once I'd gotten something to eat.

"Did you hear anything I said?" she asked frantically.

"You said you were sorry." I pushed open the doors to the dining hall and froze when everyone turned to stare at me.

My wolf's hackles raised and I twisted my hands behind my back, confused as to how I'd slept so late. Usually, I was the first to wake.

And the first at the table for food.

The room was already full and breakfast well underway. Nolan and Gertrude sat at the head of the table with their young son and smiled adoringly at my entrance. It was still a shock to know I had grandparents that didn't hate me, so I nodded, looking away. At the other end was Nolan's Beta Calder and a few of the pack enforcers. In the middle sat Sage and Coral with their mates on either side. My uncle Maddock grunted and returned to his food. Of course, there was only one open chair right across from Alpha Jareth with his delicate Luna at his side. Fate was cruel.

But I was too hungry to turn around.

I licked my dry lips, trying not to stare at him as I made my way to the empty chair. Last night had been a blur of intense emotions that I wasn't sure how to handle. I'd convinced myself he was a sleazy and ugly brute, but in the morning light with his unruly black curls mussed and dark circles under his eyes as if he'd barely slept, I couldn't help the tightness that squeezed my chest.

Why did he come to my room?

He cares about us.

My wolf wasn't helping at all.

I kept my chin raised and looked to my grandparents instead. "Good morning."

"Good morning to you too, my dear. I hope you're hungry." Nolan's kind eyes lit up and he motioned for everyone to resume their breakfast. I took the seat next to Coral and tried to ignore the pull that begged me to look at Jareth again.

I'd eat first and then handle this mate business. It'd probably turn out bloody if I ripped out half my soul and denied my future happiness on an empty stomach.

"Do you make it a habit to sleep in every morning, princess?" His voice crawled along my skin, as deep and tantalizing as it was last night. He reached for a scone on the center plate between us.

Heat rushed to my face and my wolf growled, forcing me to raise my eyes to meet his challenge. He leaned back on his seat and ripped out a chunk of pastry with his teeth as if he didn't have a care in the world.

"Normally, no." I drew on the Alpha power that was my birthright, letting it radiate through my veins and strengthen my voice. I would have done this more delicately so as not to cause a scene and embarrass his Luna, but I was in no mood to play his games. "Do you make a habit of sneaking into women's rooms and spending the night like a stalker watching them?"

The dining hall quieted as I loaded eggs and sausage onto my plate. I really needed to eat something before I said anything else.

"Touché, princess." Alpha Jareth chuckled.

The sound of it messed with my head. A part of me wanted to make him laugh harder as I bit back a smile. The other part of me wanted to stab him with my fork.

"Kera—" Coral warned through our pack link as she touched my arm.

"I won't kill him here," I cut her off. She had to know by now I'd follow the rules for visiting she'd insisted on. Gods, I was over the PR bullshit.

"Jareth, stop," Ophelia said. Even her voice was delicate. It was sickeningly sweet like honey and so feminine it made my wolf sigh.

I shoveled a forkful of tasteless eggs in my mouth, ignoring the protective impulse of my beast. The quicker I ate, the faster I could get back home and put this mate business behind me.

"My apologies, Alpha Kera," Ophelia continued in her singsong way as I bit into a hunk of sausage. "Alpha Jareth is not a morning person, nor does my brother know when to shut his mouth."

I choked on the half-chewed food, sucking it in with a startled gasp.

"Breathe." Coral pounded her fist against my back as I tried to dislodge the lump stuck in my throat. My eyes were wide, taking both of them in.

Siblings? How did I not notice that? They both had the same raven black hair and bronzed skin. The same dark blue eyes. But Jareth was fully masculine and hard whereas Ophelia… She was not.

My wolf howled in triumph while I swallowed down the food and caught Coral's hand before she punched me through the table.

"Your brother?" I coughed, reaching for the glass of juice.

"I tried to tell you," Coral muttered under her breath. I put the cup to my lips, stalling as the liquid washed down the last bit of stuck food in my throat.

39

My gaze went straight to the Alpha's face.

And as fast as it went up, the brick wall came crashing down as the mate bond flared to life.

I was allowed to look. He wasn't taken. My wolf purred in happiness, begging to crawl across the table and onto his lap. Warmth coiled low in my belly, spreading everywhere as he dabbed the napkin across his strong jaw. For one split second, I entertained the idea of having a mate.

"Now I'm worthy of your attention." Jareth folded his arms over his chest and narrowed his eyes. "Forgive me for not jumping for joy, your highness."

And that's why we don't make decisions when hungry.

I growled, returning to my breakfast. He was an asshole. I hadn't made that part up. A handsome one. An available one. But still an asshole.

I had to get this mate bond under control.

"Why don't we give them a minute alone?" Alpha Nolan stood from the head of his table.

My cheeks flamed with heat. If the scent of the bond wasn't obvious enough, they'd probably been discussing this all morning. Every shifter loved a fated mates' story.

And the juicier the drama, the better.

"No need," I spoke with my mouth full of eggs, cringing when I remembered that wasn't polite. I swallowed more carefully this time. "Secrets and games of deceit annoy me. I won't waste my time playing them. We leave for Cerberus this afternoon, but I would like to speak with you privately before then. And I hope this situation didn't ruin your plans last night."

"Oh sweetheart." Gertrude released the young Alpha heir Aiden and the tiny beast went running across the room. "You were beautiful. The perfect Alpha of Cerberus. We couldn't have asked for a better party and to know you found your mate in our home is the icing on the cake."

I took a sip of the juice, ignoring the strange burning sensation in my chest. Now was not the time to process what those emotions meant. Especially not in front of *him*.

Coral laughed as she caught the pup in her arms. "And I'm sorry for freaking out last night. I didn't know."

"A Beta's job is to protect the Alpha from liars." I grabbed a biscuit from the table and stood as I nodded to my grandparents. "I'm going to finish packing and I'll meet you both after you eat your breakfast."

Coral glanced my way, but her hands were full as the young Alpha wrapped his arms around her neck. Skoll growled at him.

The boy growled back, partially shifting as he snapped with his fangs. "She's mine."

Good natured laughter filled the room and I took that as my sign to leave. I turned on my heel, risking another glance at Jareth. But he was facing the open window, lost in thought.

Whatever.

It may hurt to end this, but even if he was available, it was never going to work. Especially not after an introduction like that. It was on the tip of my tongue to just say the words now and get them out of the way. But I hesitated, taking another step toward the door as I bit into the biscuit.

*

"Alpha Kera, wait!" Ophelia's soft voice followed me up the stairs. My wolf growled, demanding that I stop. Ophelia wasn't to blame here and I was rude to her last night.

I sighed as I turned to the rustle of black skirts hurrying up the stairs. This whole situation was so complicated and I hadn't eaten nearly enough. The mating bond wasn't leaving me clear-headed. I needed some air and a long run in the woods before I made a decision this big.

"I didn't know he was your brother." My attempt at an apology sucked.

But she didn't seem to mind as she climbed the last steps and joined me on the landing. "Oh, good. We're getting right to the point. I know he comes across as harsh, but he's stuck in his head most of the time so he doesn't interact with others very well. You'll have to forgive his quirks."

I didn't have to forgive anyone who hadn't earned it, but I held back my opinion when tears misted her eyes. Her expression was so vulnerable and trusting. Protective instinct won again.

She smiled softly, dabbing the corner of her eye with her sleeve. "You don't plan to reject him, right? Once you get to know him, I swear you'll realize he isn't that bad."

Did I? My stomach clenched as if I'd eaten something rotten. The minutes were counting down until we had to leave. My plan this morning had been simple. Reject him and go home. But now that I knew he wasn't taken, did I want to give him another chance?

I do. My wolf raised her paw as I inhaled deeply, closing my eyes.

"It looks like you're undecided." Ophelia bounced on the balls of her feet, clapping her hands as she continued the one-sided conversation. "That's okay. It means there is hope. I'd hate to see your future happiness thrown away because of a silly misunderstanding."

I wouldn't call it silly. He didn't state the truth from the beginning. One thing I hated was liars.

But maybe I had misunderstood. Intelligence on the other packs wasn't always reliable. Though nowhere was it said that Jareth and Ophelia weren't mated. Should I have known to ask?

"Why are you acting as Luna for Anubis?" The question slipped out. Better now than never.

"I'll make you a deal." Ophelia winked as she nudged me with her hip. "Let's spend some time together and I'll tell you all my dark secrets. Jareth's too."

My wolf whined as my nostrils flared, sensing him before he walked to the base of the grand staircase. The mate bond teased, growing stronger as his scent drifted up the steps, and urging me to look despite really not wanting to.

"Leave her alone, Ophelia." He leaned against the banister, staring up at her with tired eyes.

My heart caught in my throat as his gaze met mine and sensations rushed through my body that I couldn't control. I wanted an apology. If I asked, would he give it? The thought made me lightheaded with hope until I shoved it right back behind the wall where it belonged. Alphas didn't apologize.

"No." Ophelia stomped her foot on the floor. "I'm not going to let you destroy our family or your future because of your big head."

With a shifter's speed he rushed the staircase. Ophelia jumped back to give him room on the landing as he towered over her.

"Go to your room and get packed." The deep Alpha command riled my beast. I didn't have siblings so I didn't understand the dynamics, but what I was hearing only added fuel to the fire simmering beneath my skin that I'd been trying to contain since I first laid eyes on him.

"Excuse me, jerk." I stepped between the two of them, pushing Ophelia behind my back. "We were having a conversation and I don't recall anyone asking your opinion."

The intensity of the mate bond was electric this close. I was tall, but he was a few inches taller, making me look up as I glared into his eyes. Power seemed to grow, swirling between us as we squared off. Our breaths came shorter and our wolfs rose to the surface, called by the challenge.

I wasn't sure what the challenge was though. One of us needed to be the first to walk away. Or speak the words of rejection. Or did one of us need to close the distance between us and touch?

That thought warmed places I didn't know existed and I held my hands firm at my side. Instinct demanded I reach up to his lips. Just to see if they were soft or carved of stone. To run my fingers down his chest and feel the muscles hidden beneath the soft shirt. To take his hand in mine and press it to my heart. But I couldn't trust my instincts now because I also wanted to shove him down the stairs.

Jareth's fangs extended and he growled, pupils dilating as he studied me. I didn't blink.

"I like her." Ophelia poked her head around my shoulder. "Don't scare her away."

Her words broke through the trance and Jareth's fangs retracted.

I looked over at Ophelia, still keeping her brother in my direct line of sight as she danced down the hall.

"Oh, and thanks for not killing me last night." She gave a delicate little wave before disappearing into her room.

"Um… You're welcome." I finally blinked, wondering what just happened.

"I'm waiting." Jareth tapped his long fingers against his bicep, drawing my attention to his arm and the hint of inked skin that peeked out from under the sleeve of the t-shirt. I was curious to know what the artwork was. Did it cover his chest or end at his shoulder? I couldn't help wondering what he looked like naked.

The bond flared again, drawing a soft moan from my beast, and I clamped down on my lips to keep it in. This was his fault. His presence sucked all the breathable air from this massive house and made it hard to think.

A vortex of energy pulsed from him. The Alpha's impatience meeting my own and coaxing out my dominance. I cursed myself for getting swept away in the storm and knew that I should leave. He'd been nothing but awful since I'd first seen him. But I couldn't take that first step and lose.

"Waiting for what?" I growled, almost forgetting he'd spoken as I inhaled slowly to calm myself. It didn't work. Not when his scent filled my being and urged my instinct to hunt.

Jareth growled as he dipped his head down and dragged his nose up the side of my neck. My fists clenched, ready to shove him back, but not wanting him to know how much he affected me.

I shivered involuntarily as he inhaled. My wolf howled her approval, trying to force us closer. If she had her way, we'd be pinning him to the floor and forcing his submission. I lifted my chin and stared at the ceiling as if I could ignore the chills and heat that amped up with his touch.

His mouth moved lower, pressing against my collarbone, and he breathed his words against my skin. "Waiting for you to reject me so we can get on with the rest of our lives."

I took a step back and cold air filled the empty space between us. "You want me to reject you." *Gods. The audacity of this man.*

"You said you'd give me your decision later." He turned his palms up, mocking me with that stupid smirk on his handsome face. "How much longer do I have to wait for your royal approval?"

"And you don't have an opinion in this matter?" I asked, not sure if I cared to know the answer. If he could throw away our future so easily, did I even want him?

"I'm trying to be a gentleman here and let you decide." He shrugged.

"Ha." I snorted. "You are not gentle and the last thing I need is your permission to do anything."

His Alpha power surged at the challenge and I braced myself, tensing as my own emotions blazed and refusing to cower under his intimidating gaze.

"You know what?" I lowered my voice, standing on my toes so we were at eye level and watched as his focus went to my lips. "If you want that rejection so badly, go ahead and state it yourself."

I took a sick sense of pleasure in watching his face twist with confusion. It wasn't like me to give someone else control over my future, but when I turned on my heel to leave, I realized I had won this round. His beast called to mine over the mate bond, begging to be heard, while the man pressed his lips into a thin line.

"I'll be waiting for your answer, but I'd hurry. I have a pack to get back to." I took a page from Coral's playbook, flipping my braid over my shoulder as I marched away. It was a little too hard and the end smacked my other cheek. But no one needed to know how much it stung.

"But the moon sickness!" He growled in frustration, calling after me.

"That's only a problem for you." I gave him a smug smile as I threw open the doors to my room. Screw him. He could make himself sick while he fought with his own wolf. He was the one who wanted to play games. "In case you haven't heard, Cerberus pack boasts two witches that are well versed in magic of the heart. I just have to go home and I'll be fine. Can you say the same, *Alpha*?"

4
† Jareth †

She slammed the doors in my face.

You have thumbs. Open the damn things.
My beast growled with a righteous fury.

Can you shut up? I growled back at him as I leaned against the wall.

Gods. What a mess.

I shouldn't have been at this ridiculous event. The doting grandparents introducing their long-lost princess Alpha to society and pretending like they hadn't written her off along with the rest of Cerberus pack. It was a waste of time. We had bigger problems to deal with. The purist threats were growing by the minute. I kept trying to warn them, but no one listened. Instead, they threw another party. Because that's all shifters cared about.

Parties and drama.

Well, this was a party now.

I'd told Ophelia I had a bad feeling about this. She wouldn't let it alone and my wolf was anxious–like always–insisting that we go with her.

Look at what happened. I finally found my mate. Kera should have ended it. I felt the indecision through our weak bond and knew she wanted to. If she would have just spoken the words of rejection, we could forget this ever happened. But Kera twisted the narrative and dragged this out, leaving the decision in my hands. I shouldn't have expected anything less from a pampered princess.

Screw it. I'd be the one to reject her.

No, you won't. My wolf snarled.

How was this even supposed to work?

Growling, I ran my hands through my hair and stared up at the ceiling. A bitter laugh escaped my chest as something hard hit the wall behind me. Her growing anger drifted through the thin wood and plaster that separated us. *Welcome to the club, princess.*

Open the door and fix this.

No. I kicked myself off the wall and marched down the hall. She could throw her tantrum in there. It was time for me to have a chat with my darling little sister anyway.

*

Ophelia took a seat on the bed and tucked her skirts around her legs as she looked up at me through painted lashes. "What's the plan?"

"Now you ask me." I scowled, crossing my arms over my chest and leaning against the doorframe. "You've already taken it upon yourself to meddle in my affairs and try to become besties with the female Alpha."

"Someone has to show my new sister-in-law that we aren't all a bunch of jerks with trust issues," Ophelia muttered under her breath.

I looked around the room, ignoring her jab. The bags were already packed and the floor was swept clean. The *thank you* notes she always left when we visited elsewhere were sealed with wax and propped up on the nightstand by the lamp. She took her job as Luna and representative of Anubis pack seriously, making up for my shortcomings. Despite her feminine and sometimes whimsical ways, she never let me down.

"Do you lack for anything?" I relaxed my shoulders as I walked into the room and took a seat beside her on the mattress.

"Of course not, Alpha." She rolled her eyes.

"Are you so eager to give up your position?" I asked.

Ophelia snorted, covering the sound with a jingle of the bangles on her wrist as she put a hand over her mouth. "You may be the brains of the family, but you're an idiot when it comes to women. Kera is no Luna. She is without a doubt your match though."

"How can you be sure?" I stared at the wall with a million thoughts racing through my mind.

Why would fate pair two Alphas with different territories to protect? The strength of conjoined packs went against the natural balance of power. I understood inter-pack breeding to dilute bloodlines, but Alpha wolves were rarely paired. Mating bonds served a purpose. Breeding. Would mated Alphas produce some sort of super offspring?

I want to do more than breed with her.

Like what? I huffed out a laugh, knowing that was the one force driving him now that the hunt was on. I didn't blame him. It was the primitive nature of the beast. I'd be lying if I didn't say I wasn't interested in that way. Kera was a pretty woman. But the long-term ramifications of having a mate complicated the work I had to do. And it's not like we'd even had a conversation that didn't involve some kind of power struggle yet. She'd only prove a headache in the future once the initial mating hormones faded.

"Because she won't take your shit." Ophelia laid a soft hand on my arm, drawing me from my thoughts. "I have a good feeling about her. Don't mess this up."

*

My little sister and her *feelings*. I shook my head as I walked down the side staircase to the servant entrance. True, the sensitive nature of Ophelia's wolf was useful in her position as Luna which is why she held the job, but logic always trumped emotions. In this moment, I had to think with the correct head.

The council would be frustrated if I returned to Anubis as a rejected mate, but I'd dealt with their complaints for most of my life. Ophelia would get over it. My beast would learn to cope.

I'll never forgive you.

You will. In time.

I pushed open the door as I dug through my pocket for the tin case of rolled cigarettes. The bright sun glittered off the waves in the distance past the manicured hedges of the garden. I lit a match and held it to the tobacco, breathing in the familiar scent and letting it soothe my nerves. It wasn't strong enough to cover up the lingering smell of redwoods and rich soil. I turned toward the garden path as the thrill of the hunt riled my wolf, searching for Kera. The bond tugged at the center of my chest until I spotted her with Nolan and Gertrude near the hedges by the stone bench.

Her voice was husky and full of an Alpha's intensity as it drifted on the ocean breeze. "Thank you again for opening the borders and resuming trade with Cerberus. I wish I could have known my mother, but I can tell she was loved here. I'm going to honor her memory by leading Cerberus pack in a better way than Apollo did to make up for the damage he caused."

I leaned back into the shadows of the hedges. This was a private family conversation that I had no business listening to, but natural curiosity got the best of me. I inhaled another drag from the cigarette.

"There is no apology strong enough that can make up for lost time, but if you need anything, let us know." Alpha Nolan's tone was heavy with emotion.

I exhaled a plume of smoke slowly, laughing to myself. He would give her everything now; spoil his granddaughter to make up for the shortsightedness of his anger. The princess would be taken care of for the rest of her life.

I'd heard enough.

"I don't want anything from you except a normal relationship. We'll keep working on that."

Kera's words made me hesitate. She had playing cards in her pocket that any Alpha in her position would be foolish to deny. Was she really going to throw them away? Or was this some underhanded trick? I'd dealt with pack politics long enough to scent the lies. But the wind shifted, making it difficult to tell.

The mate bond flared, drawing a whimper from my wolf, and I looked over my shoulder. Kera narrowed her stormy gaze at me.

"It's time to put the trauma of the past behind us and focus on the future." Her words were directed at her grandparents, but they echoed in my head and stilled the beat of my heart for a moment or two.

Because the future was the problem here. I'd seen enough to know that the future for all of us was uncertain. There were dangers in this world that most shifters ignored.

I'll protect her. My wolf whined, still caught in the throes of the hunt.

We don't need someone else to protect.

But I couldn't make my feet take another step away. My wolf fought for control and I struggled to hold him back. I met her gaze across the hedges, sucking in a shaky drag and letting the nicotine calm my beast. Indecision was a killer. The longer I put this off, the harder it would be.

She is my future. He clawed at my mind.

We don't have the luxury of selfish choices.

How can she fight what she doesn't know? We have to warn her of the truth.

She won't listen. They never do.

"Excuse me." Kera stepped away from her grandparents and marched down the garden path. The challenge thrummed through the mate bond. I straightened my shoulders and schooled my expression as I prepared to face the brewing storm that pulsed from her aura as she approached.

"Did you make your decision yet?" She stood just out of reach, body relaxed with one foot forward in what I had to assume was her fighting stance if the emotions pummeling the air around us were any indication. The sun glittered off the gold in her hair and heated her earthy scent, tantalizing my beast.

You are mine.

I growled to silence him and my nostrils flared, inhaling more of her smell on accident and trying to hold back the primitive urge to stake my claim. Gods, it was like a shot of desire straight to my cock. More intoxicating than any drug. Had I known the effects would be this controlling, I would have studied the mate bond reaction sooner.

"You'll come to Anubis territory while I decide." The words slipped out before I thought them through, almost as if my wolf was controlling my voice.

Kera's blue eyes widened. "You are out of your damn mind."

Yes. I was. And this bond was partially to blame, but I wasn't backing down now.

"Then you make the decision, princess." I couldn't stop the threat in my tone. The Alpha in me wanted her to bend so we could be done with this game.

"No." The pulse of her power flared through our bond, coaxing mine out in response.

"Yes." I growled, stalking closer.

She raised her chin, mocking me even as she looked up to stare into my eyes. "I don't think you have the balls to reject me."

"Want to bet?" My beast surged forward and my fangs extended. The need to prove exactly what he could do with his balls overrode rational thought. A threatening growl vibrated in her chest as her fangs slid down her plump bottom lip.

The fiery female didn't flinch as I towered over her. "Name the price."

Stop. I yanked back my wolf with a firm command. She was purposefully antagonizing me and I'd dealt with enough errant wolves to know when the fight was worth it. I may have agreed that she needed to be taught a lesson, but this was not the place for it.

I turned my face to the sky, trying to breathe through the torrent of power encircling us as I pressed the cigarette to my lips. We stood in silence, both of us panting as we tried to get control of our beasts. At least I wasn't the only one struggling.

I exhaled smoke through my nose, looking back down to those stormy blue eyes that glowed with an internal tempest. "How is the graveyard this time of year?"

Her eyebrows pinched together and her mouth popped open in surprise. The delight in causing that response on her face was short lived when I realized the seriousness of what I'd just said.

"You're coming to Cerberus territory?" She cocked her head to the side, studying me.

"Maybe." I shrugged as I ran my hand through my hair. This was foolish. A pointless endeavor. I was delaying the inevitable.

"Why?"

Now she asks questions.

"It's been too long since Anubis has inspected our northern neighbors. For the good of my pack, I want to see the advancements you've made and find out what resources you lack." It was a dumb excuse. No Alpha in their right mind would allow another to come sniffing around that way. I just needed her to believe it until I could get my head on straight.

There was a good chance that I panicked too.

"Bullshit." She stole the cigarette from my fingers and crushed it on the ground as she turned to leave. "We head out in an hour. You better be ready to go then, because I'm not waiting for you."

5
† Kera †

What is happening?

I splashed cool water from the bathroom sink over my face, attempting to tame the raging inferno that was scorching beneath the surface of my skin.

This wasn't how I acted.

I made firm decisions. I didn't let macho alphaholes get to me. And I swore I'd never again put my future into someone else's hands. Yet here I was, letting my anger get the best of me. It was his fault. He was just so… *frustrating.*

I growled as I looked at the reflection in the mirror, feeling like I was seeing myself for the first time. All the female parts of my body I was used to ignoring stood out awkwardly now.

We're beautiful. My wolf sighed, content with the thought of spending more time with our mate.

We're strong, I reminded her. Gods knew I needed to be. That brooding Alpha had me questioning everything I once knew about myself. I had to keep it together. Especially now that he was coming with us to Cerberus territory.

The worst part was that I couldn't deny his visit. His reasoning was garbage, but I couldn't afford to piss off an Alpha of his standing. An alliance would be beneficial to my pack. With our numbers now, I couldn't risk a fight with Anubis.

I was doing this for my shifters.

Even as I had that thought, I realized the lie. With Fenrir and the rest of the region backing us, Jareth would be a fool to attack. Alone we were no threat to them either. Which was why his reason for coming to visit was crap.

What I couldn't understand was why he was going through all this trouble when I clearly felt his disdain through the bond. Jareth didn't want to be mated. Why couldn't he just reject me?

Unease made me growl again as I tapped my fingers against the sink, knowing I should have been the one to end it. What was wrong with me?

Better yet, what was wrong with him?

I splashed my face with water one more time and turned off the faucet.

He wants to be with us, my wolf offered like that would make me feel better. **He's our mate.**

Mate. I shook my head, giving one last look at my pained expression in the mirror. *Were the Gods really this cruel?*

*

I shouldered my simple travel bag as I hurried down the stairs. As nice as it was to have repaired the bridge with this part of my family, I'd feel steadier on my own land.

The sun was already high overhead when I stepped outside Nolan's beachside mansion. Maddock was in the back of his truck loading up the bags.

"There you are." Sage caught me by the elbow and wrapped her arms around me as a wave of soothing magic calmed my heart. "How are you doing with all of this?"

"I'm fine." I patted her back gently, trying only to touch the fabric of her shirt instead of the angry red skin on her shoulders. "But you look like you spent too much time in an oven."

Sage, my acting Luna and powerful witch, leaned back, crinkling her nose. "I might have overdone my time on the beach this trip."

"She snuck out there again this morning after breakfast even though I told her not to." Coral rolled her eyes, chastising her older sister, as Skoll took the bag from his mate.

Both sisters leaned to the side at the same time, looking at something behind me. I didn't need to turn around to see what they were staring at. The bond flared, putting the tight feeling back into my chest that I could have lived without.

"Alpha Jareth is coming home with us," I said. Sage's mouth dropped open.

Coral reached over to push it closed. "Don't say anything. This could work."

"Sure it could." I tossed my bag up to Maddock. My uncle grunted as it slammed into his gut, but said nothing after seeing my expression. I took a deep breath and turned to face this situation head on.

Jareth pushed a pair of reflective sunglasses up the bridge of his nose. Each step he took was measured and calculated. Alpha power radiated from him and riled my wolf in a confusing way. She wanted to purr as she rolled on her back. She wanted him pinned and submitting to us. He had no right to make walking down the porch steps look as sexy as he did. I hated my body's physical reaction to him.

A sleek black car with tinted windows rolled up next to my uncle's rusted truck.

"You're drooling." Coral mind-linked me.

"Am not." I wiped my hand over my mouth to check.

"I'm sorry I made a mistake," she hurried to add.

"You were looking out for me." I gave her a small smile before looking back at Jareth. Bracing myself, I straightened my shoulders and prepared for the tension to boil over again as he closed the distance between us.

He barely acknowledged me with a slight curve of his lips as he spoke to the shifters climbing out of the car. "Get her things and take Luna Ophelia back to Anubis. The convoy is waiting to escort you at the rendezvous point."

"Are you not coming with us, Alpha?" the driver asked.

Jareth responded with a pointed look of annoyance as the front doors to Nolan's home swung open. Ophelia hugged my grandparents goodbye.

Then her dainty feet pointed in my direction. I had a split second to realize she was a hugger before she threw herself into my arms.

"I'm so happy he is going with you." Ophelia squeezed me tight and rushed out the words as I tried to peel her off. "I wish I could come, but the council gets nervous when we're away for too long. Don't worry. I'll take care of them."

She leaned back and gave me a conspiratorial wink. "Take as long as you need to break him."

I didn't know what to say to that, so I just nodded at the curious creature. She seemed genuine though. I liked her. At least, I liked her better than her brother so far. Skoll joined us and she redirected her attention to him.

"Can I hug you again now that you've completed the bond with your mate and my scent doesn't make you gag?" She laughed.

Skoll echoed her laughter, looking at me from the corner of his eye. "Speaking of mates, this is a fun turn of events."

I resisted the urge to growl at him. He'd accepted me as Alpha for Coral's sake, but he never missed an opportunity to remind me that he didn't bow to anyone. Thankfully, he was good at training the troops. I could ignore him as long as he worked hard and didn't hurt my friend.

Ignoring him now, I turned to Jareth. He was busy helping load Ophelia's things into the back of the car as he talked with the driver about protective measures he'd laid out for her safe journey home. It was hard to get a read on him in this light.

Seeing him as a protective brother and watching the respect on his shifters' faces made me yearn for the other side of the Alpha I had yet to meet. Those qualities mirrored my own. What would it be like to talk to someone else about the same kind of worries?

Well, Kera, now you can. I swallowed hard, realizing this was really happening. He was coming with us, to my home, willingly. That had to count for something. He hadn't rejected me like I hadn't rejected him. We could start over and try again.

Give fate a real chance.

Jareth raised his head, but I couldn't see his eyes behind the glasses. I could feel the bond flare between us though, urging me to take a tentative step. This time I did. I let go of the worry that he'd see it as a sign of weakness and steadied my breathing. He deserved a warm welcome for taking this risk. I wouldn't be some trembling leaf on the wind.

I could do this.

He slid the sunglasses down his nose and my heart skipped a beat as our eyes met. The intensity of his gaze and the depths of the dark blue irises were like drowning in a twilight sky. My wolf howled her approval as I took another step closer.

Hi. Let's start fresh. My name is Kera.

Okay, that sounded stupid in my head.

I twisted my hands behind my back, trying to think of the words to say that would restart our introduction as I continued walking forward.

But his gaze slid past me, looking over my shoulder at Maddock's truck. His lips curled in disgust. "This is your ride?"

Seriously? What is wrong with him? I gritted my teeth as I marched forward, changing the course at the last possible second. Jareth was an asshole and I was a fool for thinking he could be anything else. This visit was going to be hell.

"Nope." I pulled my shirt over my head and tossed it back to Coral. My teeth stayed clenched as I gave a quick goodbye wave to my grandparents and leveled a glare at the jerk fate had chosen for me. Now I needed to find a way to get rid of him.

Maybe I could drop him off a deep ravine somewhere in the mountains. Really, I'd be doing the world a favor.

6
† Jareth †

Idiot! My wolf surged forward, cursing me in his haste to break free.

The pulse of desire that ran through him was almost strong enough to lose control. Kera had stood there with her bare chest heaving. Milky white breasts and rose-colored nipples on full display. Raw and feminine power crashed through our bond, coaxing tendrils of protective anger out of my beast.

Our claws extended as I turned to growl at the crowd of shifters still standing in the driveway. I was ready to rip out the eyeballs of anyone who dared to look at her. It was irrational. Crazy. We were shifters for Gods' sakes. Nudity was more common than not. But all I could think of in that moment was destroying anyone who so much as dared to glance at her flesh.

"It gets easier once you've sealed the bond." Skoll grabbed my shoulder, shaking me from the rage.

I shoved him back, not in the mood for his pacifying bullshit, and ran a hand through my hair. "This is a mistake."

"Have fun!" Ophelia blew a kiss as she slipped behind the tinted bulletproof windows of the car. I was torn, wanting to ensure her safety to the convoy at least and confused as to why Kera would put her shifters in danger with the death trap truck that looked like the bolts were about to fall out. But the reddish gold wolf seemed to think she was invincible as she howled for her pack to follow.

Hearing her call riled my wolf and for the first time in as long as I could remember, he forced the shift. I barely had time to slip out of my clothes before the beast took over.

Skoll's laughter followed me as he gathered up my belongings. His human voice echoed in my ears while my wolf set out to chase down the female Alpha. "And now the hunt begins."

*

I milled over the whole situation through the miles that stretched out before us. My wolf took the full reins for this chase. He was thriving on the freedom of being able to ignore my human thoughts as he focused on his one desire.

The gleam of the reddish gold wolf was always ahead and sometimes slipping out of sight. It urged him in a primitive way that left me plenty of time to rationalize how irrational this all was. The decision I'd made was dangerous. Impulsive. I had more important things to do.

The thrill of the run was invigorating though. I couldn't remember the last time my wolf had been this excited. There was always an undercurrent of duty and responsibility in everything we did, leaving no time for simple pleasures. Even tinkering with new inventions and rebuilding lost technology didn't bring us the joy that it once did since it was all for the good of the pack. Because that's what an Alpha was born to do. They took care of their wolves.

Ophelia and Griffon can handle things.

Maybe so. But it didn't sit right with me that my Beta and my little sister would be forced to do my job while I chased some frustrating she-wolf through the woods.

She isn't some normal she-wolf.

Right. She was our mate.

I wasn't a stranger to the strength of the love that could be had between fated mates. My own mother's heart shattered the day my father passed away, leaving me to assume the role of Alpha of Anubis pack without parents. But I had thousands of shifters to lead and I couldn't imagine abandoning them for a concept as whimsical as love. Especially not when the purists were planning something and the other packs refused to prepare.

We were on our own. I couldn't let the wolves of Anubis who depended on me down.

Maybe I could get this out of our system. Once the moon sickness waned and we'd had our fill, she wouldn't be so shiny anymore. I could talk some sense into my beast then. He'd lose interest and remember that there were bigger things at stake than settling down with a mate.

*

Skoll's wolf stayed to my right, flanking us like we were young pups again and going on an adrenaline-fueled hunt. I urged my beast to nip at his back leg for old times' sake. Skoll's wolf snarled a warning as he shook off the attack and picked up his speed. My wolf's alpha instinct bristled at the dismissal and we raced forward, ready to knock him to the dirt. The gray wolf realized what was happening and turned to brace for the hit.

Coral's white wolf darted between us and stopped my charge. Her eyes narrowed as she yipped for us to keep up.

We're not that slow.

It'd been a few years since my wolf stretched his legs and ran this far. I shook off the depressing thought as my beast continued the chase without another care in the world. There wasn't time to play when you had a pack to lead, but I could give him a few hours now.

The moon was cresting the tops of the pine trees in the untamed forest. Ophelia should be entering the outskirts of Anubis territory. Tomorrow she'd inform the elders of the reason for my absence. I was fully expecting more complaints when I yet again failed to return with my mate. At least I had a few days before they worried. My Beta Griffon could manage normal operations without me for a while. But there were other pressing issues I was anxious to get back and handle.

I urged my wolf faster, hoping to hurry the chase and get his fill of freedom so we could return to the real world.

"Took you long enough." Her human voice was a whip that slashed through the darkness. My wolf leapt into the clearing where Kera squatted over a smoldering fire. She wore only a loose shirt that hung to her thighs with the bottom of her smooth ass peeking out. My wolf turned to growl at our party, daring anyone to look at her.

Except our party only consisted of Coral and Skoll still in wolf form as they padded around the soft pine needles to make a nest for sleep. Skoll's wolf cocked his massive head to the side. There was a hint of amusement in his green eyes. The bastard was mocking me. Coral's wolf laid down and started licking her dainty white paws, but her soft wolf chortle made my pride bristle.

Down boy. I can take it from here, I soothed my beast, blaming him for the macho display.

Tomorrow I'm running beside her. He panted as he released the shift.

I stretched out my neck as I rose to my full height and eased the muscles from the long-forgotten tension of a good day's run. Skoll's travel pack was still hanging from his side as he settled down next to the fire. Coral laid beside him, looking up at me through bored and sleepy eyes while I waited for them to shift to human form.

And waited.

Skoll's wolf huffed as he laid his snout atop his mate's head and closed his eyes.

"You better not bite me," I grumbled as I opened the flap to his bag. This domesticated side of him was playing tricks with my head. I was used to a much less amused wolf and wasn't convinced he'd been truly whipped.

I dug in the pack for my pants that I'd kicked off in my wolf's haste to follow Kera, praying my tin of cigarettes had survived the journey. Luck was on my side as I opened the case and immediately lit up. With the pants still in my hand, I turned to look over my shoulder. Kera's stormy blue eyes met mine as she blew on the glowing embers of the fire.

"Do you want pants?" I offered, holding out the material that was sure to fall off her slim waist.

The thought of her in my clothes did something strange to me and I inhaled a drag off the cigarette to ignore the foreign sensation.

Her lips quirked to the side. "Does my body repulse you so much that you want to cover it up?"

That was not what I meant.

I ashed the cigarette and turned my face to the sky, calming my wolf who snarled at me. "I was trying to be nice."

"Forgive me, Alpha Jareth." Her laughter was deep and throaty. "I didn't think you knew the word nice."

"I don't." I bit back a smile.

She leaned onto her elbows and stretched out her long legs, keeping her thighs pressed tightly together. The shirt dropped over her midsection and bunched around her hips. Her red hair fell forward, wild and curling around her chin. She was effortlessly beautiful in a way that screamed she didn't care.

The thrill of the chase and pull of the mate bond were still rushing through me. Blood pooled into my groin. It was basic instinct. I tried not to fault myself as I turned around and stepped into the pants, hiding my erection against my leg.

"Those things will kill you," Kera said.

I chuckled as I looked to the burning cigarette still held in my hand. "They haven't yet. But I'd be careful, princess. Someone might think you care."

"I don't care," she mumbled softly. Her delicate ankles crossed as she watched me turn around. "Do you want to tell me the real reason you are coming with us to Cerberus lands?"

"I wanted to learn more about my fated mate." That was close enough to the truth. I still wasn't sure exactly what I was doing here and mostly acting on instinct. But if I could get her talking about herself, then maybe my beast would get bored. He despised small talk almost as much as I did.

Except now for some reason. He was silent, waiting anxiously for her to respond.

You want to hear about her pampered life?

You want to shut up so I can listen?

This mate bond was making me furious.

A soft snore interrupted my mental tirade with my wolf and I glanced back at Kera. She lay curled toward the fire with her bare legs drawn up to her chest and her hair wrapped around her like a blanket.

Did she fall asleep on me?

My wolf snickered in response.

I turned to Skoll. His eyes were closed but there was a wolfish smile on his ugly snout that rested protectively against his mate's head. I could probably coax him to shift and sit with me. But one look at his comfortable position and I knew he wasn't moving.

Instead, I looked around the small campsite. We were in the middle of nowhere, deep in the forest of Fenrir lands. I pushed out my senses to check the perimeter, but there was nothing in these woods that posed a threat to the predators sleeping here.

The only threat was in my mind which was still racing. It'd be hours before my thoughts calmed down enough to let me sleep. Kera shivered a little as she pulled her legs closer and my wolf let out a protective whine.

She's cold. Let me keep her warm.

Why doesn't she sleep in her wolf form? I smoked the last hit from my cigarette and tossed the remains into the fire.

Because her wolf wants me. The cocky beast of mine sighed like I was the stupid one.

Kera was smarter than she let on. If our wolves had free reign, they would bond quicker and it'd be harder to tear them apart. She was protecting herself from me. I don't know why that thought dropped a stone in my stomach like it did.

I wasn't a total asshole though. The least I could do was lay beside her to drive away the chill of the night. Would that be inappropriate? I was in uncharted territory here and didn't like not having a plan.

"You're making me anxious," Kera whispered. The sound of her voice in the quiet made my heart jump. "Lay down and go to sleep."

I growled at being told what to do, but slowly made my way around the fire anyway. It was late. She was tired. Sleeping beside her would keep both of us warm.

"What are you doing?" Her entire body stilled, tensing as the pull of our bond sparked when I laid on the ground behind her back. There was an inch of air between us. The bond was almost a tangible thing, electricity tingling along the muscles of my shoulders and across my spine.

"Laying down as you demanded, princess," I grumbled, giving into the bond for now. Heat flared from her skin through the thin shirt as I pressed my back against hers. My wolf let out a small howl of triumph at the simple gesture.

"No funny business," she warned in a voice heavy with sleep. The command brought a smile to my face that I didn't bother to hide in the dark.

"I don't do funny either." I pulled my beast back, ignoring the challenge her Alpha power invoked. Kera huffed in response as she adjusted her head on her arm.

But she didn't pull away.

My eyes closed and I prepared for the onslaught of random thoughts to arrive. The soft crackle of the fire and the late breeze drifted through the trees overhead. All around us was a peaceful sensation, made even more calming by Kera's rich, earthy scent. And there was nothing in my mind. No noise. No images. No worries. Just the sensation of her back pressed against mine while we laid on the dirt. I yawned as I felt myself falling asleep.

"Jareth," Kera said, the huskiness of her voice followed me to the dark depths of unconsciousness. My name on her lips was a sweet melody that must have come from a dream. "I'm serious. Keep your dick in your pants."

7
† Kera †

Dark eyelashes fluttered against his sharp cheekbones. I edged myself slowly away from the Alpha sleeping behind my back. He looked so innocent and warmly delicious in the early morning rays of sunshine that played peek-a-boo through the branches above. I didn't want to wake him.

My gaze slipped lower, taking in his bronzed skin and intricate swirl of black ink that extended up his bicep and over his shoulder. I wanted to trace my fingers along it and commit the design to memory. It seemed simple enough to paint, but I knew I'd never be able to truly capture this moment and all the carved edges that made up the muscular shape of this man. Straight lines were hard to draw.

True to his word, Jareth kept his pants on all night and didn't touch me. I'd sensed the rising flame of his arousal and the pheromones made my wolf whine with an overwhelming need. It was torture to tease him, to watch him smile, without giving into the ache for release. But since I wasn't sure what to do with his hardening cock–biting it off was still on the table–I was grateful for his control.

Maybe he wasn't that big of a dick.

A blush colored my cheeks and my wolf purred as my eyes tracked lower to his v-line muscles peeking out of the pants that hung low on his hips.

His erection pressed against the material. It was just as big as I remembered from last night.

I quickly turned my attention to the dying fire. Another few sticks had the embers roaring to life and chasing off the chill from the early fall morning.

It wouldn't be so cold if you'd let me shift.

I shivered as I held my hands over the flames. *You would have forced him to claim us.*

So what? He's our mate. You're stalling.

I wasn't stalling. I was taking my time to decide if I really wanted to be with the beast of a man who looked so perfectly handsome while his mouth was closed and he was asleep.

"This is your ride." I mocked his voice in my head, remembering exactly why we were in this position. It wasn't the plan to travel back home on foot. I wouldn't have tossed my bag into the truck if that was the case. He'd gotten under my skin with his haughty tone and my pride took over.

I wanted to make him run.

Now I wanted to curl up next to him in the dirt and forget everything that had happened; to wrap myself in that delicious warmth and scent again.

I put my face in my hands and groaned.

"Are you okay?" Coral asked as she stretched out her paws. Skoll's wolf stirred beside her.

"I'm fine. Just thinking." I straightened up and tossed another log onto the fire.

Skoll's wolf looked between the two of us before standing and shaking the dew from his fur. *"I'll go get breakfast."*

He left in a hurry and I chuckled to myself, wondering what Coral said to him. I was proud of her for learning to control her thoughts over the pack link, but I'd miss the random slipups. It'd been fun listening to her try and speak to her wolf. They argued all the time about their memories. I had a rough idea of what it was like growing up in Ethica. The people they'd left behind, like Mia her old best friend, and the weird habits of the purists. It was entertaining to say the least.

"I'm serious." Coral's white wolf padded over and laid her snout across my lap. *"How are you holding up with this mate situation? That was one heck of an introduction."*

"He's an asshole." I pursed my lips and blew out a breath as I scratched Coral behind the ear on her favorite spot. *"But coming with us has to count for something, right?"*

Her wolf sighed and relaxed beside me. *"I dug through Skoll's memories to get the inside scoop. Skoll really loves him. But Jareth is wicked smart so he might be lacking on the emotional spectrum. I think we should give him a chance now that we know he's single."*

I stilled, not bothering to point out the fact that Skoll was also an asshole. True, he'd calmed down a bit since being mated to Coral and working with Cerberus pack, but it wasn't saying much that he approved of Jareth. Coral's wolf nudged my hand and I continued scratching her ears.

Maybe that's what Jareth needed. He'd chill out once we completed the bond. That was risky though. What if his demons were beyond saving?

As if thinking about him tugged on the cord, Jareth stirred behind me. My wolf perked up and begged me to make myself more presentable if we were going to start over, yet again, this morning.

But I didn't care if I still had leaves and twigs in my hair. This was me. I couldn't be anyone else if I tried. It was better for him to learn that now.

"What are you doing?" Jareth's voice was hoarse from sleep. The dark and raspy tone made my toes curl. I bit back a moan as I looked over my shoulder, trying to give him a warm smile.

His eyes were narrowed, focusing on my hand that was nestled in Coral's fur.

"Petting my Beta." I shrugged.

His handsome face distorted with disgust and he looked away as if I was doing something wrong.

The heat of shame that washed over me was quickly replaced by anger. "Is that okay with you?"

"It's your pack." He stood and brushed the dirt from his pants. "If you want to give out special treatment and make them weak, then it's not my problem."

"Excuse me?" I growled.

Coral's wolf backed away, snarling with her upper lip curled as she sensed the tension that radiated from me.

I was going to murder this man. "When did I give you the impression that anything about my pack was weak?"

His bicep covered in the intricate tattoo flexed as he tugged his hand through his unruly hair and he blinked the sleep from his eyes. The masculine beauty of him was in poor contrast to the egotistical nature of his beast. *Damn him for making me so confused.*

I jumped to my feet in a show of dominance, not willing to sit beneath him on the ground.

"Like I said, it's not my problem." His expression darkened as he looked me over. I cursed my traitorous body for flushing with desire.

"Someone woke up on the wrong side of the dirt this morning," I muttered, taking a step away to compose myself.

He massaged the back of his neck as he looked to the spot where we'd slept. "Speaking of weakness, what kind of Alpha travels without protection?"

I'll show you weak. I would have lunged at him, but my wolf held me back.

He's worried about our safety. She whined.

No. He's worried about his pampered ass.

Jareth glared at me, saying nothing. Like I was going to stoop to his level and answer that kind of question. If he needed protection, that was on him.

Skoll's wolf came back to camp dragging a mule deer with his teeth. The tension that radiated between the two of us broke, but I was still raging mad and somehow not hungry.

"Our guest isn't used to traveling under these conditions." I turned my back on Jareth despite the cardinal rule of never putting a predator behind you. But one of us was going to end up dead if I didn't walk away. "Make sure he's well fed and then maybe he'll be able to keep up with our pace today."

*

Check out those hindquarters.

My wolf was practically in heat as she watched Jareth's sleek black wolf race alongside us through the mountain passes. Big paws stepped on branches, clearing the path for us to run, and his presence was calming in that soothing way that only Alphas could provide.

His wolf was nice enough. I was starting to like him more than the man. Maybe that was because I couldn't hear him talk. My wolf was happy with that big beast energy. It made her purr her approval.

I didn't realize you were so horny.

I mean, look at him.

That's all I'd been doing all morning, watching the wolf as we ran. His powerful muscles bunching and releasing as he leapt over boulders alongside us. The way he paused at the creek to let my wolf drink first.

The bond was growing between our wolves and I tried to distance myself from it. In a few days, the worst of the moon sickness would pass and it would be easier to get on with our lives. We'd be able to think clearly again. Or at least I hoped we would.

I don't know what the fates were thinking when they paired me with someone like Jareth. Even if he wasn't the world's biggest jerk, our match would never work.

He was the Alpha of Anubis pack for Gods' sakes. There was no way he could walk away from his pack. Hell would have to freeze over before I left mine. I only hoped the heartache wouldn't be too much for my wolf to handle once we reached the inevitable end of whatever game we were playing out here.

The minute my paws landed on Cerberus territory, I felt the power of my land roll through me. The familiar comfort of home warmed my soul and the connection with my pack grew stronger again.

I echoed their howls in the distance as Cerberus shifters breathed a cumulative sigh of relief. Some of them might have issues with the way I led the pack, but they knew I'd do anything for them. The wolves basic need for their Alpha's return fueled me. This was my purpose.

Jareth's wolf hesitated at the border in a show of respect. My wolf whined, turning to paw the ground with what I could only describe as a wolfish nod of encouragement. The Alpha of Anubis was welcome in our lands.

Would it be too much if I requested he stay in wolf form for the rest of his time here?

Ooo. I wouldn't mind that.

*

"*Set him up in the Alpha's house,*" I told Skoll as we trotted down into the valley. That was the only reason I kept my childhood home functional. For visiting dignitaries. And that's all this was. A visit.

I needed to harden myself and my wolf against the inevitable outcome. Plus, there were things I had to take care of now that I was back and having the brooding Alpha on my heels would get annoying fast.

"*He's not going to like this,*" Skoll grumbled as he moved forward to nudge his friend's side.

"*Don't care,*" I said.

But Jareth's wolf let out a sharp whine that froze my beast in her tracks. The massive black wolf puffed out his chest and moved to block me, showing his displeasure.

Alpha instinct took over and I growled, telling him to back down. I'd deal with him later once I checked on my pack. Jareth's wolf shook his thick head from side to side. His dark blue eyes narrowed with the challenge.

Did I really think the wolf was better than the man?

He wants to stay with us, my wolf whispered, lovestruck and somehow smitten.

It hit me then how messed up my wolf was if she ignored all these red flags.

"*Fine,*" I growled, even though he couldn't hear me and sidestepped the massive beast.

82

I couldn't wait to hear him mock our little cabin. If he still chose to stay with us then–and I hadn't killed him first–he was sleeping on the couch.

8

† Jareth †

Why would she dismiss me?

It's not your fault, I soothed my anxious wolf.

He was worked up hard after our travels today. Apparently, the princess hadn't appreciated his attempts to impress her sweet wolf. My beast was a perfect gentleman. No *funny business* was had. Yet she still wanted to get rid of me as soon as we arrived in Cerberus lands.

I wondered what she was trying to hide. It's not like I didn't understand the nature of being an Alpha. She'd have work to do after being separated from her pack for the journey to the Fenrir celebration. Then again, I was starting to question what kind of Alpha she was. Her strength was evident, but I wondered if she knew how to wield it.

Curling up with her Beta this morning wasn't doing anyone any favors. For all I knew, we were walking into some giant wolf cuddle puddle which strongly contrasted with the intelligence I'd gleaned of the long-lost graveyard pack.

A surge of protective instinct had me clenching my jaw as our party traveled further into the territory and I had to remind myself that Kera was an Alpha. Her issues were not my problem.

But they might be.

Even if we chose to reject the bond, I had a duty to protect my shifters. The northern gates of the purist city needed to be guarded. Kera may not like it, but I had the resources to set up an outpost here that would keep her... I meant Cerberus pack and by extension the other packs in the region safe. Being prepared for a risk would protect my shifters from joining in a battle not on our lands.

I should have checked out Cerberus territory sooner. It was my mistake for getting lax and not thinking about this area. There hadn't been any activity from the purists up north in decades. But if I were human, this is exactly where I would target.

Hit us where we didn't expect it.

Suddenly, all the sparce information that came from my source made sense. I knew the purists were planning something big and the information gathered from the Fringes was lacking. I didn't have a team of operatives in a coalition like my father did, but I'd done well enough on my own by keeping tabs on the filthy purists.

What if this was the reason fate paired us?

The gears in my brain were spinning fast and clicking into place. Fate had sent me here for a purpose. To open my eyes to the weakness in the region and make a plan to protect them. The princess could stay in her tower, petting her wolves, while I sent resources to safeguard these lands from potential invasions. I may not be a prince charming, but I was an Alpha who could protect her... I mean all shifters.

My wolf slowed to a trot outside a rustic little cabin, panting as he continued beside his intended mate. Through his vision, I took in the scenic valley with the tall pine trees and babbling brook. Another simple log cabin sat further back in the dirt yard.

Kera shifted into her human form. Her toned backside walked in front of our line of sight. My wolf was drooling as I forced the shift. Her scent was everywhere around the cabin, in the yard, and coming from the forest. It was almost as if the smells of the valley were uniquely hers.

"This is your home?" I growled. My voice was still thick with my wolf as I processed this new information. There were no guards. No security cameras. She was alone in the middle of nowhere.

Kera turned to look over her shoulder. Her gaze narrowed and my heart skipped a beat. "If you wanted better accommodations, you should have gone with Skoll to the Alpha's house. There's a king size bed there big enough to fit your ego."

She pushed open the door to the cabin and entered without another backwards glance, leaving me out in the cold. I stood there staring like an idiot and wondering what I'd done in a past life to piss off the Gods this much. Where was Ophelia when I needed her to explain that I didn't mean any harm?

I swore on my life my sister was getting a raise. She could have all the skirts she wanted.

Fix this.

Groaning, I hurried up the porch steps and caught Kera by the arm before she slammed the door. The torrent of power that rushed against mine caught me off guard.

She growled, ready to fight. "I get it, asshole. You are so much better than me. But these are my lands and you will not disrespect me when you are a visitor here."

Her words were a slap across my face. A challenge that riled my anger. I inhaled deeply, trying to calm my instinct to make her submit, but couldn't release my hold on her arm. She looked to where I touched her. I knew I should let go. But then her skin flushed. Heat intensified her scent. My beast whined as my eyes tracked down to her bottom lip which she sunk her teeth into.

Gods, I wanted to kiss her.

Do it.

I took a step back, shaking off the spell of the mate bond. "You don't have a security system."

She stepped forward with the gleam of the challenge still in her eyes and pushed her bare breasts against my chest. I forgot how to breathe for a moment as she stood on her toes to whisper in my ear.

"I dare someone to challenge me. That's all the security I need." She yanked her arm from my gasp and strutted down the hall. I wasn't proud of the way my gaze immediately went to her sashaying hips.

My beast growled with the need to spank that little ass and throw her over my shoulder, to carry her back to Anubis lands where I could keep her safe.

The shocking part was that I agreed with him. *Shit.*

This was getting too deep. Nothing was going like planned. Which was the problem with not having a plan. Winging it had never been my style and I was on shaky ground here.

Skoll shifted on the porch and stood beside me with a knowing smile. "Since when are you this bad with women?"

"Some of us stopped playing with alpha groupies younger than others," I barked at him as I grabbed his bag and dug through it for my stuff. I needed nicotine before I punched him in his smug jaw.

"Hey, it's alright." He laughed as he grabbed the back of my neck. "The mate bond makes everything heightened. Once you calm down and embrace her emotions, you'll start to understand."

I pushed him off and lit the cigarette, exhaling a thick cloud of smoke as I smirked. "I don't have time to relax."

"What is more important than taking the time to finally connect with your fated mate?" Skoll leaned against the porch rail as he waited, giving a tender look to Coral as she brushed past him and headed inside the cabin.

I didn't have a good answer for that so I changed the subject. "Is this it? Two cabins? Are the rest of the shifters holed up in caves in the woods?"

"You know that Cerberus isn't that big, but we'll take you into town where the shifters live once the girls get dressed. Kera needs to check in." He arched an eyebrow. "Does this bother you for some reason?"

I waved off his question. "How much land is there between the border and the purist city?"

"Not this again." He groaned.

"Humor me." I leaned my arms over the porch rail and flicked ashes off my cigarette onto the dirt.

Skoll's growl of frustration was a familiar sound. "Two hundred miles."

"And what are her defenses? How is she training…" The hairs on the back of my neck stood up and the bond tugged at my chest.

"Are you planning to invade my territory, Alpha?" Kera asked.

When Skoll said she was getting dressed, I'd expected to be here a while. But Kera had just… put clothes on. She eyed me warily as she gathered her hair into a ponytail and walked down the porch steps. The sight of her exposed bare neck brought a primitive impulse that excited my beast. It choked my instincts with the challenge. The aching desire to leave my mark and tell the world she was mine.

"Don't you need makeup?" I bit out too quickly as I held back the urge to extend my fangs.

Anger pulsed through the bond and Skoll barked out a laugh as my eyes widened, realizing how wrong that question sounded.

Kera's nostrils flared as she straightened her shoulders. "Watch how you talk to me in front of my pack or I'll be forced to put you down."

I tensed, wanting to call her out on the challenge, but I was man enough to admit when I'd made a serious mistake. Especially when my wolf was howling, threatening to go feral if I didn't make this right. I snubbed out my cigarette and grabbed my clothes from Skoll's pack.

"My apologies, Alpha. I meant to comment on your natural beauty." I couldn't remember the last time I apologized. A smile lit up my face as I pulled my shirt over my head. Ophelia would be proud.

But not Kera.

Her pupils dilated. A low warning growl vibrated in her chest. I leaned into the bond, trying to decipher her emotions and see what still had her riled up. A defensive wall slammed me out so hard I almost staggered back.

She thinks you're mocking her.

Well, shit.

"You're… Um… Very natural," I continued, because the hole I'd dug wasn't deep enough.

Breathe.

I coughed to clear my throat, stalling to think of the right words to fix this, and ran my hand through my hair as I looked her straight in the eyes. "You're beautiful."

She stared, blinking, as the anger dissipated and a confused expression creased her brow. "What was that? Did you have a heart attack trying to get a compliment out?"

"Whatever it was, it sounded painful." Coral giggled as she skipped out of the cabin and hurried to her Alpha's side. "Also, Maddock left the keys in the truck and Sage wants us home for dinner."

"Is that okay with you, Alpha?" Kera's blue eyes were bright with amusement as she locked arms with her Beta.

I hopped off the steps, struggling to pull up the legs of my pants. Kera and Coral were laughing at me. My dick shriveled, trying to crawl into my body, as I buttoned the top of the slacks. I looked to Skoll for support. His lips were pressed thin, trying to hide his smile. Okay. I deserved this embarrassment.

"I'm happy to experience all that Cerberus has to offer." I swallowed down my pride. "Where are we visiting first, Alpha?"

"I was going to check on the progress in town, but since you're so eager to judge my defenses, we can stop by the training grounds to catch the end of practice today." Kera gave me a teasing smile that made something uneasy twist in my stomach as she pointed to the rusted truck in the yard. "And before you complain, *Alpha*. Yes. This is your ride."

*

I'd sat in the back of the truck like some teenage pup as the wind whipped around me and Skoll. My wolf enjoyed it, wanting to stick out his tongue, while I replayed the scenes of all our interactions so far. I couldn't figure out how I'd come across as the one who needed pampering. She was the princess here.

But maybe I'd been a fool for not reading the situation correctly. People were never my strong suit. I liked to think I was a fair and just Alpha. None of my shifters had ever said otherwise. Though there was a reason that Ophelia had needed to step into the Luna role for the pack.

I wished my little sister was here now. She'd be able to mediate. I swore again I was buying her more skirts when I returned to Anubis. She had simple requests. Shiny things and clothes.

That's when I realized I had no clue what Kera would like. I'd assumed she was a pampered princess. Everything I'd seen so far was proving me wrong. She drove the old truck like she was born to do it, earned the loyalty of my oldest friend who held no allegiance that I was aware of, and stood in front of the roughest group of shifters I'd ever seen without a flicker of fear.

She was honestly a natural beauty with her fiery red hair escaping the tie that tried to contain it and the cold steel of her stormy blue gaze. Dark clouds rolled overhead as she sent out a powerful Alpha command that caused the troops on the training grounds to stop.

I tore my gaze away from her and adopted the cool poise that came with my position. My mission here was getting less clear by the minute. I was torn between wanting to spend more time next to the powerful she-wolf to learn her secrets and needing to know that Cerberus pack would be safe.

That started with learning if these shifters were willing to die for their Alpha. From the looks of it, there wasn't much they were living for now.

Females and males—some young, most well past their prime—with more teeth missing than not stood silently as they waited for Kera to speak. There was no unity in their coloring or sweat soaked clothes, but they looked to their Alpha with a deep respect.

It was a good start.

I kept my expression neutral and did a rough calculation of the numbers. There looked to be close to two-hundred bodies here which meant half of Cerberus was training to fight if the recent population report was to be believed. This turnout was commendable. If she had a larger pack and could inspire this percentage to fight, she'd be a force to be reckoned with.

"Don't let their appearance fool you." Skoll stood stoic beside me. "Kera has created a safe haven for them. There are a few retired hunters and some cage fighters from other packs. A bunch of misfit alphas who didn't have a place to belong except in the graveyard. More keep coming every day. Maddock and I train them, but they're here for her. She gives them something they can't find anywhere else."

"And that is?" I watched an old shifter with scars where one eye should be tighten his fists at his side. Bloodlust and anger ran rampant in the crowd, drawing out the protective nature of my beast.

"Freedom." Skoll shrugged.

That wouldn't work.

My blood ran cold as I thought through the implications of what he was saying. Wolves needed structure and discipline. It was one of the reasons I didn't rely on my strength alone to lead a pack as large as Anubis.

She wouldn't be safe with this many unchecked shifters. Even if we didn't complete the bond, I couldn't in good conscience leave her here to fend for herself against these rugged beasts.

"How many have tried to challenge her?" I growled as I looked them over.

"Quite a few." Skoll laughed like this was the most amusing thing in the world. "She hasn't lost yet."

My jaw clenched and claws extended at my side as Kera walked calmly into the den of vipers. She was too relaxed. Too unguarded. It reminded me for a split second of Ophelia and how trusting she always was.

Protect her. My wolf was snarling.

"Did you miss me?" Kera asked, smiling. Catcalls and vicious barking laughter echoed through the gathered crowd.

My vision turned red. This was a dangerous game. It was no way to lead a pack. She was an Alpha. They should have shown her more respect.

She stopped walking and reached down to pat a dangerous looking wolf on the head. I stepped forward, needing to do something. To be ready in case they tried to attack.

Because she was *mine*.

Curse the Gods.

Kera was mine to protect.

The knowledge hit me like a ton of bricks, crushing my chest with the force of it. I bared my fangs as the mate bond pulsed deep in my bones, coaxing out the protective instinct that nature intended. As if she could feel the strengthening call of my beast through the bond, she turned to look at me.

Her eyes flashed with warning. "Turns out I found my fated mate."

My heart slammed hard against my ribcage. She was acknowledging our fate in front of her pack. It wasn't a declaration of love. There was no pretense as she spoke the truth. But it was a start.

The whistles and shouts of the gathered shifters grew louder as my pulse thrummed in my ears. I dug my feet into the earth to stop myself from gathering her into my arms and carrying her out of here. She whipped around to face me. The challenge gleamed in her eyes.

"But I'm not sure he's worthy of being mated to the Alpha of Cerberus pack."

Thunder rolled in the distance. Electricity gathered in the dark clouds above. The crisp fall air stilled as brown leaves hung suspended on their way down from the tree branches.

She meant to embarrass me. The princess wanted me to prove myself. She needed to know I was worthy of her time.

I grinned as I pulled my shirt over my head.

Challenge accepted.

9
† Kera †

He thinks we're beautiful.

My wolf was still riding that high while I felt the compliment like a thorn in my foot, irritating to the point where I wanted to rip it out and throw it away. Looks weren't the problem here. Even without the cursed mate bond making him glow, I'd have to be blind to deny he was handsome. If I were someone else then I could look past his arrogance and enjoy the view. But I couldn't.

The challenge simmering below the surface of each of our interactions was making me crazy. He was an Alpha wolf. I was an Alpha wolf. Those were the stone-cold facts. We'd never have a life where we weren't butting heads. I didn't want him to want me.

Or maybe I did.

This was all too complicated. The only way to calm my irrational response was to fight. I felt most alive and in control when there was violence.

It may not have been a healthy coping mechanism, but I was an Alpha.

We weren't always sane.

Jareth circled me with his hands raised and a playful smirk on his handsome face. I didn't care if he taunted me. Reaching deep inside and tugging on the strength of my wolf, I found the center that kept us steady in the face of any challenge.

Here was the place we survived.

I exhaled slowly and the world focused in sharp detail as I watched him move in slow motion. His bare feet were surprisingly nimble on the cold grass despite his muscular build. The predator watched my movements too and the thrill of the hunt pulsed through the bond.

I had to ignore that bond and the strange emotions coming through if I was going to win.

My hands relaxed at my sides and my pulse slowed to a steady beat as he jabbed with a right hook playfully, mocking me. It was a punk move.

I leaned away at the last moment, missing his outstretched fist, and drove the heel of my foot into his knee. His painful grunt echoed in my bones and a sharp pain shot up my leg.

My wolf howled in agony and I had a moment of panic. *How could I fight him if I felt his pain?*

Jareth took advantage of my distraction and threw his arms around me. I reacted out of instinct, slamming my elbow into his solar plexus before he could lock his wrists to trap me against his chest.

The pain was instant. It took my breath away.

I shoved him off and spun around to face him. There was a knowing gleam in his eyes as he staggered back. My pack was howling around us, egging me on. Cerberus shifters loved a good fight.

The noise of their cheers formed a vortex around us, pushed back by the heightened sensations of power that pulsed between us.

"You can't hurt me." Jareth smiled as his fangs extended. He raised his hands again.

"That goes both ways." I feigned right to his dominant side and slipped to the left when he lunged.

I leapt onto his back as he moved forward. My arm caught around his throat. I locked my elbow into place, catching him in a headlock.

"Submit." I growled.

He chuckled as I squeezed my legs tighter around his chest. I may not be able to draw blood without feeling it, but I would make him bend.

"Never." He stilled.

I held tighter, expecting him to throw me off. His hand moved slowly, rubbing my knee in a way that was almost tender, and continued up my thigh.

My leg burned where he touched, sending a spasm of heat to my core. I gasped as my eyes widened. One second was all it took to send me flying off his back as he spun.

Jareth toppled to the earth with me. His hand cradled the back of my head before it hit the ground as his massive body crashed onto mine.

I pulled up my legs, catching him with the balls of my feet, and kicking hard against his chest. He flew backwards, tumbling as he caught his footing.

We locked eyes as I jumped to my feet and crouched as we circled each other.

"That was dirty," I hissed, still reeling in shock from the way he touched me.

"You're telling me this isn't your idea of foreplay." His smug grin had me seeing red as he sniffed the air. "I can smell your arousal, princess."

My whole body was slick with sweat so I paid no attention to the moisture gathering between my thighs. But my nostrils flared when I caught the heat of his rising pheromones and my eyes dropped to the bulge tenting his pants.

"I'm not a princess." Growling, I charged as I pulled more strength from my beast who was howling in confusion.

A roundhouse kick connected with his jaw, sweeping him off his feet. I rubbed my chin as the pack scattered out of the way of Jareth's fall. Greg, the one-eyed mean bastard of a wolf, growled as he took a step back. I ignored the concerned whines of my shifters, barking at them to stay out of the fight, as I jumped on top of Jareth's chest.

"Submit," I yelled as I pinned his arms above his head. The kick to his jaw had to hurt because I could still feel the vibration of it in my teeth.

Jareth panted, smiling up at me through a busted lip. "Will you go out with me?"

"Whaaa—"

The asshole flipped me in a solid move until my back crashed against the dirt. Panic roared its ugly head as his weight pressed against me. I would not go down like this.

He dragged his teeth up the side of my exposed neck as I squirmed beneath him. "I'm asking you to go out with me on a date."

I ignored his tactic to derail my concentration, claws extending as I dug through the dirt between my legs and wiggled my hand free enough to grab the rod pressed against my thigh. There was a sick sense of pleasure as his eyes widened. I pulled. Hard.

It may have hurt him, but I didn't have that part and could ignore the phantom ache.

"Submit."

"You didn't need an excuse to grab my cock." Jareth arched one of his dark eyebrows, pressing into my grasp like he enjoyed the pain.

Damn this Alpha!

I twisted hard, using the leverage to flip him over onto his back. My hair had come undone from the tie and surrounded our faces like a curtain. I pinned him with one hand still firmly holding his dick and catching his wrists above his head again.

"What is wrong with you?" I growled. His wolf shone through his eyes, hungry with need, and my wolf howled in my head.

I had to stop this. I was losing control. That thought was terrifying. I wanted to spit in his face. Wanted to kiss his bloodied lips. The bond between us sparked, power arcing between our chests.

I needed to let him go, but one soft move and he'd have the upper hand. Then I'd be pinned again. He knew it as well as I did.

And I knew he was holding back.

"Is that a no on the date?" He licked the blood from his lips as he stared at my mouth.

I rolled my eyes and released him, scrambling backwards. Curse the mate bond. This was never a fair fight. As much as I wanted to force Jareth to submit and possibly break a few of his bones, I wasn't actually fond of pain.

"Do you want us to handle him, Alpha?" Greg was still growling. The rough shifters that hung out with him at the tavern moved closer to my side. You'd think after challenging me and losing he'd keep his distance. Instead, I'd grown a team of protective and slightly unhinged wolves.

"He's handled." I sighed as I rose to my full height, glancing over at the shifters who'd chosen to make Cerberus their home. Most of them were smiling. The pheromones of... whatever that fight was... still hung heavy in the air. I was half surprised an orgy didn't break out on the training grounds.

My cheeks flamed with heat as I realized the show we'd just put on.

Jareth grinned like he knew it too as he brushed the dirt from his pants. "Is that a yes on the date then?"

I yanked my hair back into the ponytail, looking to Coral with wide eyes. She stood back with Skoll, tucked under his arm, and tried to hide her amused expression with her hand over her mouth.

"Just say yes." She giggled over the mind link.

My Beta was a traitor.

I turned to my pack instead. Shifters chuckled softly, avoiding their direct gaze as they looked to their feet and baring their necks in respect.

"Ah, just say yes, Alpha Kera," someone shouted. I flared my nostrils trying to sniff out the dead beast when the rest of the pack chimed in.

"Give him a chance!"

"He didn't die!"

"Let's see what he can do."

Jareth's confused face as he looked over the group of Cerberus warriors made me laugh.

"Your people have voted?" It was more of a question than a statement.

"Maybe." I turned to leave with the adrenaline from the fight still pumping through my veins. His scent was everywhere on my body. The dusty sage and sharp spice seeping into my pores and mixing with my sweat.

It smells soooo good. My wolf was drooling.

"Maybe isn't an answer," Jareth called after me. There was genuine worry in his tone. I may not have beat him in a fight, but that submission was enough to sate my desire to win.

I bit back a smile as I turned to look at him. The wolves on the training grounds were hanging on our every word. I couldn't let them down.

"I'll schedule you in for tomorrow night." I resumed walking up the hill.

The howl of triumph that erupted from his chest set off a chain reaction with all the Cerberus warriors howling in response.

Even mean old Greg joined in.

*

The rest of the day was a blur. I'd only been gone a week, but the issues had piled up. I stared at the mass of complaints before me, feeling Jareth's swirling presence take up too much space in my office, before I broke down and told Skoll to take him away.

It wasn't a stretch to realize he was gloating. Since our stalemate on the training grounds and his date request, he hadn't said another word. I should have been grateful for the lack of teasing, but it just made me nervous instead.

Skoll had muttered something about fishing as he pulled Jareth outside. I'd hoped I'd be able to breathe once he was gone. But I felt anxious. Like I should have been anywhere else besides work and taking care of this pack which had grown even bigger in my absence.

It was their fault I had to agree to the date.

Though it was kind of sweet that they cared.

I rubbed my temples as I read over the treasury report for the hundredth time. Nothing was sticking. This was Coral's area of expertise anyway.

Let's get out of here, my wolf whined.

Smiling, I gave into her request.

*

I wanted to hurry home, but I still had a job to do. Showing face at the training grounds wasn't enough. Though I'm sure the rumors had spread like wildfire about that little show this afternoon.

The rest of the pack needed to see me. It set their wolves at ease. I swore to myself I wouldn't be an aloof figure like my father, and that required me to actually be there. Even if it was for a brief moment.

My wolf trotted through the housing units, nodding to the few shifters that waved.

If I wasn't this out of sorts, I'd stop to chat with the newcomers and ask how they were settling in. Our pack seemed to get larger every day. That meant more jobs were needed than I could provide. I made a note to hold another town meeting to see what we could come up with as a pack to make sure everyone was doing their part.

Uncle Maddock and Skoll were quick to point out that I walked a delicate line here. Other Alphas weren't so relaxed about taking in strays for a reason. But I wasn't like other Alphas. My hope was that everyone would work for the community we were building here. So far, we were doing alright.

My wolf passed through town quickly and made it to the edge of the woods, ready to release her pent-up aggression with a run straight to the cabin.

"Alpha Kera, can I speak with you for a moment?"

My wolf huffed her frustration as we turned toward the rolling hills at Kathryn's soft request.

I don't know why you're so worked up, I grumbled at my own wolf. *I said we'd go on a date.*

But what if he misses us now?

I chuckled at her enthusiasm. It was likely that he'd grown bored already and was looking for an escape. My wolf didn't think so as she picked up the pace, heading to Kathryn and Stockton's farm.

The old shifter woman sat on the front porch shucking corn. She saw me coming and waved.

"Are you alright?" I took a deep sniff, checking for any lingering tension or fear.

"More than alright." Kathryn smiled as she leaned back into her rocking chair and picked out another husk. "Ava said Owen saw you tumbling with your fated mate on the training grounds today."

My wolf's fur covered the blush that heated our skin. We raised our snout higher, not letting weakness show. *"And?"*

"My apologies, Alpha." Kathryn bent her head to the side to show submission as she worried her bottom lip. "You know how fast rumors spread. Will we be seeing more of Alpha Jareth around here?"

As if I would continue to feed the rumor mill. I huffed at her statement.

Then again, this was Kathryn. Her family may have not been strong enough to challenge Apollo, but I'd be forever grateful for the baskets of food left in the orchard when I was small and my father forgot growing pups need to eat.

I tossed her a bone. *"Maybe. If I don't kill him."*

Kathryn's laughter followed my wolf as she turned and raced back to the woods.

The quiet of the forest in the early evening was normally a soothing balm at the end of the day, but as my wolf ran, I felt the unease and doubt creeping back in.

It would be impossible for Jareth to stick around much longer. He had a pack to lead. My place was here, in the graveyard, with all my rugged shifter beasts. I knew we didn't have much, but this was home.

"Princess." I snorted to myself, remembering what he called me. Some princess I was.

He was the one who'd been given his Alpha title by his father after he passed away. I had to fight and bleed for mine.

It wasn't his fault. My wolf whined, trying to stand up for her mate. She was right. I couldn't blame him for having a normal family.

Except Jareth was anything but normal.

I'd understood him as an asshole and made my peace with it. The bond would be easy to reject because I wasn't about to be mated to an Alpha with that dark and tumultuous energy. He was deeper than the persona he projected though. Something had shifted and it bothered me.

Why was he acting this way?

He'd asked me on a date for Gods' sakes.

Who does that?

And he said we were beautiful.

Are you going to forgive him that easily?

It's time we found our happily ever after.

Life isn't a fairy tale.

I didn't want her to get her hopes up any more than they already were. Wolves were simple, ruled by basic instinct, but they couldn't understand how cruel people could be.

I had to protect us both because no one else would.

10
† Jareth †

My wolf was oddly silent as I sat in the shade beneath the oak tree near the rushing creek. He seemed to think we'd won the challenge against Kera and was content that things were moving in the right direction now that we were taking her on a date. I, however, couldn't understand what had prompted me to blurt out that request. In the heat of the moment, it felt like the right thing to do. But now I was questioning everything.

Like always.

To settle my racing thoughts, I started sketching out plans on some paper I'd swiped from Kera's office. The tree coverage in the area would make solar power unpredictable. Along the hike out here, I memorized the flow of the creek and mapped the hills to try and plot the best course for a hydro-electric station. It was all theoretical for now, but the initial concepts were my favorite part to work on. It'd been years since I started something new.

"I'm assuming you aren't going to fish." Skoll sighed as he reeled in his line.

I looked up from my sketch to the forgotten pole lying at my feet with the line drifting downstream. "Nothing's biting."

A grumbling growl was followed by heavy footsteps up the bank. The pack enforcer, the Sigma

Maddock, muttered something about *"idiots"* under his breath as he carried a stringer with eight fat trout slung over his shoulder. The golden sun sparkled off their rainbow scaled skin.

"What's his problem?" I tucked the pencil behind my ear and filled the space in my fingers with a new cigarette.

"He doesn't like you." Skoll chuckled as he took a seat on the boulder beside the oak tree. "Can you blame him?"

"I've long since grown past the stage of caring if people like me," I spoke through clenched teeth, holding the cigarette between them as I lit it with a match. On the exhale of smoke, I cast a side glance to my friend. "Why doesn't he like me?"

Skoll stared at me like I had two heads. He was the only alpha my wolf would tolerate outright challenging him and getting away with it. We had too much history to be offended by his antics now.

"Better you than me I guess." He tossed a rock into the creek and leaned back on his elbows. "But you should know that Maddock is protective of the girls. Kera is his niece so he has double the reason not to like you. Can't say that I blame him with the way you've been acting lately."

"What's that supposed to mean?" I crushed the cigarette in the sand. A bad taste coated my mouth. Since when did Skoll care about feelings? Much less talk about them.

"I'm saying you haven't made the best introduction to your fated mate." He stared at the water.

The bugs danced on the rapids and reeds of the shoreline. Crickets chirped in the forest behind us. A soft breeze rattled the orange and red leaves on the trees above.

"I have no clue what you're talking about."

Skoll choked on his laughter. "You can't be serious. Sometimes I wonder if that twisted brain of yours isn't screwed down tight enough. What happened to the Jareth I once knew that could whistle any shifter woman into his bed? If he could see you now, he'd be laughing with me."

A smile crept onto my face as I remembered how young and dumb we once were before I learned the truth of this world. It wasn't just the purists and their motives that made me cynical. I was tired of dealing with shifters too. Females especially.

None of them held much substance. I did have fun with the alpha groupies a long time ago until I could no longer play their games. Hence another reason my sister was acting as Luna. It helped keep the power-hungry women at bay.

I didn't fault them though. A young unmated Alpha ruling over the largest pack in the region was too good an opportunity to pass up. Wolves loved a good challenge just as much as they loved sex.

An image of Kera sweaty and gripping my cock in her fist stirred a deep longing in my groin.

She was different. I didn't realize it when I first saw her, but I was curious to learn more now.

Told you. My arrogant wolf smiled.

I growled to quiet the beast.

"I think if you'd have said who Ophelia was in the beginning, things might have worked out differently," Skoll mused.

"Be careful." I chuckled. "You're not used to thinking. Besides, it wasn't my fault that she assumed. And I did just ask her on a date."

"Yeah." Skoll rubbed his jaw. "I'm surprised she said yes. I'm also surprised you asked."

"Me too." I folded up the drawing and tucked it in my back pocket.

"What changed? Why did you ask?" Skoll's eyebrows lifted as he studied me. Coral was really wearing off on him. He didn't use to talk this much.

I grabbed the pole from the ground, slowly reeling in the fishing line. The worm had fallen off the hook. No wonder I didn't get a bite. "I'm not sure. There was a moment there where I knew I had to take care of her and wanted to make her smile. It was an overwhelming urge."

"Welcome to the start of the rest of your life. That feeling only gets stronger." Skoll jumped to his feet. "Do you know where you're taking her?"

A flicker of nervousness made my beast whine and I rubbed the back of my neck. "I don't suppose you could help me with that."

"The Alpha of Anubis is trusting someone else with a task this great." His face lit up with amusement and he dramatically winked. "I know just the place, but you're going to have to trust a witch to help us out too."

*

It wasn't that I didn't trust witches. I didn't trust most anyone. But plans were quickly settled for our date tomorrow night. Sage and Coral seemed excited to help. When that was taken care of, I paced the inside of the small cabin and inhaled Kera's scent to calm my beast. It was strange to be on the other side of an Alpha's time. How long was I supposed to wait until she got done for the day?

My wolf wanted to shift and go find her, but I'd already taken the first step by planning out the date. Alpha pride wouldn't let me act like some needy pup. She'd come to me when she was ready. I wasn't known for my patience, but I held to what little I had and waited.

Ophelia wouldn't believe it.

I smirked at the thought. All of this was so out of character that I was starting to surprise myself. Maybe I needed this. I'd think of it like a vacation. We'd done some fishing, slept under the stars, and I'd made enough rough sketches to get some of my engineers here to bring Cerberus out of the dark ages.

They needed to reduce their dependence on bio-diesel. My wolf was not comfortable with Kera continuing to do business with Alpha Oscar of Cadejo pack on a regular basis and being indebted to that shifter.

I'll feel better when she wears our mark.

If she wears it. But I didn't bother to correct him. My thoughts were racing enough without starting another fight with my beast.

I continued to pace, casting random glances at the closed door at the end of the short hallway. That's where her scent was the strongest. Kera's bedroom.

My curiosity kept edging me closer.

What kind of secrets would I find inside?

I thought back over the past few days, realizing Kera never shared anything about herself. If she was a private person, her room would tell me more.

This is a bad idea. My wolf scolded as I leaned against the door.

I'm not going in. I only wanted to take a quick peek. The temptation was too great to resist. Slowly, I edged the door open and was rewarded with a stronger wave of her earthy scent.

I scanned the room, looking for something to stand out and reveal her secrets to me. Her smell was the perfect drug. It soothed my beast and grounded my body, keeping me rooted to the spot.

There wasn't much to look at though. Everything in the simple bedroom was tucked neatly into place. The drawers were closed. The bed was made. There wasn't even a speck of dust. If it wasn't for her intoxicating scent, I wouldn't think anyone slept here.

Which only riled my curiosity more.

No one lived this plainly.

My bet was on secrets hiding behind the closed closet doors.

Don't do it, my wolf warned as my feet itched to take another step.

The hairs on the back of my neck stood up. I yanked on the handle, slamming the bedroom door shut just as the front door to the cabin swung open.

Kera, in all her feminine Alpha glory, stood like a fiery archangel in the hallway with her arms crossed over her chest. "Looking for something?"

"I…" I was out of my element here, caught red-handed like an errant pup.

Told you, my wolf voiced his disapproval.

I straightened my shoulders, meeting the challenge head on like a man. "I wanted to see what you were hiding in your underwear drawer."

I admit, it wasn't my smoothest line. Another female would have eaten it up though. Someone who wasn't the tornado barreling toward me with murder in her eyes.

"That's none of your business," Kera snapped as she shoulder checked me out of the way and opened her door.

Apologize now. Make this right.

"Isn't it?" I smirked. "I mean, you are my fated mate. Shouldn't I know what kind of underwear you own?"

Her face flushed with anger. Or maybe it was embarrassment. The emotions coming through our growing bond were still too hard to read. But her pretty pink cheeks did something to me, pulled out a desire to make them flush deeper.

"You haven't earned that privilege." She moved to slam the door in my face.

I laughed, catching it with my forearm as the wood splintered with a small crack. "You're fun to tease."

Kera took a step back, looking me over as the flush spread down her neck and dipped below her shirt. "If this is how a date with you is going to be, consider my consent revoked."

No... No... No. My wolf panicked.

I leaned against the doorframe and smiled. "We can skip the date and go straight to bed." I motioned to the mattress behind her.

Please shut up, he begged.

Kera growled and her eyes flashed with her wolf. "You haven't earned that privilege yet either."

Another challenge?

My wolf and I froze, cocking our heads to the side. Both of us were intrigued.

"And what will it take to earn that privilege?" My voice came out huskier than I intended.

"Don't sneak into my room for starters." She moved to close the door again.

I caught it easily, hoping I didn't smash it this time. "You are hiding something."

"What? No." Her gaze flicked to the closet briefly, a tell that even the greenest Alpha should be able to hide. It dawned on me that she sucked at lying, which only fueled my burning curiosity about this woman.

"If that's true, let's look in here." I strolled into the room with renewed confidence.

"Don't you dare." She growled, leaping onto my back as her arm locked around my neck. The signature move was cute.

"Too late," I choked out, laughing as she cut the air to my windpipe and marched forward with her clinging like a monkey to my back. She was solid muscle, but weighed nothing. Stars danced in my vision as I zeroed in on my target. I wanted to see what was behind those closet doors.

Kera yanked my head to the side with a frustrated snarl and used the momentum to spin us. She landed on her feet. My back crashed against the wall, making the plaster crack as she pinned me with her forearm across my neck.

"This is my room. Get out." The Alpha fury in her voice spoke to my beast, but not in the way she intended.

It was too good. The challenge drew at the primal part of my nature that craved submission. Our wolves shone in both of our eyes as I pressed my neck harder against her arm.

My nostrils flared as I inhaled her delicious scent. "Make me."

With a furious growl, she hooked her ankle behind my leg, intending to sweep me off my feet. Points to the fiery minx. It might have worked if she had my height advantage.

I caught her calf and lifted, intending to toss her onto the bed. She twisted hard, dislodging my grip, and I staggered forward. Kera jumped behind me.

A grin spread across my face as I whirled on her, only to see her fist as it connected with my nose.

She'll get hurt. My beast whined.

I wiped the blood from my mouth, watching as she pinched the bridge of her nose and stumbled back.

Like in the training grounds this morning, the adrenaline and logic warred within me. I didn't want her to hurt, but my instinct was to teach her a lesson.

The fight wasn't the problem. I'd had my fair share of them. But it physically destroyed me to see her in pain. I raised my hands, opting for a defensive position as I calculated the best way to safely pin her in submission.

She used the moment to kick me in the ribs.

As pain exploded across my chest, I realized she was schooled at hiding her own weakness. She had to feel it. Yet she didn't flinch as she charged forward.

Someone has hurt her, bad. He snarled, clawing at my mind.

I lost all sense of rational thought as my beast rose to the surface and growled with a protective fury as I wrapped her in my arms.

We fell back to the bed. The frame cracked beneath us. Kera screamed. The sound of her cry broke through the blinding bloodlust and cleared my mind.

"Are you hurt?" I jerked away to look her over.

She drew up her knee, slamming it into my side. As I was flipped to my back, stunned, Kera landed on top. Her pelvic bones slammed into my stomach.

She punched the pillow next to my head, sending goose feathers flying. "Gods! What is wrong with you? Stop holding back."

My vision tunneled as I slowed my breathing. Soft white feathers drifted down from the busted pillow and fell around her fiery red hair like snowflakes. Her eyes were intense, storm clouds brewing in a clear blue sky. The image was gauzy, angelic, and burned into my memory. I'd be a lucky bastard to wake up to this every day.

"Why are you smiling?" She grabbed my shirt, fully intending to shake some sense into me. I needed it because I couldn't help the hope that this might end with a kiss.

I licked my lips, keeping my hands pressed at my sides instead of rubbing them up her legs like my beast was urging me to. "You proved it."

"Proved what?" Kera groaned as she scrambled off the bed. She stood with her chest heaving, looking around the damage in her room.

We'll fix it.

I know.

"Proved you have something to hide." I jumped to my feet and shrugged, intending to leave it at that. I had my proof. Though I wasn't sure what I was trying to prove anymore. The mate bond pulsed stronger, settling in my bones, and I rubbed my chest as I turned to leave.

The closet door creaked open behind me and I froze. Maybe I wasn't ready to leave just yet. I wanted more secrets from the graveyard princess and was curious to know what skeletons she kept.

I want to know who hurt her so we can kill them. My wolf growled.

I stuffed down his anger and turned back. Kera was staring out the window at the setting sun. The weight of the world seemed to hang on her shoulders and she looked older, more tired, than she should have been. The kind of dejection that could only come from an abused pup. My heart squeezed in my chest as I realized just how deeply she'd been hurt.

I think she already killed him.

I wish I would have done it first.

Me too.

"You don't have to show me anything, Kera. I was playing with you." I coughed to clear my throat.

The creases of her face smoothed out as she smiled and the hope in her gaze made the heaviness in my chest lighter. "If you mock me for what I'm about to show you, I swear I'll castrate you."

*

"These are…" My voice trailed off with a whistle and I rubbed the back of my neck, holding the canvas up with my free hand as I angled it to the window to see the swirling mass of…

"Garbage," Kera mumbled as she snatched the painting back.

120

I was never one to mince my opinion, but watching her hug the canvas against her chest and the blush creeping onto her cheeks that she tried to hide behind a scowl had me searching deep for a diplomatic thing to say.

"Really, they're not that bad. What's this one supposed to be?"

"Shut up." Kera groaned as she shoved the canvas into the closet with the others. "I was trying to paint my favorite lake."

Oh, that's what it was. There was blue. And a lot of black. Maybe a stick in the mud. "I can definitely see that now."

I bit down on my lip to hide my smile as her pretty pink cheeks reddened further.

"You're mocking me, Alpha."

"I wouldn't dare." I placed my hand over my heart. "How long have you been painting for?"

"A few months." She closed the closet door and refused to meet my eyes. "No one knows, so don't say anything."

"You're trusting me with your secrets." I arched an eyebrow. She growled, looking at her feet.

That knowledge floored me. I wanted more. More secrets. More moments. More of a connection through the bond. More time before I had to go back to my pack.

I reached out to touch her chin, tilting her face up as those intense blue eyes glared at me. Her power pulsed with the need to fight, but there was a vulnerability there beneath the surface that I ached to dive into.

"Have you had any lessons?" I asked softly, staring at her rose-colored lips and the freckles that dotted her nose so our wolves wouldn't challenge each other through direct eye contact.

"There's not enough time for them." Kera pushed my hand away and drew in a ragged breath.

She was right. There was never enough time.

I hated that for her.

"We have some artists in Anubis that teach classes. I could send them here or you can come there." The words slipped out. The air between us stilled as we both recognized them for what they were. A hint of a promise for an uncertain future. It wasn't something I wanted to take back.

"Maybe." She sighed, giving a small smile that had my wolf howling. Kera took a step away and shook her head, breaking whatever spell was being cast between us as she sniffed the air.

"Come on. Dinner is almost done and I don't like to be late."

11
† Kera †

There was something seriously wrong with me.

No there isn't.

My wolf shook out her coat with a huff and continued her run through the woods.

Something *was* wrong though.

My stomach was in knots and an anxious twitch had me twisting my hands behind my back all morning. My wrists freaking ached.

I had to finish checking the repairs on the northern roads to hold up my end of the treaty with Cadejo pack and then I was done for the day. But the minutes were ticking by so slowly and also going faster than I wanted them to. I'd promised to be ready at five o'clock.

Why had I agreed to go on this stupid date?

Oh, that's right. My pack had betrayed me and the mate bond wouldn't leave me alone. That frustrating Alpha had gotten under my skin. It was my wolf's fault I wanted to see him again.

You were the one who wanted to give him another chance. She rolled her eyes.

I did because normally I trusted my gut instincts, but with the way my stomach ached now, I wasn't sure if that was the right thing to do.

Last night I'd seen a completely different side of him. It shocked the hell out of me. He'd been playful almost, and so sweet to Sage by offering to help with the dishes. Even my uncle thawed a little and sat at the table after dinner with us. Skoll liked him. Coral did too. Now I needed to figure out what I thought.

He was handsome. We all knew that. I did hate that he held back in a fight. He spoke like a true asshole, but his actions didn't mirror that part of him. I liked the way he touched me.

And I didn't like it at all.

Curse this mate bond. My head was as messed up as my stomach. I didn't know if I needed to eat or throw up.

You're nervous. My wolf teased as she slowed to a trot beside the construction crew.

Am not. I ignored her.

They'd made a decent amount of progress. If this pace kept up, it'd be finished by the end of the week. Then I could give Alpha Oscar the go ahead to start transporting his bio-diesel through our lands again.

Greg stood at the end of the line with his team and wiped the sweat off his brow as he waved to me.

"Everything looks great." My wolf nodded at the burly old shifter. I still hadn't asked how he'd got the injury to his eye, but he'd been a beast to fight in the challenge so I knew it didn't come easy.

"Thanks, Alpha." He bared his neck in respect. "Also, me and the boys got to talking. If you need some help with that slick Alpha, we know some deep holes in the hills."

"Good to know." I chuckled, shaking off his misplaced concern. This was one thing I had to handle myself.

I can't wait to handle his wolf.

Her enthusiasm made me laugh. At least one of us was having fun. She spun on her paws and took off through the woods, howling her delight.

I tried to shove my worry down deep so it didn't bother her. It was one night. That wouldn't kill me. I'd survived much worse.

*

"What are you going to wear?" Coral screeched as soon as I opened the door to the cabin.

I hesitated with one foot on the threshold, ready to make a run for it, but Skoll caught me by the arm and yanked me inside.

"Good luck," he whispered as he made his escape. I expected the betrayal from him, so I didn't growl at his retreating form.

"Coral…" I started, sucking in a calming breath.

"No arguing." She moved quickly, grabbing my hand in a vicelike grip and dragging me down the hall before I could process what was happening. I cursed myself for helping her come in to her shifter strength.

"I have the curling iron heating up, but we can do braids if you want. I know the makeup needs to be minimal. I do love it when we outline your eyes though. It really makes them pop."

Gods. Did she ever breathe?

Coral stopped walking as she turned to face me. "I laid out some clothing choices on your bed."

Frowning, I peered over her shoulder to the disaster of a bedroom I'd slept in after our scuffle last night and tried to think of a quick explanation. Everything was fixed and set back to place. Even my blankets were tucked the way I liked them.

"Did you fix my room?"

Coral's eyes widened as she took a step back. "No. Was there something that needed to be fixed?"

I inhaled deeply, picking up Jareth's lingering scent. It was strongest on the couch where he'd slept, but still fresh as it drifted from my room. I ran my hand over my face to hide my smile. If Coral noticed, she didn't comment.

"Anyway, we have less than an hour to get you ready. Do you know what you want to wear?"

"Clothes." I shrugged.

Coral grimaced. "Casual chic it is. Now get your frustrating butt in the shower, Alpha."

*

After arguing with my Beta for far longer than necessary, I ended up in a pair of dark jeans with a loose-fitting scooped neck gray t-shirt. She wouldn't relent on the hair though.

I stood in front of the bathroom mirror looking at the reflection that wasn't quite me as she curled the last few strands. The hair and sheen of sticky lip balm weren't the only things different. My eyes seemed brighter and more open even without the mascara she didn't get to use. I inhaled deeply, closing them.

Coral whistled as she laid the last warm curl against my back and ran her fingers through all the work she'd done. "Hot damn girl. You are a natural beauty."

Her use of the term natural made my lips twitch. That's what Jareth had said. But I wasn't sure if he meant it. And I wasn't sure why I cared.

She's right. We look nice. My wolf stretched herself out languidly when she saw our reflection.

I shook out my hair like I was drying my fur coat and tried to ignore that twisting feeling in my stomach again.

"Coral, I…" I searched for the words, looking to my Beta and best friend.

"Whatever it is, you can tell me." She hopped onto the counter and swung her legs off the edge. "We've already dealt with the keeping secrets thing and that did not turn out well, so I respectfully demand that you spit it out. I'm not leaving here until you do. We can add more makeup while I wait."

Coral reached for the palate of blush to prove her point. I cringed as I raised my arms to ward off the evil powder. She growled and grabbed the brush in warning.

"Fine." I laughed, feeling a little anxious as I looked to my feet. "I've never been on a date before."

"You've never…" Her jaw dropped but she quickly snapped it shut. "Of course you haven't. Not with that asshole father of yours scaring everyone away."

She paused. "No offense."

"None taken." I shoved my embarrassment down deep so she wouldn't feel the need to comfort me. Sage and Coral were quick to jump on the reassuring Kera train. At times it was a little too much. Don't get me wrong, I loved them. But I was still learning to accept their kindness.

"Okay." Coral blew out a breath so long that her lips vibrated. Always the diplomat, she gave me a playful swat with the brush to lighten the mood. "Any other secrets I should know about?"

I shook my head, not ready to discuss more about my lacking love life and experience. There was also my little painting hobby, but she didn't need to know that until I got a little better.

You let Jareth see, my annoying wolf reminded me.

That was different. He'd somehow discovered the truth and I couldn't flat out lie.

Coral nodded, ignoring my inner turmoil like the perfect Beta she was. "It's just a date. Nothing sexual has to happen. Try to have fun and get to know one another."

"Alphas don't really have fun—" My statement was cut short by the knock on the door.

The bond flared, sending that fluttering feeling back to my stomach, and I knew it was him.

He'd slept on our couch last night. I didn't see why he needed to do the formal thing by knocking. But it was cute. I twisted my hands behind my back.

My first date.

Coral said I should have fun.

"He's here!" She shrieked, jumping off the counter and dragging me back down the hall.

Each step felt leaden. My insides were churning. I swallowed dry spit and raised my chin.

"Don't worry about impressing him," Coral said through the mind link as she fluffed my hair a final time and added out loud, "He should be trying to win you over. You're the catch here."

My smile was genuine and some of the tension I was carrying eased. Coral threw open the door. This was it.

"Flowers?" I arched an eyebrow, looking to the bouquet of late season sunflowers Jareth held in his hand. It was easier to focus on those instead of the way he leaned against the porch post. His posture was relaxed and he made the dressy black slacks and black button up shirt look effortless. The masculine scent of his made my wolf want to howl.

His easy smile dropped and a frown tugged at his lips as he raised the bouquet to his nose. "You don't like flowers?"

I made an awful giggling snort sound and wanted to smack myself.

"She loves flowers." Coral shoved me to the side. "I'll put them in water. You two have a nice time." She snatched them from his hand.

"Hey. Those are mine." I spun around, nearly colliding with the door as she slammed it in my face.

"They'll be here when you come home, Alpha. Go get something to eat before you get mean."

I smiled sheepishly and looked back to Jareth.

He stood with his elbow raised. "Shall we?"

I hesitated. A cold sweat broke out onto my skin. I had to grab his elbow. Let him lead me down the porch steps. It was a simple gesture.

Why was this so complicated then?

He watched me expectantly as if he could sense my dilemma. Hell, maybe he could through the bond. Relaxing, I tried to sense his emotions. The normally turbulent tension was gone.

Because he wants to take you on a date.

I nodded, getting myself together with a deep inhale as I slipped my hand through the crook of his arm. The connection through our mate bond sparked. But this was nothing like fighting or the accidental touch where it felt so intense that it almost burned.

This was a gentle breeze. The first stroke of a brush on canvas. A soft sigh escaped my lips.

I didn't know what to think about that.

"Where are we going?" I blurted out, trying not to read too deep into anything. "I have a place I could show you since this is my territory after all."

We walked arm in arm across the yard. Jareth remained silent. A small smile played on his face. If I thought I liked him quiet before, I was wrong.

"Are you going to tell me?"

"No." He opened the passenger door to my uncle's truck. "It's a surprise."

"I'll drive." I motioned for him to get in.

"What part of surprise don't you understand?" He folded his arms over his chest and waited. The challenge in his tone stoked my need to win. We hadn't even started this date and I already wanted to fight. This was a bad idea.

The flash of the curtain closing in the window of the cabin caught my attention and I cursed under my breath. Coral would never let me live it down if her work on my hair went to waste.

You can do this. Give him a chance.

"Fine." I growled as I climbed onto the passenger seat. "Have you ever even driven a truck before?"

*

I swear on all the Gods that he had never driven a truck. This old thing wasn't built for speed. I clung to my seatbelt, too stunned to reach out through my pack link and get the details on this *surprise*. I was surprised alright.

Surprised we didn't die.

Jareth careened onto Main Street and slammed on the brakes outside of the Witch's Tavern.

"Who taught you how to drive?" I closed my eyes and thanked the moon that we made it.

"I taught myself." He was so damn smug. "I've always had an affinity for mechanical things. And I only went that fast so you didn't have time to ask around and ruin the surprise."

"How did you know I would…" I blinked, looking up to see him smiling at me.

If the near-death experience didn't take my breath away, the way the golden rays of the setting sun that played on his bronze skin and the smile that lit up his face sure did.

He was so handsome that it wasn't fair.

And he is dangerous, I reminded myself.

We're still alive. My wolf sighed.

At least one of us was having fun.

"Sage is in on the surprise?" I unclipped the seatbelt.

"Is that okay with you, princess?" A lock of his unruly black hair fell forward, covering half his face as he looked away. It was the first time he'd seemed unsure of anything since I met him. My instinct was to push his hair back and reassure him that his doubt wasn't necessary.

But I couldn't let the insult slide.

"I'm not a princess." I pushed open the door, grateful to be on the steady ground again, and glanced back to make sure he was coming. "Besides, I already told you that if Sage is cooking, I'm there and not late."

Jareth's laughter was making me nervous. I'd grown used to his snarky comments and general asshole-ness. The Alpha who stood next to me now and insisted on opening the door was like a beautiful stranger. My wolf was loving it, convinced these were his true colors, but I was waiting for the mask to fall.

"After you." His hand swept to the side as he stepped back. I ignored the urge to growl as I walked into the tavern. And I'm glad I did.

The family picnic style tables were cleared out, leaving a small circular table draped with a white linen cloth in the center of the room. A bread basket and fine China with glass flutes reflecting the amber light sat on top. Every surface in the rest of the space held pewter candle sticks and vases of sunflowers.

I looked down at my clothes, suddenly feeling underdressed in a place I visited every day.

"You're beautiful," Jareth said softly as he closed the tavern door.

There it was again. That compliment. At least he hadn't choked getting it out. I sniffed, sensing Sage and Ava in the kitchen, grateful it was only the two of them here to watch me look like an idiot.

Jareth moved to pull out one of the two chairs by the table. He stood beside it with an encouraging smile. Steam drifted from the fresh baked rolls in the basket and I groaned, forgetting my awkwardness in favor of bread as I pulled out the other chair and plopped down on it.

Jareth coughed to clear his throat.

"What?" I spoke over a mouthful of bread.

He looked to the empty seat he was still standing beside and shook his head before finally sitting down.

"Ophelia usually sets up my events so you'll have to forgive me if I forgot something." He pulled the napkin from the table and put it over his lap.

I chewed thoughtfully, grabbing a second roll. It was sweet that he set this up for me, but I had to wonder how many other dates he'd been on like this one. The thought of him with someone else made my stomach a little queasy. I sniffed the roll discretely, wondering if something was wrong with it.

He better not be seeing anyone else. My wolf growled possessively.

The bread was fine. It was the mate bond making things strange. I took another bite.

"Why didn't you tell me Ophelia was your sister the minute we first met?" I asked. The question was still bothering me.

He poured water from the pitcher into the crystal glasses. "I never hid it from anyone. Those who know us, know the circumstances. Anyone else is free to ask."

"You wanted me to ask you." I took a sip from my water. There was something off about it. A hint of mint. Thankfully I was used to Sage sneaking strange herbs into her food so I didn't spit it out.

"Weren't you curious?" He arched an eyebrow, studying me.

"I tend to take people at face value. If you wanted to be honest, you would have." I shrugged. There were four rolls still in the basket. I grabbed another and left the rest for him so it would be even.

His gaze dropped to the table and the silence was made even louder by me swallowing a piece of bread. I tried to make it quieter and failed.

"My apologies, Alpha." He raised his eyes and looked at me with a sad smile as he reached for a roll. "I didn't realize you trusted people. Ophelia is a lot like that too. She makes a good Luna."

I didn't point out that I didn't trust many people, but I did give the benefit of the doubt until someone proved themself untrustworthy. It seemed toxic to keep going around in circles about this though. If we were going to move on, I had to put it in the past.

"I understand needing a good Luna. Sage has really stepped in for me." I laughed as I tried to change the subject. "I wasn't sure if I'd ever meet a mate that could handle the duties of Luna for our pack."

"I'm glad you have the witch then." The knife in his hand gleamed as he speared the bread with a slab of butter. A growl vibrated in his chest, but his eyes were clear with an apology as he pushed another roll in my direction.

I leaned into the bond, trying to sense his emotions. When the same sick feeling twisted in my gut, I could put a name to it. Jealousy.

He's struggling because he wants us.

135

I smiled, sensing the truth as I took another bite of bread. Actions did speak louder than words.

Now I needed to figure out if I wanted him too.

12
† Jareth †

Don't screw this up… Don't…

My wolf was on a frantic loop as he paced the confines of my mind, driving me crazy. No amount of reassurance could convince him that we were doing alright. At least I assumed we were.

Nothing had been broken yet.

I wanted to use this time to really get to know her. My expectations hadn't been that high, but Kera had already surpassed them. There was no pretense to her. No ulterior motives. She wasn't trying to impress anyone. The girl was just hungry.

It was easy to… relax.

I couldn't remember the last time I'd felt this way, but sitting in silence with her was as natural as breathing. I didn't find myself drifting away like I normally did. The lack of mindless chatter was a pleasant distraction. If anything, I wanted to know more about what she was thinking.

I tried to lean into the bond and discover the power behind it. Scientifically, I understood that feeling each other's emotions had a survival benefit. It made sense to be able to sense danger for our mate.

But it was more complicated than that.

The emotions came with feelings and those were another puzzle altogether.

I did love a good puzzle though.

The blissful expression on her face when she tasted the apple crumble served for dessert was mesmerizing. Was it pure joy? Reminiscent of a childhood memory? I tried to remember what my father had said about the mate bond with my mother, but all I had were fuzzy images of how they seemed to share everything. I wanted to experience that.

She pulled the clean spoon out of her mouth and her moan of approval almost knocked me out of my chair. Her zest for life warmed an empty place in my soul. I had to taste this pie.

Her stormy blue eyes met mine across the table and the soft candlelight reflected in them. "Why are you smiling? Is there something in my teeth?"

I shook my head as I took a bite of our shared dessert. She'd left me exactly half like she'd done with the bread rolls. I don't know that she was even aware of what she was doing. She was taking care of herself, but also taking care of me.

Try as I might to sort through what was true and what was enhanced by the mate bond, I couldn't help but think that Kera was the realest person I ever met. I wanted more time with her. But even as I let myself enjoy being in the present, doubt crept in.

It wasn't only our future that was uncertain. It was the future of the entire world.

"Are you alright?" Kera reached across the table and laid her hand on top of my arm. The touch was grounding and soothed my beast.

I took a deep breath as I put down the spoon and passed the rest of the pie her way. "What defenses do you have in place against the purist city?"

You idiot! This is how you screw it up!

Yeah, I know. I exhaled, wishing I had a cigarette to calm my nerves.

Kera leaned her elbows on the table and smiled. "Coral told me you were paranoid about the human city. Why is that?"

I growled, hating that look on her face more than anything. It cut deeper than the others for some reason. I was used to being called crazy, but I'd hoped… I don't know what I hoped.

I hoped you wouldn't scare her off.

"I don't think being proactive about our natural enemy is paranoia." I blotted my lips with the napkin, ready to make an excuse to step outside.

"I'm listening." Kera rested her chin on her hand and picked up the spoon for the pie.

"Listening?" I smirked to hide that my heart was racing. I desperately wanted to cling to that glimmer of hope that she wasn't like the others. Kera would hear me. Even my wolf was silent in shock.

She set down the spoon and gave me her full attention. "If there is a threat or a problem I should be aware of, I'd appreciate you telling me what it is."

The breath rushed from my lungs as I looked into her stormy eyes. "Are you sure you want to know the truth?"

*

The candles had burned low by the time we left the tavern to walk the streets of the quiet backwoods town. True to her word, Kera listened.

She made it too easy to talk. At some point, I took her hand in mine as we walked past the buildings and into the woods. The moon lit up her pale skin and the faraway look in her eyes.

I'd been emboldened by her silence, but now I was nervous. "What are you thinking?"

I tried to sense her emotions through the bond and felt the guarded wall shutting me out.

She looked down to our conjoined hands like she just noticed them. "I've studied our past with the purists. Only an idiot would think history doesn't repeat itself. I can see why you're worried."

I let out a breath I didn't know I was holding, playing off the moment of weakness as I ran my hand through my hair. "It would worry me less if we had eyes inside the city walls. When my grandfather was Alpha, he started the coalition and kept shifters rotating through for intelligence. Now all I have are sources from what they call the Fringes. I've also been able to hack the government computer software, but some of the new code doesn't make sense."

"I'm not going to pretend that I understand a word of what you're saying." Her eyes met mine. There was no judgement, but a fierce protectiveness shone through. "You won't put Coral in any danger. I don't want her to go back to that place."

Her command caught me off guard and I fumbled for words. True, I had that thought, but I'd never force anyone to work for me. "I'm not stupid."

"Are you sure about that?" she teased as she nudged me with her elbow.

"It doesn't have to be Coral," I hurried to add, worried I'd lose Kera when we'd finally arrived at this point. "It was only an idea, but if we can't go on the offensive, then we should at least be building up our defenses."

Kera nodded, looking out at a distant point in the southern direction half obscured by the trees. "It's been over a hundred years since we've had any trouble from the northern gates and at least seven years since there were any problems down south."

"Which is why the shifters are getting lax," I practically begged her to understand. "But I'm telling you there is a frenzy of activity on their servers. Parts are being manufactured in excess. Training schedules are more frequent. Something is coming. Something big."

"What are the other Alphas saying about this?" It was an innocent question.

I shouldn't have growled. "They'll send me reinforcements if—when—something happens, but they can't be bothered with prevention."

"Why?" She sounded sad.

My happiness in getting through to her was muted by the pain of telling her the truth. "Because they're lazy. No one wants to leave the comfortable positions of power in their packs."

"That's not what I meant." Kera chuckled. My pride stung a bit, but she put her hand in mine again, calming my beast as she tugged us forward. "Why are the purists going to attack us? Or why did they do it before?"

I wanted to howl at the moon and thank the Gods for pairing me with this beautiful creature. These were the questions we should be asking. "I have a theory."

She looked to me from the corner of her eye and nodded for me to continue.

"Overpopulation. Their cities can only hold so much. Wiping us out would allow them to expand."

Kera shook her head. "Ethica isn't the only purist city on the continent. There are others out there surrounded by shifter territory."

"And they have these same problems too," I explained. "Which makes me think my theory is solid. Purists built their bubbles hundreds of years ago. Nothing lasts that long without rotting."

"You think they want more land," Kera mused. "I don't buy that theory."

"Do you have a better one?" I laughed.

"No." She shoved me playfully with her shoulder. "But if they wanted us dead, why haven't they tried harder?"

"We're not an easy enemy to defeat."

"Spoken like the arrogant wolf you are." Kera winked. She released my hand and looked to the southern night sky again. The constellations above twinkled as she twisted her wrists behind her back.

Some deep part of me thawed in that moment, realizing how calm this conversation was. I was used to yelling and denial. Shifters didn't like the idea that there was an enemy bigger than them. I

142

would have expected Kera to be the same with her fiery disposition. But the curious she-wolf continued to surprise me.

"Thank you," I said, really meaning it.

"For what?" she asked.

"Listening."

Kera sighed. The sound of it tugged at my heart. "You've been carrying this alone for a long time, haven't you? The least I can do is listen."

She gets me.

I didn't see that coming.

Neither did I, but I wasn't going to let the moment pass. This woman was perfect. More so than any wolf I'd ever met and not only because of her looks. Her soul was pure. She was a calming presence in the midst of a storm.

And she was strong.

Strong enough to be an Alpha's mate.

I could only hope I was strong enough to be her mate too.

I reached out, driven by the urge to touch her, and tucked a lock of hair behind her ear.

"What are you doing?" She wrapped her hand around my wrist as I stepped into her space.

"I'm going to kiss you if that's alright."

Her breath caught and her pulse quickened, thumping hard at the spot below her collarbone where I ached with a primal need to leave my mark. She was everything. I wanted this more than anything.

My lips caressed the smooth skin of her neck as I inhaled her earthy scent, breathing it in like air.

Kera gasped as she took a step back. The moonlight reflected off the wolf and challenge in her glowing eyes. "If you want to kiss me, you have to catch me first."

13
† Kera †

So… he might be crazy.

But if that was true, what did that make me?

Spies in the purist city, really? Those were shifter tall tales. If Coral and Sage had never showed up, I wouldn't believe half the things I'd heard. Hearing them now, coming from Jareth's gorgeous lips, was another thing entirely.

Gods, stop thinking about his lips.

It was kind of hard to do since I literally took off running through the forest like a scared rabbit when he'd tried to kiss me.

Get control of yourself, Kera.

I wasn't scared. I needed a moment to think. Because the sad thing was, I believed him. Or at least believed that he believed what he was saying. He spoke with so much conviction it was hard to dismiss.

The longer I sat and listened, the more I wanted to give into illogical impulses. Like seeing what his lips tasted like. Or storming the purist city. Or throwing caution to the wind and giving fate a chance. That's basically what I'd done by giving into the wolf's instinct to chase.

I was a mess.

This is fun. My wolf howled.

At least she was having a good time.

I leaned into her instincts, staying in human form as I raced through the familiar terrain. I wasn't even sure if I wanted to kiss him or if the mate bond was putting ideas in my head. Jareth was a raging storm and I needed distance before I got swept away. My one consolation was that I knew he couldn't catch me unless I wanted him to.

I leapt from the soft forest floor, grabbing the nearest branch of a pine tree, and hoisted myself off the ground. Silently, I crawled through the canopy. Arm after arm, I climbed until I found a branch steady enough to support my weight.

Then I jumped. The air rushed around me as I fell. It drowned out the noise of my other worries. I extended my claws and bark shredded beneath my fingers, catching the limb of a neighboring tree.

I didn't get much of a head start. His confusion only bought me a few seconds. A deep howl echoed through the silent woods, exciting my wolf and making my heart skip a beat. I launched myself into another tree, clinging to the trunk when the branch swayed beneath my feet.

Running wasn't my style anymore, not since I was small, but I had homefield advantage so I didn't let the opportunity go to waste. Everything was happening too fast. I needed a minute to breathe. He couldn't track me out here, not when my scent was everywhere. These were my woods. My territory. My home. My people…

What if he is right?

I balanced on the balls of my feet on the unsteady branch, testing my weight just long enough to pull myself up to a stronger limb.

If there was even a small chance that the purists would attack Cerberus, I had to entertain the idea. I refused to believe none of the other Alphas worried about this. It didn't make sense for them not to care.

Except Anubis and Cerberus were the packs closest to the human city gates. Any roads that led in or out came through our territories. Maybe we had to worry more because of our proximity.

I had to speak with Maddock and my grandmother. They'd know more about this. My uncles fought the purists a long time ago down south with the Anubis pack while my father stayed here in Cerberus.

I crouched down low on the branch and breathed deeply to calm my racing thoughts.

My father never once mentioned anything about what the purists did. I'd snuck into every meeting as a child, learning about my birthright, because he wasn't going to teach me. Apollo was too caught up in the power of being an Alpha to think about a future where he wasn't the one in charge.

But his own mate, Coral's mother, had abandoned him to work for the coalition. She'd recognized a threat and fought against it. I admired her for that.

"Come out, come out wherever you are, princess. You can't hide from me forever," Jareth's deep voice echoed through the trees, raising the hairs on my arms and sending a delicious shiver to my beast. Alpha males were so damn cocky.

I cupped my hands over my mouth to project a *coo* across the distance. The leaves on the ground crunched as he turned, disorientated, and I silently pulled my body up to a higher branch.

This was my legacy and what made me different from the other Alphas. I refused to be arrogant or blind. We'd strengthen our defenses and prepare in case Jareth was right.

"Caught you."

I startled, looking down from my treetop perch to see him staring up into the patch of moonlight.

"Doesn't seem like it." I laughed. "You're down there and I'm up here."

"I can't even remember the last time I climbed a tree." He grunted as he grabbed the lowest branch.

I waited for him to hoist himself up higher. His fangs extended as he reached for me. My feet hit the ground and I took off running, loving the thrill that raced through my body. The night wind whipped through my hair as I flew through the woods.

"You'll have to try harder than that if you want to kiss me!"

*

It was getting late and I was starting to get tired. If he'd hurry, he could catch me where I wanted to be found. There was a rocky outcropping overlooking a hidden lake in the middle of nowhere.

148

It was one of my favorite places. The one I tried to paint and failed miserably.

I figured the least I could do was show him what it really looked like, but the moon was about to drop below the mountain ridge. If we didn't get there soon, it wouldn't be as beautiful.

Slow down, my wolf urged.

I put my hands on my head and tried to catch my breath as I stopped running. We were moving too fast anyway. That nervous feeling sank in the pit of my stomach again. If I let him catch me–and if I gave into the mate bond–I'd be jumping into a future I couldn't walk away from.

Did I really want to kiss him?

It was silly to be nervous about this. A kiss wasn't that big of a deal. I'd grown up watching shifters openly display every type of sexual expression. It wasn't anything to be ashamed of.

I only wished this wasn't the first time in my life I knew someone wanted to kiss me. It made every feeling more intense. Add in the fact that he was my fated mate, the one I'd kiss for the rest of my life if I sealed the bond, and it seemed like something more than it was. What if I made a fool of myself?

I cupped my palm over my mouth and checked my breath, thinking I should go back to the cabin and brush my teeth. While I was there, I could change into pajamas and crawl into bed...

Don't you want to see what it's like?

Gods help me, I did.

Which was terrifying.

Somehow, during the past few days, the asshole had thawed my reaction to him. I wanted to see what it was like if I pulled down some bricks in my wall and let him in. But I was afraid.

I swallowed hard, admitting that to myself. Mate bonds didn't always work out like they should. I'd seen the way it destroyed my father. I didn't want to end up like him.

You'll never know if you don't try.

True. I nodded, straightening my shoulders. I was Kera, Alpha of Cerberus, and I could do this. I'd give fate a chance because I wasn't afraid of anything.

"Is this your lake?"

The sound of his voice in the quiet night made me screech a high-pitched girly noise that I blamed on Coral's influence. The outline of his shadowy figure was perched on a rock overlooking the moonlit water below.

"I figured you should see it," I said a little too loud, trying to cover up the weird sound I made that was still echoing through the valley.

"Come sit with me." He held out his hand.

It was a little rude and presumptuous in assuming I'd take it.

"Unless this spot is too rough for your princess behind." The teasing tone ruffled my fur.

"I'm not a princess." I growled, free climbing the rock face with little effort as I crawled up next to him.

We sat in silence, breathing in the crisp fall air. My heart was beating faster than I wanted it too. I wasn't sure what I was supposed to say. The heat radiating in the space between us was the only warmth on the chill night. Unconsciously, I edged closer and he did the same, drawn by the magnet of the bond.

"You don't talk much."

I tensed, and then forced myself to relax as he wrapped his arm around my shoulder. The touch sent a soft swirl of butterflies dancing in my stomach and my wolf relaxed in his masculine scent.

"I talk a lot when I get to know someone." I focused on the reflection of silver moonlight rippling across the lake in the breeze.

"I want to get to know you more." I felt his eyes on me and didn't dare look. The sincerity of his words made my palms sweat.

I rubbed my hands against my lap. "How is this going to work?"

He was silent for a beat and I turned to him, not prepared for the intensity in his gaze.

"Do you want to make it work?"

This was an unfamiliar dance and I wasn't sure how to step. He'd answered my question with a question, redirecting the focus on me. It was almost a challenge. I didn't want to back down. What did that say about our future? Would everything be a fight? Was love supposed to be this hard?

I lowered my eyes, staring at his mouth, as the uncertainty and desire swirled within me. "Jareth, I…"

He leaned forward, capturing my words with his lips, and stealing the breath from my lungs.

I sat there, stunned, as his lips worked my mouth open. A delicious magic rolled over my skin, making me shiver. Tentatively, I tasted his bottom lip. The explosion of his masculine scent and spice warmed my core. Jareth groaned. The sound of it awakened a new power in me.

I growled as he deepened the kiss. His fingers curled through the back of my hair, pulling me closer, as his tongue expertly possessed my mouth. My lips pushed harder against his and I met the demands of his tongue, wanting more. I wasn't even sure of what though. All I knew was that the warmth devoured me and a fire stoked deep in my soul.

I gave into the sensations, meeting his kisses with an intensity I'd never felt before. Then I was drowning, lost to the real world, and needing this like I'd never needed anything.

Without breaking the kiss, I straddled his lap. He growled as his hands slipped down to latch onto my hips. My back arched. He dragged me closer, pressing me against his hard body. Tension tightened in my stomach as I fisted my hands in his hair.

I wanted this. Deeper. Harder. More friction.

He moaned into my mouth as he rocked me against him, giving into my demands and taking for himself. The pulsing sensation started low in my core and set my blood on fire.

My body shook, pained at the loss, as he released my hips. His hands traveled up the bare skin under my shirt. I arched into him as his palm slipped around my ribs and cupped the fullness of my breast.

His kiss became more possessive, a dance of dominance, and I returned it greedily. Need shot to my aching core as his thumb brushed over my sensitive and hard nipple.

I gasped as I tore my mouth away. "Wait."

"What's wrong?" Jareth let out a ragged breath and ran a hand through his messy hair. His lips were swollen, still wet from our kiss, as his heady gaze swept over my face.

Thankfully it was dark enough to hide the blush on my cheeks, because I was already embarrassed enough. "I haven't done this before."

"You've never done what?" His eyes narrowed in confusion.

Ugh. He's going to make me say it.

I shoved him back, needing to get away.

"Hang on." He caught me by the arms and held me in place as he blinked. "You've never done any of this before. I didn't realize. You seemed so confident."

"I am confident." I growled at him. "And I didn't need a dick to become this way."

He chuckled. I debated kneeing him in the crotch to drive my point home.

"Were you saving yourself for me?"

"Could your head get any bigger?" I cried, shoving him onto his back and yanking my arms from his grasp. I leapt off the rocks and landed in a crouch on the forest floor.

"Wait, princess." He jumped after me.

"Not a princess," I growled for what must have been the millionth time. The rage was taking over which felt a hell of a lot better than the unmet need still pulsing through my body and the embarrassment that made me want to cringe.

"Stop," he spoke with an Alpha command.

Yeah, well, I had one of those too.

"No." I kept walking.

"Kera, please. I'm not good with words. I didn't mean to upset you." He laced his hand through mine. "I'm sorry."

I stopped dead in my tracks.

Did he just apologize?

He sure did. Even my wolf's mind was blown. I wasn't sure what was happening here. Was he the asshole? Or was I?

"Thank you." Jareth let out a heavy sigh as he pressed his face against my neck, inhaling my scent. I melted into him and the rage dissipated, leaving me hollow and empty inside.

I closed my eyes and breathed deeply. "It's not that big of a deal."

"But it is." He pulled back and touched my chin, tilting my face so he was looking deep into my eyes. "We have time. We don't have to rush things."

Now I knew he was lying. I huffed out a laugh, feeling my heart twist in my chest. "We're Alphas. There is no such thing as extra time."

"We'll make time." The conviction in his growl made me weak in the knees. I clung to him as he moved to whisper in my ear. "And I'm not rutting my princess in the dirt for her first time. You deserve more. I'm going to give it to you."

"Your princess?" I bit my lip, trying not to let his sweet words overwhelm me.

Jareth nodded and smiled as he caressed his hand along my cheek. "Mine."

Something in me snapped. The wall came crumbling down. I wanted to try. Wanted to feel what it would be like to be Jareth's *mine*.

"Alpha, we have a problem." I stilled as the border patrol connected with me through the pack link. *"There are some wolves here from Anubis requesting entry."*

Jareth growled as I glanced back up at him. His fists clenched at his side as he listened to whatever he was hearing through the link with his pack members at my border.

I blinked back the burning sensation behind my eyes and raised my chin. "It seems that our time is up, Alpha."

14
† Jareth †

Every nerve ending of mine was misfiring, leaving me jittery and high strung. I lit a cigarette as I marched to the Alpha's mansion of Cerberus pack with Kera by my side. The past few days of this *vacation* felt like a dream where I was operating on a slower clock. Dinner tonight, chasing the fiery redheaded she-wolf through the woods, and the few blissful moments spent by the lake would have to be enough to fuel me on the return to the real world.

I was an Alpha.

And I'd seriously misjudged the amount of time I'd be able to escape my duties since two runners from my pack were out of breath and urgently requesting my presence.

"Those things will kill you." The lights coming from the windows of the Alpha's mansion cast shadows over Kera's soft smile.

I gave her one last wistful look as we both hardened our expressions and crushed the cigarette under my boot. "It's a good thing I'm hard to kill."

Her fingers brushed along mine and she nodded, before we both marched up the stairs.

"This better be important." I growled.

The sound of my voice echoed in the mostly empty house. A scent of death still lingered here despite the recent cleaning. I looked to Kera, but she didn't seem bothered by it. The graveyard princess wasn't afraid of ghosts. I ignored the newfound ache in my heart. There wasn't time right now to ask why.

My anxiety was growing when the runners failed to respond. I reached through my pack link, trying to sense who they were. In a pack as large as Anubis, it was difficult to know everyone's name, but I recognized their scents as belonging to the new group of younger wolves Griffon was training.

Kera pushed open the door to the sitting room. The décor was something that belonged in my late grandmother's house. She'd lived past one-hundred. On the red velvet couch lined with gold trim sat the two Anubis shifters guzzling water. A Cerberus shifter hurried past us with a tray of food, baring his neck to Kera in respect.

"I assumed you were injured since you didn't respond to me." The strength in my tone cowered the young wolves.

"Apologies, Alpha," the skinnier male barked out as he dropped his cup. "We've been running since this morning without stopping."

"And they're probably thirsty." Kera rolled her eyes at me as she bent to retrieve the cup.

Later, I'd have to speak with her about disrespecting me in front of my pack. But I wasn't ready to fight her again until after I figured out what was going on. Most of this furniture looked like it was one bad crack away from disintegrating anyway.

Though the thought of pinning Kera under me in the middle of her childhood home was making my wolf…

I shook my head to clear those thoughts. Kera's piercing blue eyes glared my way like she knew what I was thinking as she refilled the cup.

I took the glass pitcher from her hand and turned to focus on my runners, ignoring the pulsing tension in her stare. "Why are you here?"

Both shifters looked to each other with grim expressions and I felt the whine of their wolves. Fear leaked from them in waves. The pitcher shattered in my fists, causing the runners to drop to the floor and show submission, as I sensed the reason for their distress.

Gods. No.

My claws extended and my clothes ripped as my beast took over. The furious howl that erupted from my chest shook the windows. Alpha power roared through my voice and I commanded the whining wolves to speak.

"What the fuck happened to my sister?"

*

Blinding rage had me tearing at my own mind as my wolf sprinted through the forest. She should have been safe. The convoy was armor plated and the strongest warriors in Anubis were her escorts.

Nothing should have happened.

I urged my wolf faster. Spit frothed in his jaw and his muscles were burning. The only thing keeping him from turning feral and destroying everything in his path was Kera's red wolf running alongside him.

She didn't turn back, trusting that Skoll and Coral were following, but I couldn't bear to look at her. This was my fault. While I'd been playing romantic in the graveyard, my sister was taken.

I screamed at nothing, beating my fists against my head in the darkness of my wolf's hold.

Ophelia should have been back in Santa Lindo, safe and protected in our home. But according to the runners who were lagging behind us on the race through Cerberus territory, my sister made a pit stop on her journey.

Gods damnit, Ophelia!

The foolish girl had commanded them to stop. I should have known she'd do this. All the times she spoke of the little villages at the desert borders where she sent extra humanitarian aid despite me building agricultural waterways and electrical grids, doing everything in my power to give them a better way of life. I could still hear her pest-like voice begging me to show face. Of course she would take the opportunity of my absence to dance around in her skirts, kissing babies and giving gifts.

My little sister had a bleeding heart. It was my job to protect her from the poison in this world.

And I'd failed.

I was probably fishing for Gods' sakes while the purist scum sent out a raid on that forsaken little town. I wanted to rage. To kill. To beat my fists against my chest and burn this world to the ground.

The purists took my sister.

159

If I could gouge my own eyes out, I would. My wolf howled for us both, letting his pain and anger echo to the world as the red sun rose above us. Kera's wolf didn't break stride as she pressed her body against his, trying to give comfort.

But we didn't need comfort.

We needed blood.

*

Fueled by adrenaline, I marched barefoot and naked through the smoldering ashes that covered Junction City. The northern town in Anubis lands bordered the Fenrir territory. Scraggly trees bent under harsh high-desert winds, grown by seeds that drifted down from their maternal lineage which flourished in the rich soil of the Fenrir mountains in the distance. The trees still remained, hardened as they were, despite the explosions that had destroyed most of the few dwellings.

The Anubis shifters who lived here still answered to me and the council though they clung to their independence being so far removed from the rest of the population. Those that remained didn't seem to relish in that distance now.

Grime-streaked bodies met me in the street; shifters baring their necks in respect as I stood shaking and let out a vicious howl. Their livelihoods were reduced to ash. Crumbling structures lined the street. Smoke still hung heavy in the air as they dug through the rubble of the small town.

Still miles away, I listened to the rumble of aid trucks coming from Santa Lindo and a few more southbound from Fenrir pack. Alpha Nolan's response to our plight.

With my heart beating hard in my chest, I scanned the destruction. Two downed purist flying machines sat smoking on the desert horizon. In the buildings that remained, bullet holes peppered sagging walls. Rapidly healing wounds were on each of the shifter's faces that gathered around me.

"What happened?" I spit through gritted teeth, trying to contain my beast as I worked to piece together the situation.

"We fought, Alpha Jareth." An old shifter with a hobbled leg lowered his head to hide the tears in his eyes.

"Did you?" I asked, searching their faces for the truth as the guilt tore my stomach to shreds.

"That's enough." Kera growled.

She stepped beside me.

Of course, she was naked.

My beast surged forward, chomping at the bits, and needing to protect. To kill. To make it stop.

"Put some clothes on," I barked at her as my vision tunneled.

"Screw you." She squared her shoulders. Betrayal was written on her face. There were bags under her eyes and she was breathing heavily.

It was another punch to the gut.

I'd put them through hell by running hard all night. But it wasn't their fault. It was mine. If I'd been here, this wouldn't have happened. I turned from Kera so she couldn't see the shame on my face and addressed my pack instead.

"You fought, but they won." No shifter met my eye. They didn't have to. I could sense their defeat. It tasted like the bile rising up the back of my throat. "Why did you let your Luna sacrifice herself?"

*

She'd begged them to take her.

I stood next to the pyre as they burned the bodies of my fallen shifters. My voice didn't break as I delivered a prayer to the Gods. The smoke drifted to the clear desert night sky, obscuring the stars overhead. I kept it together as the survivors told me their stories and tried to separate fact from fiction.

The purists had dropped some kind of gas at first that rendered the shifters blind and thrust their wolves into a frenzy. A few hunters had the instinct to run to the armory. The coward humans didn't set foot on the ground until chaos had taken over.

Unlike the other packs, Anubis shifters were trained in mechanical warfare. My grandfather insisted and I carried on the tradition. The weapons of your enemies should be familiar enough to turn on them.

They managed to shoot two of the flying attack vehicles down from the sky before reinforcements came airborne. The purists still didn't touch the ground until they'd destroyed the small armory and every major building in the town center.

Then the bullets started.

Hard and fast, the shifters were blind as the humans swept through in waves. It was coordinated. This served some kind of sick purpose. But I couldn't tell my people that without worrying them further.

The flames of the pyre danced higher as more bodies were piled on. The ashes of my people drifted down and coated my skin. I'd carry them with me for the rest of my life.

"It reminds me of Lone Pine." Beta Calder of the Fenrir pack stood beside me in a show of support since the council had called out the signal for aid. I liked the old man. He was one of the few who saw through the bullshit and understood the precarious balance in our world. But he wasn't an Alpha. He could only take orders. Nolan had ordered him here.

"How so?" I wasn't in the mood to talk, but I humored him anyway as I stood in solidarity while the shifter's bodies burned.

"They came for the children." Calder spit on the dry earth. "The bastards knew just where to hit us to make it hurt."

"You forget they also took our Luna." The rage still boiled under my skin, making my beast howl with a feral pain.

We'll get her back.

I'll kill them all.

Stormy blue eyes met mine from across the fire. Kera's brow furrowed with concern. I forced myself to look away.

*

All through the night, I sifted through the rubble alongside my people to clear the destruction. I couldn't stop or rest. The anxious energy fueled me to hurry, but I had to compartmentalize it.

I needed to get these shifters on the road to recovery. My Beta Griffon was on his way with trucks to load up the purist vehicles. Once we cleared this up, then I could go.

The need for revenge was so strong it was splitting my skull in two. I focused on the task at hand so I didn't lose myself to the beast.

And I had to stay busy so I didn't run to Kera.

She worked twice as hard as any shifter throughout the night, casting stolen glances my way that I pretended not to notice. I couldn't deal with her pity now. Later, once I'd rescued my sister and burned that purist city to the ground, then maybe I could face her like an Alpha.

*

The sun was barely cresting the horizon when I finished directing the first of the construction crew to the most urgent sections. The wailing cries of a female shifter drew my attention. I handed off my shovel and followed the sounds of pain, hardening myself for the situation I might find.

A trailer riddled with bullet holes sat at the edge of town. The metal door was bent, hanging from its hinges. The woman continued to cry inside, unaware of my steps into the house.

I walked over the broken window glass and smashed furniture, finding her in the back bedroom. She sat on the edge of a small bed rocking a stuffed wolf in her arms as if it were a child and howling like a banshee.

I forced myself to keep moving forward and took her pain as mine, reaching through the pack link to ease her worries with my presence, as I crouched down beside her. "Did you know this child?"

Red-rimmed eyes turned to look at me. Even the Alpha couldn't take away this pain. "They stole my baby boy."

My fist tightened on the blue bedspread as I mentally ran through the list I'd been given. I didn't think I could feel another surge of anger this strong. I was wrong. "What's his name?"

"Logan," she choked out, burying her face against the toy as she sobbed into it. "He's two. I was out hunting. I wasn't here to protect him and die alongside my mate trying to keep him safe."

"It's for the best." I drew on my inner strength to look the grieving mother in the eye as I repeated the child's name to myself, committing it to memory. "I will find him and I will bring him home to you."

She nodded and sucked in a shaky breath. "I know you will, Alpha. Our Luna knew it too. That's why she went with our babies."

I rose to my full height slowly. One wrong step and I'd fall apart. I forced myself to touch her head, sending a wave of reassurance that only an Alpha could give. My beast howled, his heart ripping in two, as I turned to walk away.

There'd been no demands. No ransom. No communication. The children they took could already be dead. But I refused to cower and let my pack lose hope. It was my fault. I didn't protect them.

Outside the trailer, I put my fist in my mouth to bite back my silent scream as the ashes continued to rain down on the destruction of my land.

I would find them all if it was the last thing I ever did.

15
† Kera †

My heart was shattering.

Opening myself to the bond allowed more of his emotions to come through and it was breaking me. All night, I'd fought the instinct of my wolf to go to him. Duty, honor, regret, revenge– his feelings pulsed like a siren call. A song that my own soul sang. It hurt worse because I knew these emotions intimately and there wasn't anything I could do to change them.

We worked in close proximity, but I didn't approach him here. I didn't know how. Love and comfort weren't my strong points. I could only hope my presence proved that he wasn't alone in this, just as Coral and Skoll stayed beside me.

I knew my place.

As an Alpha, the other wolves looked to us for guidance. If we remained calm, they'd draw on our strength. Though I wasn't sure if I should technically be here. It wasn't my pack. This wasn't my land. I didn't know if Jareth had even declared us as formal allies. But I couldn't leave him alone in his hour of need, fated mate bond or not.

And I had selfish reasons for being here too.

I needed to see this with my own eyes, to bear witness to the truth. This was what he'd talked about. All the doubts I had were washed away.

The purists attacked us.

They'd left their emerald city to lay waste to a small, defenseless town. Purists killed shifters.

And they took the kids.

My fangs and claws kept trying to break free every time I thought about it. Throughout the night, I'd listened to the stories of what happened here. The chaos, the choked voices of shifters still hoarse from screaming, and the realization that no matter how hard they'd fought, it wasn't enough.

I pushed down my rage and focused on the one story that stood out as a beacon of hope. It'd been told so many times that I could almost envision it in perfect clarity. Ophelia walking with her hands raised through the thick smoke and flying bullets, begging them to take her too as she stated her title over and over again. All the reverent whispers of the shifters said she'd gone with the pups to make sure they weren't alone.

Gods, that woman was brave.

I was so glad I hadn't killed her. If Jareth didn't go save his sister, I'd do it without a moment of regret. But that was my ego talking.

There was still so much unknown and it plagued me. I couldn't let something like this happen to my pack. Jareth was right. We needed to strengthen our defenses. All the packs needed to wake up and fight together.

Jareth said they didn't care, but after this, they would have to. My grandfather wasn't here, but he did send his Beta to show support. That had to mean something. Then again, I didn't know my own grandfather enough to speak on his response. Hell, I didn't know any of the other Alphas all that well. Even Jareth was still a mystery to me, but I decided it was time someone started to trust him.

I scooped the last bit of debris from the pile we were working on into the back of the dump truck and wiped the sweat off my forehead. Now that the sun had risen, it was bearing down brutally on our heads. The thicker clothes Coral packed in a hurry did nothing to help with the heat. She sagged onto her shovel beside me, shaking her neckline to let in some air as Skoll offered her water.

"Why don't you two get some rest?" I scanned the work efforts, looking for Jareth. A sense of profound loss echoed through the bond but I couldn't see him anywhere.

"In a minute." Coral guzzled some of the cool liquid and handed me the jug. "I'm going to talk with Beta Calder and find out what Fenrir's response is."

I smiled at my friend. Our thoughts were aligned more often than not and there was no other Beta I'd rather have by my side.

"Call an emergency meeting with all the Alphas in the region. We can host it in Cerberus lands that way no one has to travel too far. I want to be ready with a plan of attack, so Jareth doesn't have to stress about setting it up."

"Roger that, Alpha." Coral gave me a mock salute. I shook my head as I handed Skoll the water jug, still having no clue who this Roger guy was that she insisted on talking about.

*

The sun was so bright that I had to squint until I finally picked out his broad shoulders and messy head of black curls in the distance. He stood where the remains of the purists' contraptions were being loaded up onto a long semi-truck by a crane.

The shifter next to him was a beta wolf about my uncle's age. His salt and pepper hair was cropped close to his head and his actions were militaristic and sharp. From the way he addressed Jareth, I assumed it was his Beta Griffon who I had yet to meet. I hung back, not wanting to interrupt them, until the last strap was tied down.

The Beta issued a whistle to roll out and climbed into the lead truck. Jareth stood alone in the desert, staring at the mountains as he lit a cigarette. Still, I hesitated, sensing his inner turmoil, and searching for the right words to say.

He blew out a cloud of smoke as he turned his face to the brutal sun. "What are you thinking, princess?"

"Not a princess." I smiled despite the circumstances and finally closed the distance between us.

"Not an answer." A slight smile twitched his lips that did nothing to lighten the darkness in his eyes.

"I'm thinking we need to set up an emergency meeting with the other Alphas." I said it like it was no big deal, like we wouldn't be risking the lives of hundreds of shifters and declaring war on the purists, like I wasn't suggesting putting my own people in harm's way for another pack.

"You haven't been an Alpha for very long." Jareth's laugh was humorless. "You still have faith in people. It's cute."

I let the insult roll off my shoulders. He was in a tough spot right now. "We have to try."

He looked down to the cigarette in his hand like the glowing ember held all the answers in the world. "They won't act. They never do."

I glanced over my shoulder, seeing the destruction of the little town we were struggling to clean up. I could still hear the cries of those who lost pups and their loved ones.

"We'll convince them," I said. No Alpha in their right mind would let this go unpunished.

"You do realize it isn't the first time this has happened." Jareth shook his head.

"Has a Luna ever been taken?" I thought back through our history lessons, forgetting myself for a moment until Jareth turned to fully face me.

Those darkened eyes, bloodshot and begging for tears that would never fall, pulled at the pain hidden deep in my soul. Every fiber of my being ached with the need to end his suffering.

Touch him. My wolf urged me forward.

I stumbled, and panicked, reaching for the cigarette in his hand. "Can I have some of that?"

He arched an eyebrow as he slowly passed it over. My fingers grazed his skin and I let them linger there, sending reassurance that he wasn't alone. I'd seen him. The truth of who he was as a man and a leader. He took his pack's pain as if it was his own.

Being an Alpha was a lonely position and even his Beta hadn't given off much warmth. I had Sage and Coral and my uncle and grandmother. If all he had was his sister and she was gone…

I understood and wanted to be there for him.

He closed his eyes, shuddering as if my intention reached his heart, and a feeling of peace washed over my beast. Awkwardly, I took the cigarette from his hand and pressed it to my lips.

It tasted like burning death.

My tongue, my throat, and my lungs filled with a thick disgusting cotton evil and I immediately started coughing, trying to rid my body of the taste.

"Damn it, Kera." Jareth grabbed me by the shoulder and patted my back. "How are you this innocent?"

"Innocent?" I coughed, still choking on the hellish death stick smoke. "You know what? I'm going to pretend you aren't always a jerk."

I wasn't pretending. I'd seen the sweetness he was capable of, but it seriously hurt to breathe.

"Don't pretend." He sighed as he took back the cigarette. "I'm always a jerk."

The urge to challenge him shot through me, but it wasn't the time or place. The world was changing. We were surrounded by chaos. And I didn't know what our future was going to look like.

But I refused to be afraid. "We'll get her back, okay? I promise I'll do—"

His lips crashed against mine possessively, stealing the rest of the words I wanted to say.

The kiss was angry and dominating. My lips were bruised. The pain of it left me breathless. He clung to me like he was drowning while fire raged within me, hot enough to compete with the scorched earth beneath my feet.

Too soon, he ripped his mouth away and stared at the distant horizon where the mountains signaled a different life beyond the barren high-desert.

"Don't make promises you can't keep." He flicked the cigarette onto the ground and rested his forehead against mine. The tired ache that drifted through the bond from him fueled me with new energy.

"I'll convince them to help." I growled, thinking through everything I needed to do. I'd have to hurry to Cerberus pack. Once I called an emergency meeting, they'd come quick. The other Alphas would see reason. We'd stand together.

Jareth wouldn't be alone.

"We'll see." He pressed a tender kiss to my lips, so soft it was almost apologetic, and turned away.

I'll show him. I stomped out the burning ember of the death stick he left behind.

We sure will. My wolf let out a little cough. **Also, don't ever smoke that shit again.**

173

16
† Jareth †

"What's the plan?" Skoll's jaw was clenched as he stared at the map of the human city projected on the wall of my garage.

I tossed the wrench onto the workbench and wiped the grease from my hands onto my pants. The machine the shifters had shot down ran fine now that I'd fixed the propeller and straightened out the back wing. The other one was shot to shit and the engine wiring was fried beyond repair. After spending all morning talking with the council, I needed something to do with my hands before I started wringing necks.

"The plan is to get Ophelia and the pups." I held a cigarette between my teeth as I patted my grease-stained pockets, looking for matches.

My wolf whined, remembering how Kera coughed yesterday. Seeing her in pain like that made me physically sick. I slid the unburned cigarette back into the tin and tossed it next to the wrench on the workbench.

I missed Kera.

It'd only been a day since she headed back to Cerberus territory while I came home to take care of my pack and appease the council. The anxiousness in being away from her added to my wolf's constant frustration. It'd been three days since Ophelia was taken. Six hours since the council meeting where the coward members refused to launch an attack. And three hours since my last cigarette. Each minute that ticked by was grating on my nerves.

"Why are you looking at me like I stepped in shit?" Skoll growled.

"Stepped in it? I assumed you slept in it."

His wolf flashed in his eyes, mirroring mine. I considered fighting him just to release some of this pent-up aggression.

"That's enough boys." Coral came in with a tray of food from the kitchen. My nostrils flared. She still smelled faintly of Kera, like they shared clothes or something, but the scent on her was wrong.

If she sensed my frustration, she didn't comment. "So, your council is annoying. How much control do they have anyway?"

"More than they should," I spit the words through clenched teeth, remembering all the painfully long turnaround times it took to get their approval. My father, Gods rest his soul, wanted more of a democratic society. As our population continued to grow, I'd carried on the tradition.

"But I have the final say," I muttered.

My Beta Griffon was ready to go when I gave the word despite the council's caution. Our army was trained and dedicated to their Luna. I could have been storming the gates to the purist city right now. But as much as it pained me to admit, the council was right.

Even with the size and strength of our shifter army, it wasn't enough to fight against the millions of humans they had crammed behind those walls.

"Not all of them can fight. The people are taught not to use violence," Coral said, picking back up on the conversation we'd already rehashed. "And I don't think many of them will even if they are told to, but let's go to the meeting with the other Alphas first. I want to get Kera and see what she has to say."

Frustrated, I ran a hand through my hair. This was a waste of time. I couldn't understand how everyone was so calm when I wanted to smash the workbench in two.

"The wards are going to be a problem." Coral chewed her bottom lip as she studied the map.

It was a bit sad how little she knew about the place she'd grown up. "The wards are always problematic. That's why they won't notice when my source fries the electrical current for me."

Her eyes widened. "I thought we didn't have spies in the city anymore."

"We don't. He has a *source*." Skoll growled. *Possessive bastard.*

"Chill out." I growled back at him.

He was right. I didn't have spies. No one needed to know who my source was. A sixteen-year-old hacker who lived in the Fringes wouldn't inspire much confidence. But I'd been working with him for years and he'd never let me down. Which was more than I could say for most of the shifters I'd dealt with.

Skoll continued to glare at me. I didn't need a pack link to read his mind. Yes, I wanted to see if the daughter was like her mother, but it wasn't like I'd force her into it. Besides, we had bigger things to worry about now. I didn't need more inside information. I needed to get my sister and the pups out of there.

Coral hummed, lost in thought. "I wonder why all the attacks have been down past the southern gates."

Her words broke through our staring contest and I ignored her mate, turning to her instead. It was something I often wondered myself. "My guess is that we're more populated here and seen as the bigger threat. It makes sense that they'd try to whittle down our numbers."

"Maybe." She tapped her finger against a cluster of buildings projected on the wall map. "I'm sure it's only a coincidence that the government research facilities are located near the southern gates."

"What are you talking about?" I moved to her side, ignoring Skoll's growl as I leaned over her shoulder. "There are more government facilities here and here." I pointed to the buildings in the center of the city and the ones slightly to the west.

Coral huffed, looking at me from the corner of her eye. "Some sources you have. They relocated the government buildings for the university apartments and for as long as I've been alive, this is the hospital."

She circled the building to the west before dragging her finger back to the southern cluster. "These are the government research facilities. They're off limits to the general public, but everyone knows that's where they take mutants... er... shifters."

My wolf was silent as I stared at the map, processing this new information. I knew they eradicated Lycan DNA from the populace if it cropped up and studied those who had it, but not in a singular location. One spot on a map. My eyes burned, glowing with my wolf, as we focused on the point like an X was marked on the building.

I could almost see Ophelia sitting there locked in some cage. For the first time since I'd learned she'd been taken, I had real hope. This changed things.

"Where are you going now?" Skoll growled, turning to follow as I marched out of the room.

My thoughts were racing too fast to give a concrete answer. I needed to pull code for those systems, see if they had security cameras I could hack the footage to, find blue prints and layouts...

"Jareth, stop." Skoll laid his hand on my shoulder. "Whatever is going on in that crazy brain of yours, you aren't doing this alone. She is like a sister to me too."

"I know that, brother." I pushed his hand off me. "But I don't need a babysitter. Go back to Cerberus. I'll meet you there for the meeting tomorrow."

If I started now, I could have all the data before I returned home. Maybe I didn't need the other Alphas after all. I could assemble a small team and...

"I can't do that." Skoll sighed. "Kera wants—"

"What does Kera want?" I snapped. Hearing her name spoken stopped me in my tracks. It was already hard enough with a part of my soul stretched across the distance and ignoring the need to be with my mate. But my sister was taken because I'd given into that primitive desire.

Skoll's shoulders slumped as he looked away. "Kera doesn't want you to be alone."

My wolf whined at the confession, but I couldn't let it get to me. "You and Kera of all people know that to be an Alpha is to be alone."

The challenge flared in his eyes, unspoken words hanging in the air between us, because he did know. Skoll was the only one I confided in. After all these years of being an Alpha and the politics we'd been forced to deal with, he understood more than most why I couldn't trust anyone.

"Yeah, that's not going to work for me." Coral smiled brightly as she poked her head between us. "We don't do alone in our circle. And if you're mating Kera, you're stuck with us. So go do whatever you need to quick and let's get out of here."

*

"This is what I'm going to need." I handed Griffon the set of instructions, knowing he'd pull it together before I got back.

He was an efficiently mean old brute who'd served my father as Beta. The shifter may have looked rugged and uncaring, but he'd been kind to me and

Ophelia growing up when he wasn't beating my ass in training. My sister had him wrapped around her finger though. I still remembered the day she tripped over his boot and spilled her ice cream cone on the pavement. She'd wailed and he gathered her in his arms, rushing back to the vendor to buy out the whole cart. The other shifters didn't dare tease him. Ophelia was his one soft spot.

I scratched the back of my neck, trying not to choke up at the memory of Ophelia riding on his shoulders with her long black hair half covering his stern face.

Griffon read over the list. "Are you sure about this, Alpha?"

"I'm sure." He didn't often question me, but I didn't usually use his services for things of this nature. Like the others, he was old school and methodical. I'd long ago learned who was adaptable to change and who preferred to do things by the book.

"And what about them?" He looked over to the armor-plated black sedan where Coral and Skoll sat waiting, sweltering in the desert sun.

"We'll try it their way first, but when it fails, this is what we're doing."

Griffon nodded as he folded the page. "Then let's hope for all our sakes that their plan will work."

*

The wind rushed through the open window blowing Coral's blond hair around like a dust devil as I gunned the sedan to 120mph. The thrumming of the wind drowned out my rampant thoughts and the incessant howling of my beast.

He was torn and chaotic, wanting to save his littermate and pulled by the bond to return to Kera's side. The instinct to protect was overwhelming when there were so many that needed saving. I ignored him as best as I could, focusing on the road ahead and the rumble of the engine as I tested its limits.

What I couldn't ignore was Skoll's death grip on the back of my seat. If he wasn't careful, he'd rip the custom leather.

"I think you're scaring him," Coral screamed to be heard over the sound of the wind.

I checked the rearview mirror, noticing the green tint to his skin as I accelerated around another bend in the road. He'd be fine.

It was the loss of time I was worried about and what that might mean for my sister. I had to believe Ophelia was taken alive for a reason. If they wanted her dead, they'd have killed her on sight. It was the only reason I was entertaining this foolish plan to get in touch with the other Alphas.

My fiery red-head of a fated mate might think this would work, and I was curious to see what she could do, but I'd been burned too many times before to have the hope that Kera still did.

17
† Kera †

"Did you get any sleep?" Sage met me in the cabin, smelling like heaven as the scent of food wafted from her hands.

I grunted my thanks as I snagged a breakfast sandwich from her and slipped into the bathroom, biting into the biscuit and eggs as I stared at my reflection in the mirror. "No time to sleep," I spoke around a second bite.

My eyes were swollen and bloodshot. I could almost see my wolf pacing within them, eager to be near her mate again. Little butterflies danced in my stomach, but I chalked it up to hunger. Or nerves. I hadn't been Alpha long enough to make a solid presence in the region. Yet here I was, sending runners out for the past day to arrange an emergency meeting and calling on pack treaty to demand their presence in Cerberus lands today.

I tried not to focus too hard on what failure would look like. Coral would be here with Jareth soon. I had to make this work for him. And for Ophelia. I barely knew his sister, but the thought of her sacrificing herself for those pups pulled at my protective instincts. The other Alphas would feel it too. I was sure of it.

We wouldn't let Jareth down.

I shoved the rest of the sandwich in my mouth and yanked a brush through my hair. Sage stood in the doorway, radiating a comforting magic that helped take the edge off this morning. Unlike Coral, Sage never spoke her opinion freely unless I asked for it. She made a good Luna, handling the pettier problems in the pack with a tender and nonjudgmental heart.

I didn't know what I'd have done if the fates hadn't sent her here. Killing shifters for arguing over rumors and gossip wouldn't earn me any loyalty. Even if it would make me feel better.

Just kidding.

"Let me help." Sage took the brush from my hand and smoothed down my hair. I sighed as I leaned against the sink, letting her calming magic work its way over my scalp as she twisted the strands into a braid.

"Thank you." I chewed my bottom lip, not wanting to meet her eyes in the mirror. She'd done so much for me and this pack. I needed to figure out a way to make it up to her.

Sage waited until she finished tying off the braid and pulled her hands back, not wanting to push me with her magical gift of being able to bend people to her will. She'd gotten so strong with her magic lately that it even scared me a bit. "Is there anything you want to talk about?"

I raised my eyes to hers, seeing the warm expression on her face. Maybe this would have been a better conversation to have with Coral, but I'd left her with Skoll and Jareth because I didn't want him to be alone. The question had been gnawing at me though and I didn't know when I'd get another chance to ask.

"Why did you hesitate to act on the mate bond with my uncle Maddock?"

"A few weeks isn't that long for humans." Sage chuckled. "I know by shifter standards that can feel like eternity. To answer your question though, I hesitated because I wasn't sure if I could survive the intensity of the feelings between us. And I didn't know if I deserved them or if I was hurting Coral somehow by acting on them."

"But you did survive," I pressed, a little too eagerly, and lowered my voice in embarrassment. "The intensity of the emotions. They weren't too bad when you gave in."

Sage gave me a knowing smile as she rested her hand on my shoulder. A burst of energy filled my chest, making me almost giddy and lightheaded.

"It was the best decision I ever made and I shouldn't have waited a whole two weeks, but your love story is your own. You're going to have to follow your heart to see where it takes you."

"Well that didn't help," I muttered under my breath.

"Looks like it did to me." She laughed as she patted my arm. I glanced up at my reflection. The bags were gone and my eyes were clear. I looked well rested and felt amazing.

Witches were so weird.

And cool.

But why did they all have to talk in riddles?

*

I rushed outside, burying thoughts of fated mates down deep, and met Maddock in the yard. He'd already shifted into his massive brown wolf and was ready to go. With a meeting this important, neither of us had gotten much sleep between setting patrols around the perimeter, organizing arrival escorts, and making sure the Alpha's home was ready to receive guests.

Maddock's wolf let out a low growl. He was more irritated than usual this morning. Something had been bothering him since we left Alpha Nolan's house in Fenrir. Sage must have worn off on him though, because he hadn't said anything to me.

"Do you think this meeting is the wrong thing to do?" I asked as I set off on a jog with my uncle's wolf by my side.

"No. It's important," he spoke through the link.

The birds were chirping and the morning fog was lifting from the trees. The slowly rising sun was like a clock ticking backwards, drawing each minute out painfully long. I preferred action, not sitting around and talking like this, but being an Alpha came with so many rules.

We make the rules. My wolf let out an agitated growl.

On our land, we do.

I blew out a sweaty breath and picked up the pace, trying to ignore the direction my thoughts were taking me. "Are you going to tell me what's wrong?"

Silence.

Growing up, I'd always sought out his quiet solitude. It was a welcome relief to the constant chaos and shitshow that was my life. But my patience was wearing thin and my wolf was restless.

"If it'd work on you, I'd use an Alpha command to make you spit it out."

Maddock's wolf looked over his shoulder and huffed.

"Fine. Don't tell me." I ignored my uncle and focused on the song of the waking forest instead.

The crisp breeze filled my lungs, refreshing as they burned for oxygen. I ran harder, pushing my muscles and limits with the need to be doing something more than sitting still. Prey scattered through the fallen leaves off the paths I'd made through these woods. I needed this moment of clarity and peace with nature to stay centered. Everything was going to be okay.

The other Alphas would help us.

I knew it.

"Kera, wait." Maddock slowed to a trot as we approached the orchard of the Alpha's mansion.

"I knew you had something to say." I put my hands on my head, breathing heavy as I started to walk.

"Don't be disappointed if this meeting doesn't go like you planned."

187

I almost tripped over an exposed root as I whirled around to face him. "You said it was the right thing to do."

"It is." Maddock shifted. His voice was still throaty with his wolf as his bones rearranged. "But I've seen this happen before with the attack on Lone Pine. Even though the town bordered Fenrir and Anubis pack, making it an interterritorial crisis, our rules of engagement were not to give chase into the purist city."

I still didn't know much about Lone Pine other than it was a large attack at Fenrir's most southern region, cementing the relationship between Fenrir and Anubis as powerhouses. I knew my uncles had fought there and that Skoll was rescued as a pup from the destruction. But they didn't talk much about the details.

"This is different. The purists took children."

"They went for the pups in Lone Pine too." Maddock scratched the beard on his chin, giving me a look so full of pity that my defenses raised.

"They also took the Luna of Anubis pack." I growled. "Maybe the Alphas have grown a pair of balls since then."

"Maybe." Maddock marched past me.

I pressed my palms into my eyes, willing my temper to calm down. "Then what do you suggest we do?"

"What you're doing now." He shrugged.

"You know, you used to be more helpful." I rushed forward to keep up with his pace.

"That was when you were a kid. You're an Alpha now. If you want my advice, you have to ask for it."

"What do you think I'm doing?" I almost screamed in frustration.

"You want my advice?" Maddock stopped walking and folded his arms over his chest.

"This conversation is hilarious." I deadpanned. "Yes. Sigma. Advisor. Please advise."

He let out a heavy sigh. "Sometimes all you can do is try, even if it won't work out."

The rumble of a foreign engine and tires squealing, going too fast on loose gravel, drew our attention toward the house. Maddock gave a warning growl that was full of deadly promise.

I shot him a look to shut him up as my heart leapt into my chest and my wolf howled her approval.

He's here!

"Do you still want my advice?" My uncle glared at the sleek black sedan.

"If it's about my mate, you can keep it to yourself." I smacked his arm when he started growling again.

*

I inhaled deeply, calming my beast, and tried not to look too eager as I walked to the front of the house. This wasn't a fairy tale. We were in the middle of a really messed up situation. Lives were at stake. We had jobs to do.

But in that moment, with the sunlight reflecting off his dark glasses and his head turning in my direction as if he knew just where to find me, my heart skipped a beat. It was like I was ten years old again and still had hope for a brighter future.

We didn't have time to be alone, but I couldn't tamp down that overwhelming desire. Just one minute. I'd steal it if I could.

Gods. What is wrong with me?

It was the bond drawing us together. Nothing more than that. We were both strong enough to not act on our impulses when there were more important things at stake. But my body still ached and my soul yearned for more moments like we'd had the other night at the lake. With his hands on my…

That thought sobered me.

What kind of future would we have? Stolen moments in a chaotic world, and that was if we survived the battle with the purists first.

I stood steady, resisting the urge to run to him as he walked slowly, like a predator, towards me. His presence seemed to suck away all the air as he drew closer. The swirling vortex of power and pain and adrenaline dimmed the morning sun.

My wolf whined and panted, basking in the masculine scent that enveloped us. The dusty sage, pepper, and hint of tobacco would be my undoing.

I already wanted to rip off my clothes.

Get it together, Kera. I forced my breathing to calm down as I looked up at Jareth. "Hey. Are you okay?"

Real smooth. Of course he wasn't alright.

Jareth growled, slipping his hand under the back of my braid and leaning down to inhale my scent. I wet my lips, preparing for another kiss as anticipation swirled low in my belly.

But he didn't kiss me.

He lowered his forehead to mine and breathed deeply as his heartrate slowed to a steadier pulse. "Thank you for trying to do this. Let's hurry up and get it over with."

It wasn't a kiss, but seeing him calm down and knowing it had something to do with me was enough to bolster my confidence.

I disagree. My wolf grumbled.

Ignoring her and her primitive urges, I straightened my chin and took a step back. A limousine pulled in behind Jareth's sedan. The woods were alive with the rustle of leaves as more shifters came through. Later, I'd steal another moment.

It wasn't the right time now.

*

Alphas Nolan, Uki, Oscar, and Jareth were the only people in the dining room with me. All their guards and escorts milled about the property, enjoying the meal Ava had prepared. The treaty said there could be no magic used at these meetings. Sage had grown too powerful lately and I was worried some of her magic would slip through despite her best intentions, so we had bland food and equally stoic faces discussing the fate of the region.

It wasn't going well.

"What I don't understand is how you think this is a rescue situation. Didn't the Luna go with them willingly?" Alpha Oscar was a beautiful man. Dark and clean cut, he was the exact opposite of Jareth despite their similar build and hair color. Where Jareth was rough around the edges, Oscar was polished with an angular face and eyes that glinted with humor. I'd have admired him more if the overpowering scent of unmated male musk wasn't making me gag.

Jareth growled beside me as if his wolf could sense my thoughts and his foot started tapping against the floor. "My sister went with the pups who were taken. The plan is to rescue them all like we should have done before."

"Lone Pine was different." Alpha Nolan stared at the door as if he could sense Skoll behind it. My grandfather had been cagey since he set foot in this house. Like the ghosts of his daughter still haunted him here. "We were prepared to attack and we slaughtered them. Only a few got away."

"Obviously they didn't get the message." I growled as Jareth's foot began to tap faster. His anxious energy was riling my wolf and getting under my skin. "We won't make the same mistake again."

Jareth smirked, looking to me from the corner of his eye, but I was too heated to look back at him.

"These are passionate words, young Alpha." Uki leaned back in her chair, cleaning under her claws with the blade of her knife. "Are you sure you're willing to slaughter your own shifters in a war we cannot win?"

I placed my hand on Jareth's knee to stop it from bouncing. If Coral was allowed in here, she might be able to talk some sense into these jerks.

Jareth's anger simmering through the bond washed over me and I grit my teeth.

"Are you saying we are weaker than humans?"

That did it.

Growls sounded around the table as the other Alpha's wolves surged forward at the challenge. The tension thickened and my own beast extended her claws. Now I understood why only Alphas were allowed in a meeting like this. We were going to tear each other apart. Gods help whoever got in our way.

"I understand your frustration, granddaughter." Alpha Nolan retracted his fangs with a tired sigh, regaining control of himself faster than the rest of us could. "But a war between the shifters and the purists will cause heavy losses on both sides and they have technology we don't."

I wanted to yank my hands through my hair. "They've already declared war by attacking us first."

"Not all of us." Alpha Oscar's eyes still glowed with his beast as he smoothed down the sleeves of his suit. "They attacked Anubis territory and the Luna willingly went with them. I fail to see how this is Cadejo's problem."

"You're joking, right?" My jaw about hit the table.

Jareth slammed back his chair. "If this meeting of cowards is finished, I'm going to save my sister."

It happened so fast, I barely had time to react. Oscar's eyes flashed red and Jareth's fangs extended. Both men lunged across the table, going for each other's throats. I leapt between the two of them, not sure who would win, but overcome with the protective urge to keep Oscar away from my mate.

Jareth's power was thrumming feral and I didn't want blood coating this room.

"Calm down," I hissed as I slammed Oscar against the wall.

His eyes were still glowing red, but he gave a perfect smile with straight teeth as he inhaled my scent. "My apologies, Alpha."

The growling behind me intensified. I glanced back to see Nolan gripping Jareth by his arms. His face was twisted with rage and a possessive jealously punched my gut through the bond.

Quickly, I released my hold on Oscar when I realized what I'd done.

"Get off me." Jareth growled, raising his hands to show he meant no threat.

"Jareth... I..." I whispered as he stormed past me, not waiting to hear my apology.

I'd failed.

And while the power of his raging presence had filled the room, when he left it was sucked into a void of cold emptiness.

Go to him, my wolf begged.

"Let me talk to him." Nolan squeezed my shoulder as I turned to face the other two Alphas.

Oscar buttoned his suit coat that hadn't popped a single seam. "I trust this won't put a damper on our negotiations, but you have to understand that I weigh the cost of any action I take that affects my shifters."

I nodded, too numb to speak, and still trying to process how this all happened.

He paused at the side door, probably the safest exit at this point, and gave me a warm smile. "I do enjoy speaking with you Kera. It's a shame we only got to meet in person today. If you ever find yourself in need and it doesn't require the blood of my people, let me know what I can do to help."

What the hell was I supposed to say to that?

I turned to Uki as the door closed behind Oscar, wondering how everything had gone so wrong so fast.

She chuckled, putting her boot up on my table, and continued cleaning her claws with the knife. "I admire you, young Alpha, but you still have a thing or two to learn about pack politics. The next time you call a meeting like this, you better have something to offer in exchange for help."

"Isn't doing the right thing enough of an incentive?" I growled. Coral would probably tell me

I'd catch more flies with honey, but this was just… wrong. Uki folded her pocket knife and put it away.

"I believe you think you're doing the right thing by following your heart." Her gaze slipped to the door Jareth had exited before looking back at me. "But not all of us have the same emotional investment in this situation. I would have come to aid in the fight on pack lands. Sacrificing my shifters for love is an entirely different matter."

I dug my nails into my palm, tasting the bile that rose in the back of my throat. Jareth was right. All Alphas were selfish assholes. They only thought of themselves. And their land. And their people…

Was I in the wrong here?

I shook my head, refusing to go down that path. They were twisting words and playing games. I wouldn't fall into that rabbit hole.

This was wrong.

They should care.

"A word to the wise," Uki untied the top of her white silk blouse as she stood, "just because you are mated to someone, doesn't mean your whole life revolves around them."

I stared in confusion at the claiming mark scarred on her shoulder. "You're mated?"

Duh. Kera. That was obvious now, but I hadn't thought to ask before and didn't remember anyone mentioning it.

Uki covered her shoulder and retied her shirt. "I am and we have an arrangement. He prefers his life of solitude and I spend vacations with him yearly when I'm in heat. It leaves time for both of us to explore our other pleasures."

She smiled. "But that's not why I showed you my mark. I want you to understand that life is never as black and white as we think it is supposed to be."

What's that supposed to mean? My wolf was hyper-focused on Uki's words as I tried to process them myself. We both admired her as a strong female Alpha. Had I known she was mated, I might have sought her out for advice on my situation.

It didn't change anything though.

She was wrong.

Or was I wrong?

I was so confused.

"Um, Kera. What happened? Jareth is going nuts out here." Coral's voice through the pack link snapped me from my thoughts.

"I'm coming." I nodded to Uki, taking my leave. It wasn't the time to dwell on what ifs.

It was time to act.

18
† Jareth †

My pulse was drumming in my ears, drowning out the words of encouragement spoken by Skoll and Nolan as I fumbled to light a cigarette.

Fucking Oscar.

Let's kill the rat bastard.

I hated him.

Cadejo lands were some of the richest in the region and it was because of his export of bio-diesel which he kept the other packs dependent on. For years I'd tried to get the other Alphas to use more sustainable resources, even offering to produce custom equipment myself, but they didn't want to be in debt to me for the short run. They'd rather line that asshole's pockets instead. They were all cowards, scared of change, and he played them like the fools they were.

As if I didn't have reason enough to hate him already, watching Kera rush to protect him…

Watching him inhale her scent…

My hands shook as the match caught.

I'd never known this kind of anger before. My beast was snarling, begging to be set free to hunt the dickhead down. I had to get out of here before I did something that would change the future of all our packs, because I was going to rip his throat out and bathe in his blood and claim the Cadejo territory as my own.

Which was terrifying.

I shouldn't be thinking like this.

My sister was a captive, young pups had been taken from my lands, and I was wasting time with this bullshit meeting.

Kill the Alpha... Kill the purists… My wolf continued to pace and chant.

My eyes shot up as Skoll took his meaty hand off my shoulder. Kera walked out of the gaudy Alpha home and stood on the porch staring at me while she communicated with her Beta.

The look on her face drove a splintered stake through my heart. This morning, I'd seen the flicker of hope. Now the light was dimmed in her eyes, replaced by a disappointed acceptance.

Welcome to the club, princess. I inhaled a deep drag off the cigarette before crushing it under my boot.

*

"Walk with me?" Kera asked.

I nodded, inhaling her scent to calm my beast, but keeping enough distance so I didn't reach out and touch her. "Not too far. I need to get back soon."

Kera's lips pressed into a thin line, emotions warring. I tuned them out.

"I hate that you were right."

That caught me off guard and I smirked a little. "Not used to losing, princess?"

"Not a princess." Her response lacked the usual bite I was growing to love. This world was already wearing her down. The truth was a hard pill to swallow.

I shoved my hands in my pockets, staring at the outline of her face. One step at a time. I'd get my sister out, make the purists pay and think twice about attacking my lands again, and then come back to work through this mate bond with Kera.

"What's your plan?" She looked to me as if she could see my gears turning.

"Anubis will take care of their own." It wasn't like I expected anything different. But this was the right thing to do, no matter how useless it had been. It just killed me to watch them crush her innocent hope.

"I stand with you." She straightened her shoulders, power rushing from her like the warrior she was. "We go together."

"No, you won't." I couldn't help it. I tucked the piece of fiery red hair that escaped from her braid back behind her ear.

"Are you telling me what I can and can't do?" Her eyebrow arched.

The challenge reignited her spark.

There she is. I swallowed past the lump in my throat. At least she didn't stay down for long.

"They're right." The truth of it weighed heavy on my shoulders. "My own council agreed. The risk is too great. The loss would be too much. There's no way we could storm the purist city with all their technology without destroying ourselves. They've had hundreds of years to prepare for something like this. It's why we haven't attacked before."

Kera shook her head. "I refuse to roll over and show my belly. There has to be a way to fix this."

"Would you still feel that way if Ophelia wasn't my sister and was my chosen mate like you first believed?" I didn't mean to dredge up the fight, but I needed to show her this bond wasn't making her think clearly just as much as it was affecting me.

The conviction in her eyes spoke directly to my soul. Kera couldn't lie. "Yes. And if I'd been Alpha during Lone Pine, I wouldn't have stopped at that battle either. This is *wrong*."

I wasn't much older than her, but five years of experience in this world seemed to make the age gap stretch for decades. I was tired.

"I'm sure you would." I pressed my lips against her cheek. "Stay here and work on trying to convince them if you want. I'll be in touch soon."

She placed her palm against my chest, pushing me back. "What are you not telling me?"

I smiled. She was smart. Or maybe the bond was making me easier to read.

"Don't worry. I've got to get back to Anubis, but I'll send word once I have a better plan." If everything went according to plan, I'd be here myself in a few days.

"You're not giving up?" Kera breathed a sigh of relief, leaning into my touch. I let my hand linger on her face, memorizing the feel of it, and drawing in her undiluted strength that pulsed through the bond.

"No." I kissed her gently, breathing in her grounding scent. "I have to go now."

"Am I supposed to sit here and wait?" The frustration in her tone almost made me laugh.

"Don't you have a pack to take care of?" I ignored the desire of my beast to keep her by my side.

"That's not what I'm talking about." She growled. "I have plenty of things to do, but I'm going to go crazy waiting to hear what the plan is."

"Careful, princess." I lightly flicked her forehead. "Someone might think you're falling for me."

"Don't let your head get any bigger while you're gone." She laughed.

I caught her hand, brushing my thumb over her knuckles as I hardened my heart and forced myself to walk away. "Paint me something, okay?"

*

"This is it?" Sweat dripped down the crevice of my shoulder blades as I stood under the brutal sun on the desert sands of Anubis. Up North, autumn was changing the leaves on the trees, but we still had endless days of warmth before winter lightened the temperature.

I forced myself not to think that far ahead, to forget the way Kera's lips tasted as I kissed her goodbye. My mission was here with the crew Griffon had thrown together at my request.

The brute of a Beta stood stoically by my side. "This is what you asked for, Alpha."

I surveyed the four shifters standing at attention and waiting for my approval. Jimenez and Shelby were the elite of our fighting force. Both men had fought in Lone Pine and helped trained newer recruits. They were large and bulky. Shelby was covered in similar tattoos as the Anubis design I had inked on my shoulder. Jimenez was cleaner cut and polished, but he had the steel eyes of a ruthless killer. I'd fought with both of them enough times to know these two would be a problem in an official Alpha challenge.

Thankfully, it never came to that because they were loyal to the pack.

The other two were green as hell. Their faces were unmarked by the brutality of training in the harsh desert though their bodies were lean and well-toned. I searched through the pack link, trying to recall their names and weaknesses.

On cue, Griffon stepped forward. "Foster and Neil. Aced at the top of their training groups and the fastest runners we have."

Both young men stood up straighter, even as they bared their necks in respect. I took a step back, lighting a cigarette, and exhaled the smoke through my nose.

"Do you understand this is a suicide mission?" I asked. It wasn't, but I needed them to think that to judge their loyalties and see if they were willing to die for their Luna. "You're free to go home if you want."

Their growls of disapproval riled my beast. I smiled grimly. At least we were all on the same page.

I walked in front of the men, stopping in front of Foster who was the youngest of the bunch. He couldn't be more than seventeen. Only a year older than I was when my father took me on my first mission. Looking at his eager face and freshly trimmed hair brought me back.

I still remembered Skoll at my side. The nerves. The fear. Our jokes to try and lighten the tension. Even though Mojave turned into no more than a skirmish, that fear stuck with me and made me who I was today.

"Are you scared?" I asked Foster, waiting to sniff out the lie.

He exhaled slowly, focusing on my eyes in a way most wolves wouldn't dare. "Yes, Alpha. But our Luna needs us to save her so it doesn't matter if I'm scared. I'm here to fight."

I nodded. It wasn't the first time my pack's loyalty made me question if I was good enough to lead them and it wouldn't be the last. But there was no time for doubt or self-consciousness. It was time to act.

"Fall out. Grab the packs prepared for you. We leave tonight."

"Yes, Alpha," the shifters spoke in unison as they rushed to follow orders. Their bloodlust and howls of anxious energy heightened the drive of my beast.

When they were gone, I turned to Griffon. "I asked for five."

"And here I am." He grunted.

I shook my head. "You're not coming."

"Alpha, with all due respect, I can't let you–"

I cut him off with a warning growl. "There's no one better to protect the pack in my absence. If anything happens, I need you here."

My Beta snarled as his biceps flexed and his wolf shone in his eyes.

"I know," I spit the words through clenched teeth. "I don't make this decision lightly."

"Then send me in your place." The beast of a man stood his ground. He'd sworn to serve me like he'd done for my father and I knew he was struggling with the possibility that we wouldn't return. But I also knew the responsibility for this mission was mine alone.

"I have to do this." I sighed, running a hand through my hair as I issued an Alpha command he couldn't refuse. "You will stay here and protect the pack. And I need you to do something else for me."

"Anything, Alpha." He begrudgingly snapped to attention.

Give it to him.

I felt in my pocket for the note I'd jotted down earlier and handed it over without ceremony. I didn't expect anything to happen, but I wasn't foolish enough to think I was invincible. Preparing for everything was what I did. I'd seen enough bad things happen to those who didn't. Which was why it was my fault that I hadn't anticipated this particular attack. And why it was my responsibility to make things right.

"Just in case, this is for Alpha Kera. You'll continue an alliance with Cerberus pack and make sure she always has everything she needs." I inhaled another lungful of smoke. My vision grew darker with my wolf's intensity. "Understood?"

"Of course, Alpha."

*

I pushed the thoughts of the future away and focused on the task in front of me. It would have been nice to have Skoll here now, but I wanted him there with Kera in Cerberus in case something went wrong. Still, his crude sense of humor had kept the terror at bay the last time I stood this close to the purist territory.

That seemed like a lifetime ago. Years before he'd taken a job as a hunter and I had to fulfill my role as Alpha. Back when we still had that youthful spark. Foster and Neil joked around with each other, reminding me of those days long past.

I growled to shut them up.

While we waited for the signal, I closed my eyes and mentally ran through the blueprints for the research facility until I was familiar enough with the layout that it'd be as if I'd walked the floors a hundred times. The rest of the team had maps, but I didn't need them. There were times I resented my brain for its quirks.

Memorization wasn't one of those things.

We don't need a brain to kill them all.

I chuckled at my wolf as I checked the younger shifters' packs and ensured they still had everything. We carried human weapons which they'd all been trained on, but the real strength laid with their beasts. Jimenez was already in position after running through the checks on the purist flying machine. He was almost as good with mechanics as I was. I made a mental note to upgrade his position in the pack when we returned home.

I didn't want to separate Foster and Neil, but I needed another body to come with me and Shelby inside. It was too late to worry about that now though. We'd adapt with what we had and make it work.

I rechecked their weapons a final time before we moved to the next mark.

*

Night fell slowly, easing the desert heat, as we drew closer to the fence. Magic sparked when Shelby touched it. With our faces painted, we nodded at each other, and slipped back into the shadows of the boulders on the side of the broken road to wait.

The signal through the handheld radio I'd rebuilt when I was nine came as three short bursts.

Even on the lowest volume setting, the shifters startled as if a fog horn had blasted.

He's on time. My wolf was pleased.

As was I.

I held up three fingers.

"Ready?" I asked through the pack link.

The shifters moved into formation, steeling their nerves as bloodlust ran hot through their veins.

Two... One...

The crackle of energy faded, leaving nothing but the quiet, unassuming night as the predators stalked alongside me into the enemy purist territory.

19
† Kera †

This painting sucks.

The lines were all wrong. Crooked eyes with one a little larger than the other. Paint dripped down onto the too thin upper lip. If I squinted and leaned back it almost looked like...

A big fat booger was leaking from the bulbous nose on a monster.

I slapped the brush against the canvas, leaving a black streak across the center of the *not-really-a* face.

"It's abstract art." Coral looked up from her book as she laid on her stomach on my bed.

"That's what you said about the last one." I groaned in frustration, realizing there was no way I could salvage this monstrosity. I really didn't need an audience to my shame, but after I'd showed Jareth my secret hobby, it felt wrong to keep her in the dark. She hadn't judged me for it. Except for the word *abstract*. If I didn't know her better, I'd assume that was a thinly veiled insult.

"I'm tossing it." I unclipped the pins and ripped it from the easel. Coral jumped to her feet.

"Don't do that." She grabbed for the canvas. Our silent tug-of-war lasted a whole two seconds before I let her have the ugly thing.

Coral skipped away, gloating from her win as she studied the painting in the lantern light. "It's him, isn't it?"

"It was supposed to be," I grumbled, setting a blank canvas on the easel. I was almost out of the ones I'd bought in Amarok at the market. This was a waste of time and resources. I didn't know why I kept trying to paint his likeness. I could barely paint a tree, let alone capture the look in his soulful eyes like he held all the secrets of the universe. Or the curve of his hand as he caressed my face. Or the strength of his lips, pressed against mine in a way that made my knees weak.

I let out a pathetic whine, praying Coral didn't hear it as she ran from the room carrying the bad art to safety.

"Do you want to talk about it?" Her voice called from down the hall.

I stared at the blank canvas. "Where's Skoll?"

"Way to deflect." My Beta laughed at me from somewhere in the kitchen. "He and Maddock did an extra run to mark the southern borders. You know this. You requested it."

I cleaned the brush in the jar of mineral spirits. Maybe I should have gone to the border with them instead of doing whatever this was. But after running the pack harder than normal in training today, my Beta strongly encouraged me to take a step back. We needed numbers to prepare for the coming days and whatever plan Jareth was brewing up.

Killing my own shifters was apparently frowned upon if we wanted to keep up morale.

The bossy Beta skipped back into my room carrying two steaming mugs of tea. "Is that a no on talking about your fated mate?"

"What is there to say?" I sighed, rolling my neck to ease the tension from my shoulders as I dipped the brush into the brown. The color was nowhere close to his deliciously bronzed skin tone. I couldn't even mix paint right.

"You could talk about how you are feeling." Coral set one of the mugs down next to the paints.

"Feeling?" I asked.

"You know, that completely normal emotional response one gets when they are going through something." Coral smiled as she blew on the steam from her mug.

"Oh that." I tried not to smile. "I don't like those. I'd much rather kill something."

She snorted so hard tea went up her nose and her face turned red. Once I was sure she could breathe again, I turned back to my painting.

"There isn't much to say. We're both Alphas. There is a war coming. Time isn't on our side." I clung to the facts, nodding to myself as I carefully placed the first line of his cheekbone on the canvas.

"Hold that thought." Coral laughed as she ran out of my room.

It took a second of confusion before I caught the scent of cinnamon and earthy magic mixed with the smell of fresh baked sweets. Coral opened the front door to the cabin.

"Operation girl's night." Sage beamed as she held up a basket on the front porch. "I've got the goods. Where is she?"

*

I laid on the couch wearing a pair of loose sweatpants, completely at the mercy of the Luna witch and my Beta while they stuffed me full of cookies. But in this moment, they were just Sage and Coral. Their laughter and inside jokes they tried to include me in filled the small cabin. My world had been turned upside down since they arrived, in a good way. I never had close friends or people I could relax with.

Being the Alpha's daughter separated me from the rest of the pack. I chuckled to myself, taking a sip of tea to hide the internal amusement.

Jareth kept calling me a princess as if I'd been locked in some ivory tower instead of isolated and kept on the outskirts of my pack, forced to fight my way through the ranks and take the brunt of abuse from my unhinged father.

Jareth thought he knew everything. Typical Alpha males and their giant… egos.

I didn't want to think of what else he had that was oversized. Not the feel of it pressed against my stomach when I'd sat on his lap. Not the way his hands cupped my…

"Sage, what did you do?" Coral's worried whisper snapped me from my thoughts.

212

The room was too hot. I looked up to see both of their eyes on me, blushing as the scent of my arousal hung heavy in the air.

"What?" Sage frowned as she looked to what was left of the basket of cookies. "You said we were going to talk about boys tonight."

The red flush burned hotter on my skin and I squeezed my legs together, definitely not thinking about any boys. Jareth was a man. His growl sent vibrations straight to my core. The taste of his tongue as it swept my mouth. The confidence in which he…

I moaned, bolting upright.

"Oh no." Coral's eyes widened. She leaned closer to her sister, whispering as if I couldn't hear her, "Did your love cookies maybe have a hint of passion in them?"

The rush of blood brought sweat beading on my face and I swallowed hard. "Love cookies?"

"No," Sage started, looking to the basket as if it was to blame and not her. "I was thinking about fated mates and wanted us to be able to relax while we were talking about them."

I was not relaxed.

Oh Gods. I want my mate.

My wolf panted, urging me to run, as a wave of desire crashed over me. It wasn't the same intensity as a heat—thankfully—but it reared up just as fast.

I tugged at my clothes, thinking about what I'd do next year. Now that I knew Jareth, I wanted him there and not my grandmother standing guard a respectful distance away while I took care of myself alone in a cave. I would be loud next time. Feral. Give into every desire of my beast.

Which conjured up images I did not want to be having while sitting on this couch.

"Love cookies?" I barked louder this time, delirious as I pictured melting chocolate dripping down the delicious dips and curves of Jareth's muscular chest. I wet my lips, almost tasting it. Sage and Coral jumped to their feet.

"This is all your fault!" Coral was screaming. "Could you not think about Maddock in the bedroom for one freaking minute?"

"I'm sorry," Sage cried.

I squeezed my eyes shut. My uncle was the last thing on earth I wanted to think about now.

"Hang on. I can fix this." Sage raced to the kitchen.

A glass of water was pressed to my lips and I drank deep, grateful for the cooling sensation that eased the fire burning my body from the inside out. My breathing slowed and the tingles started to fade.

I took another sip, making sure I was back in control, and cracked open one eye to look at them. "That was so not cool."

Both Sage and Coral were statues, watching me as if I might explode. I tossed the rest of the water onto them to break the trance.

They burst into laughter, clutching their sides as they sagged against each other. I couldn't breathe through the fit of giggles rocking me too. It took forever to get them to stop.

Sighing, I rested my head back against the couch. "Okay, I needed this."

"I really am sorry." Sage was still trying to hold back her laughter. "It's like a funnel opened up these past few months and the magic flows out stronger than I want. It must have been a quick moment when I was infusing them with thoughts of love that desire slipped out. I swear I didn't mean to make them this potent."

"No. It's fine." I waved my hand in the air, choking down another laugh that wanted to escape. "Your magic only works if the intent is there and I might have been suppressing that part of myself a bit."

Sage and Coral shared the same knowing look, waiting for me to explain. I shrugged it off. There were many things I didn't mind talking about, but my lack of experience wasn't one of them.

"You do like him though," Coral said, changing the subject to something less intrusive.

"I do," I admitted. "He's strange and a little weird, but there's something about him that calls to me on a deeper level. I don't think it's all the mate bond either."

"Maddock thinks he's an asshole." Sage chuckled.

"Jareth is an Alpha. We're all assholes." I looked to the window, hoping they wouldn't see the worry on my face. I didn't want their pity, but I needed to get these words out. "I don't think Alphas are supposed to be paired together."

Coral reached for my hand and gave it a gentle squeeze. "I've honestly been thinking about that and I figure fate knew you'd never settle for anyone less strong-willed than you."

"Is that your way of calling me an asshole?" I teased.

"If the shoe fits…" Her face lit up as she winked. "I'm kidding. You need someone to take care of you too. I'm happy fate paired you with an Alpha strong enough to do that."

I blinked back the burning sensation behind my eyes. It'd been years since I cried and I wasn't about to start now. Especially over something so trivial as a future relationship. We had bigger things to worry about.

"Fate paired me with an Alpha. Neither of us have time for each other. There are too many issues and there always will be." Those were the facts.

"None of us know the future." Sage moved to my side and put her hand on my shoulder. Her magic was a soothing balm. "Except Lisa, of course, but even she can't see everything. Fate paired you for a reason. You're going to have to trust the bond if you choose not to reject it."

The thought of rejecting him, of living a life without him, slashed against my heart as my wolf let out a painfilled howl. I couldn't even entertain the idea now that he'd buried his essence under my skin and given me a taste of what could be.

I cleared my throat and nodded.

Sage was right.

He's mine.

But how is this going to work?

"What's the plan to rescue his sister?" Coral changed the subject again, sensing my unease.

As if war was more comfortable for me to talk about than love.

I'd process that later.

"I'm not sure. He's going to get back to me in a few days. Tomorrow I'll talk to the troops after we finish setting up the outposts down south."

"And what will you say to them?" Sage worried her bottom lip, probably thinking of what she'd have to tell the families.

"I won't force anyone to fight," I told her, recalling the stance of the other Alphas. "They'll be allowed to make their own decisions. If they want to stand with me and Anubis, it'll be their choice."

"You're a good leader." Sage smiled. "The pack is lucky to have you."

I blushed under her praise, turning to Coral who was lost in thought. "What is it?"

Coral blew out a long breath. "None of this seems right. The purists aren't fighting some war against shifters unless there is a secret most of the citizens don't know. Which may be true. Everything we thought we knew was a lie. But I tried to tell the council in Anubis about this. Hardly any of the purists know how to defend themselves. They aren't trained for battle. We were taught not to fight each other. I'm not sure the threat you all imagine is there."

"Jareth knows their weapons capability. He's been seeing…" My voice trailed off. Those were his words, not mine, and I couldn't understand them enough to use anyway. "The purists did attack Junction City. They took the pups and Ophelia. We have eye witness reports."

"I'm not denying that." Coral held up her hands. "I'm saying we need more information. Maybe I should find a way back. I could talk to Mia."

"No." Sage shook her head. I glanced between the two of them, realizing they'd already had this conversation. The worry in Sage's eyes bothered me. I didn't want either of them to go back there either.

"Let's shelve this for now." I sensed Maddock and Skoll returning as both women looked to the door wistfully.

And that was my cue to leave.

I stood, making my way to my room, but had to issue a final Alpha command as I pointed to the basket. "And Sage, take those *love cookies* back to your own damn cabin."

*

Alone in my bed, I tried to get comfortable. Every touch of fabric against my skin and each little lump in the mattress was making it hard to sleep. I sighed, reaching out with my senses to check the web of connection I had with my pack in Cerberus lands. All of them were settled now, lost to their dreams, except for the few distant souls still moving and stationed at the lookouts we'd put in the southern part of the territory. The distance made it harder to connect with them, but they were safe.

I laid my head back on the pillow and listened to the soft snores of Coral and Skoll in the other room, wondering if Jareth was sleeping now too.

Groaning, I pulled the warm pillow out from under my head and put it across my face.

You should have told him.

Told him what?

That we want him.

Would that have changed anything?

We could be wearing his mark.

It still wouldn't change anything, I grumbled.

If we sealed the bond, I'd be able to sense him wherever he was. We'd share our soul, our healing capabilities, our memories, and our emotions. But even complete, I wouldn't be able to communicate with him over this vast distance. There would be so many nights spent like this.

Alone in my bed.

An empty ache settled deep in my core as I wondered what it would be like to have him here.

Sage's love cookies were still messing with my head. I could smell him. The lingering masculine scent hung in my room and called to my beast, bringing back images of his hard cock in my fist while we'd wrestled. I smiled, touching my lips, and remembering the taste of his mouth on mine.

My hand traveled lower, imagining his hands on my breasts as I kneaded them gently. His eyes darkening with desire. The feral growl of his beast.

A shock of pleasure shot through me.

I trailed my hand lower, dipping under the waistband of my pants, and rubbed against my clit. His hands were so rough and calloused. I pressed harder, wondering what his fingers would feel like if he touched me here. I cupped my center and rocked against it, pretending it was his body that pressed against mine as I bit back a moan.

It wasn't enough.

I squeezed my eyes shut tight as I spread my legs open, searching for something. A connection. The image of his face. A whisp of our growing bond to cling to as I pushed one finger inside.

There. I gasped, sensing the slightest hint of a flame. A spark from a match jumped in the darkness of my mind. I curled my finger, dragging it up slowly.

"Jareth," I whispered, tasting his name on my lips. The flame grew brighter. My soul called to it, begging for him to hear me.

I pumped my finger faster, chasing the brightness of that light as the heat continued to grow.

Come for me, princess. The sound of his voice was a teasing my own mind conjured. Stars edged my vision as I danced alone toward the call of it.

Red and orange flames burst as I exploded.

I buried my face in the pillow to muffle my scream as I rolled to the side. The light began to dim, but still I held to it, not ready to let go yet as the aftershocks vibrated through me.

It was him. Somehow, I knew it. Or maybe it was wishful thinking, but I wanted it to be.

I wanted Jareth here with me.

The light blinked out just as fast as it came. A cold breeze blew across my back from the open window. My wolf snarled as my eyes shot open.

No.

A connection in my pack snapped into place. One soul waking as it reached out to me. The sound of my grandmother's voice came over the link.

"Kera. Something is wrong."

20
† Jareth †

Kera.

My wolf let out a long sigh, distracted for a moment. I forced myself to push away thoughts of the fiery she-wolf and her sweet earthy scent. There'd been something there, a brief flash of a spark, but it was too dangerous to focus on now.

Sticking to the shadows, we moved with inhuman speed and picked our way through the rundown buildings that sat outside the looming walls of the purist city. The stench was overpowering. No wonder I wanted to remember Kera's smell instead. Trash buildup and decay, unwashed bodies and muddy streets. There were bursts of magic here and there that smelt burnt–*wrong*–as if the users were scorched by their own weak power.

Every now and then, we'd get a whiff of shifter blood, but even that was diluted and tainted somehow. Wondering eyes looked straight through us without recognizing the predators in their midst.

If this was how the humans lived, clinging to the walls in the decaying outskirts, maybe an invasion would be doing them a favor.

But that was a problem for another day.

My sole focus was on keeping my team alive and extracting my people safely.

"Everything still quiet?" I asked Jimenez.

He had the purist flyer parked near the outcropping of boulders inside the fence line and we'd disabled the homing trackers.

"I'm set. Waiting on you, Alpha."

"Twenty minutes after I give the signal." I growled, directing my senses toward the wall to try and grasp the connection to my pack hidden within. The webs were there, dimmed by the human buildings and the blur of technology, but I touched each string to the pups. I sent out a calming reassurance, hoping the little ones would know I was coming. It took a moment longer to reach her presence, still too far away to communicate directly with, but I finally felt it.

Her aura was strong.

I'm on my way, Ophelia.

Breathing a sigh of relief, I checked the rest of my team and headed deeper into the Fringes.

We came to a stop in the darkened doorway of a two-story building with sectioned off rooms. The scent of so many humans crammed into a single space made my wolf agitated. The unease of the shifters beside me came first though and I focused on sending confidence their way. I touched Shelby and Foster's shoulders, sending them up the rickety stairs, and motioned for Neil to take his location watching the street.

So far so good.

Phase one of the mission was complete.

*

Blue light glowed from the panel of computer screens over the stale chips and wrappers that lined the desk. Heavy black curtains hung from the windows to keep in, or out, the light. Shelby and Foster were still on edge, even after I explained what we were looking at. It really blew their mind when he pulled up the holograph projections.

I had a vintage laptop model I'd refurbished at twelve, but it wasn't something I went around showing everyone. I'd also set up an amplifier allowing me to pick up the signal from the Fringes.

Try explaining that to a bunch of wolves.

Please don't try again.

The fact that Ethan was a teenage boy who smelled like a diluted mutt of some sort under all that funk wasn't helping matters. Thankfully, my shifters knew better than to question me. I didn't have time to explain. The goal was to get out of here as fast as possible. Any longer and the council would get wind of what I was doing.

I had enough headaches to deal with.

"Here are the main security camera feeds." Ethan drew up another window on the screen. Shelby and Foster growled at the sudden flash.

Sweat beaded on the kid's pimpled brow and he sucked in a deep breath. "No one is going to believe this."

"No one will because we were never here." I rested my hand on his shoulder, infusing my tone with an Alpha command that I hoped would reach through the generations of his DNA and speak to that missing part of him.

"Oh, yeah. Of course." Ethan nodded eagerly. "But I wanted to ask, are you guys like real mutants? Can you…um…change?"

I lifted my hand and extended a claw, using it to tap the screen. "Back to the footage."

"Wicked cool." His wide eyes reflected the blue light as his fingers flew over the keyboard. More video windows opened and with a few clicks, he sent them as holograph images to float in the air.

Feeds came up in all directions with cameras pointing at different angles. Hallways appeared in the same order of the blueprints I'd memorized, filling in the 3D details to the reconstructed layout I'd envisioned.

"I've tried hacking any hidden systems, but it doesn't look like they have cameras on floors five and six. Those top two floors are secret clearance only access from the elevators. And then we have the rooftop cameras at the landing pad." Each new window popped up as a holograph image at Ethan's command, filling the cramped room.

Shelby growled and smacked one that neared too close to his arm like it was a bug. I ignored his unease, focusing on the feeds playing back at high speed and slowing them down in my mind's eye.

"Circle back." I pointed at the camera labeled Floor Four. Ethan rewound the video and replayed it on a slower speed.

The bangles on her wrist caught the reflection of the florescent light. A quick flash from the cage entering the elevator, going up.

"Pause it again." Rage tinted my vision red as I stared at that sliver of a bracelet. The same ones our mother wore when we were young.

They put my little sister in a cage.

I'm going to kill every last one of them.

"And no one has left?" I growled along with my beast.

Ethan clicked to fast forward the feeds. "I've been monitoring them since you sent me notice. They have to be on one of those two floors still."

"Alright." My fists clenched at my sides. I had the layout of every floor in that building memorized. Screw the cameras. "And you're sure the service exit for trash is open?"

"Oh science, you guys are really going in that way. This is some James Bond stuff." Ethan's face lit up in wonder.

"Who?" all three of us asked.

"Never mind." He shook his head. "The chute opens from two-AM to seven-AM when they offload all the trucks. If you go now, it should be less congested."

"Let's move." I nodded to Shelby. "Foster, you'll stay here."

"Alpha," Foster choked out, looking to the kid. He wasn't much older, but the years spent behind a computer screen gave Ethan a younger looking stature.

I placed a second radio in Foster's hand. "If something happens, you get in touch with Jimenez. We get them out one way or another."

"And watch him," I added through the pack link.

Foster nodded, holding the radio out from his body like it was going to explode. "What do I do with this?"

"I'll show you." Ethan slid his rolling chair back, eager to help. One day, I'd see what I could do to get him and his grandfather out of this place. After all our years of communicating, he'd never told me it was this bad.

One step at a time.

I hurried down the stairs with Shelby at my side, sending up a silent prayer to the Gods that they'd watch over us tonight.

"Alpha, are you sure we can trust him?" Shelby asked, stepping onto the dirty street behind me. "He's just a kid."

I smirked, adjusting the weapon on my back so my claws were free, and whistled for Neil to join us. "That's what they used to say about me."

*

This was too easy.

I knew it, but I wasn't going to sit around thinking about why. The trash service exit was unguarded, devoid of life except for the few scavengers with flashlights who picked through piles of rubbish. They barely glanced at us once they realized we weren't there to hunt alongside them.

If what lay beyond the giant walls was better than the Fringes, you'd think there'd be more protection at the entry. But maybe they'd grown complacent. There is no reason to fight for something better if you roll on your back and accept your lot in life.

With our shifter vision, we didn't need the dim lights from the buildings in the distance to make our way through the darkened industrial complex. Empty parking lots and the sharp smell of steel lay around us black as night.

The government research facility stood like an ominous beacon up ahead. Security floodlights illuminated the metal fences topped with barbed wire.

"There." I pointed it out to Shelby and Neil. They growled. Their wolves were dangerously close to the surface and itching for a fight.

I held them back a moment longer, reaching out with my senses to get a feel for the land and scent out any hidden traps. There was no magic here. It was clay baked and toxic, stifling in its grandiosity.

A guard tower stood on the wall to the right of the compound. By the soft grunts and smacking sounds, I hoped he'd be occupied for some time.

Satisfied we were undetected for now, I leaned into my pack connections and sought out my shifters in the building.

Ophelia always wore dark clothes, matching her long black hair, but her aura, the essence of her soul, shone like a rainbow to me.

I latched onto the brightness and smiled now that I was close enough to communicate. *"You dumbass little wolf."*

"Jareth?" Her thoughts were muddied, waking from sleep, but her voice was strong.

I could have howled in relief if I wasn't silently racing toward the looming facility with Neil and Shelby on my heels. *"Are you hurt?"*

I'll kill them.

"What? Why? How?" She gasped, coming fully awake.

"Did you think I wouldn't?" I growled and resisted the urge to scold her. There'd be time to do that later once all of them were safe. *"Do you have any details on your location?"*

"No. You can't." Her voice was a whisper despite speaking in her mind. *"You have to go back. The pack needs you."*

Of course she would say something stupid like that. Shelby and Neil skidded to a stop behind me as we reached the fence. We crouched in the shadows where the floodlights didn't reach.

"Twenty minutes." I spoke into the radio tuned to the frequency for Jimenez and Foster.

Shelby and Neil growled, claws extending as they gripped the metal links.

Three…

Two…

One…

The floodlights blinked off.

Damn, that hacker kid was good.

Silence stretched before us as the government research facility effectively powered down. Security systems turned off with the touch of a button. The whir of technology useless now.

I dug my bare feet into the metal links and hoisted myself up. We could have torn the fence, but it wasn't that far of a climb. Shelby ripped the barbwire off the top with a shake of his wrist. His hand was already healing before he dropped the wire to the ground below.

"You're here!" Ophelia's high-pitched shriek rattled in my head as I landed silently in the parking lot on the other side of the fence.

"I told you I was." I moved fast, breeching the side door that would lead to the security office and the service stairwell beyond it.

Shelby lunged at the sentry who struggled with a flashlight on his belt. Claws extended, the shifter punched through the purist's guts and ripped out his entrails as easily as the barbed wire. The gore squelched under my feet as we scanned the office for more bodies.

"Clear." Neil pushed forward, his voice betraying none of the nervousness I knew he felt.

I rushed to the steel door at the end of the hall that led to the stairwell, sensing for movement behind it and finding none. I didn't hesitate. We leapt up the cold concrete steps in the darkened stairwell, only stopping to chain the first door.

"Jareth! Stop!" Ophelia cried. *"They're listening."*

"Listening?" I put out my arm, stopping Shelby and Neil from crashing into me as we slid onto the second-floor landing. My wolf lent me his hearing as we *listened* back.

There was a commotion on the levels above us. Boots stomping along linoleum floors. Hurried shouts of "intruders." Not a problem. I didn't think we'd keep up the element of surprise for long.

Seventeen more minutes.

I slowed down my heart, counting as each boot hit the floors above in slow motion. Eight steps. Four guards. We slunk back into the shadows and pressed ourselves against the wall as the metal door on the landing above us swung open with a loud creak.

Flashlight beams swept the stairwell on the floors above and below us. Humans were loud, clumsy, as they barreled down the steps.

"Jareth, you idiot! They have these devices…"

I tuned out my sister's frantic cries as the first of the guards came within arm's reach. I wanted them close. Their weapons were only useful until I pulled them from their grasp.

Screams echoed around us. Bursts of shots from guns fired in close quarters rang in the darkened stairwell. I sank my fangs into the first guard's neck, ripping out his carotid artery and spraying blood over the concrete walls as I shoved him back.

His body crashed into the group of purists that followed. I leapt over the fallen guard and reached for another, my fist inclosing around his neck. Brain matter splashed as I slammed his skull into the stairs.

The other two guards turned tail and ran. Shelby and Neil gave chase while I locked out the second floor with another chain from my pack.

Thirteen minutes.

At the third floor landing, I shoved what remained of Shelby and Neil's kills out of the way to chain the entry doors. The shifters stood panting by my side, wiping blood from their chins.

We weren't coming back this way. I didn't want the pups exposed to the gore. But I covered our bases anyway and gave the purists something to work at. Let them think we were as stupid as they were.

Ten minutes.

We raced up to the next floor landing, chasing the sound of chaos raining above. Neil got there first and shoved his shoulder against the door as more booted feet came running down the hall beyond it.

The door pushed outward, but the effort of the purists wasn't enough to budge three grown shifters as I latched the handle with another chain.

"They finally figured out we were here." Shelby chuckled.

"Took them long enough." I grunted, locking the chain.

"How much time do we have?" Neil panted as he raced up the stairs behind me. The young shifter was holding his own. Griffon had picked them well.

"Eight minutes left, but we don't need it." I pressed the button on the radio, giving Jimenez the go ahead to fly to the roof as we rushed out of the stairwell onto the fifth level of the building. If Ethan was right, it'd take a while for any of the night guards to get secret clearance passes to access the elevators to this floor. He'd earned my trust by now.

"What room are you in?" I tapped into the link with my sister now that the doors in the hallway stretched out before us. The hall was illuminated by the dim red emergency lights that kicked on with the generator after the power failure. There were six offices, a lab, and eight patient rooms.

Floor six had a similar layout.

Ophelia was crying softly.

"Answer me!" I snapped at her, kicking open the first office door to the right as Shelby rushed in to clear the room. *"Do you know where you are?"*

"It's too late," she sobbed. *"Damn you for being a hero."*

My blood ran cold, hearing the defeat in her voice, as my wolf snarled his bloodlust to the world.

I will kill them... I will...

Growling, I forced myself to focus. The web of my pack pulled toward the lab and I could sense the pups. Ophelia wasn't there though. I closed my eyes, calming my breathing, to seek her presence out.

And located it on the floor above.

233

Shelby kicked in the deadbolt of the lab door and stepped inside. Neil swept the hall before ducking in after him. The grieving howl of the two shifter males had me sprinting forward, ready to destroy the threat to my pack.

I came to a stop just outside the lab door.

Instant nausea overcame my beast as I stepped past the vomit that spewed from Neil's mouth onto the floor. Fecal matter and chemical agents tainted by the haunt of death.

Cages. Tiny cages. Rows of bars stretched the length of the room. Silent machines hooked up to tubing. I placed my fist in my mouth, biting back a growl. For the first time in my life, my brain couldn't process what was happening fast enough.

Bony, fur covered elbows. Half starved newborn wolves. The mewingly whimpers and weak yips as we stared at cage after cage of terrified golden eyes that peeked out from behind the bars. And those were just the ones that looked at us. Other's had eyes swollen shut, barely moving. Rows and rows of abandoned baby pups, separated from each other by cages so they couldn't even pile up to keep warm.

I will burn this place to the ground.

My claws extended and clothes ripped from my body as my beast tried to force the change. I ground my teeth, struggling to keep him contained as Shelby and Neil looked to me for support. Their wolves were rising too, drawn by the bloodlust of my beast, but we needed hands for this.

"There's so many." Neil wiped the vomit from his mouth. "Where are they all from?"

I blinked, getting control of my wolf.

"Ophelia, what is going on?" I jumped into action, tearing through the locking mechanisms on the cages, and holding back the burning rage that threatened to turn me into a feral creature.

"Just leave me here!" she screamed.

With a frustrated growl, I ripped off the bolts on the first row of cages. Shelby and Neil followed, sniffing out our pack members and placing them into a sack. The radio beeped at my hip.

Shit.

Jimenez was almost here, ready to land on the roof. I needed to go and find Ophelia.

I reached into the first cage, locking eyes with the little pup. He couldn't be more than two and he barked excitedly, tiny claws digging into my arm when he felt my Alpha presence surround him. His scent was familiar. I breathed it in, remembering the bullet ridden bedroom and the toy stuffed wolf.

Logan.

I made his mother a promise.

Holding the pup to my chest, I looked at the others. There were so many of them. More than those of my pack. Motherless. Alone. No one to demand a promise for.

"Get them all out," I barked, handing Logan over to Neil. He quickly tucked the pup in with the others.

"But, Alpha…" Shelby turned to look at me, motioning to the rows of cages as I dumped my pack on the floor.

"Get every single one of them." I growled, issuing the strongest Alpha command I could muster. Anger and beastly nature rode me hard. My protective instinct clouded rational thought.

"What about Luna Ophelia?" Neil whined, compelled to turn back to the cage as he tried to coax a blind newborn pup out.

"I'll get my sister. Take all these pups to the roof. If we're not back before the lights come on, go and don't look back."

Their growls of disapproval followed me down the hall, but they had no choice but to obey.

*

Ophelia's scent grew stronger as I raced down the hallway on the sixth floor to the patient rooms.

My heart beat harder in response and my wolf howled, demanding revenge.

"We're leaving!" I screamed at her to get ready as my feet slapped against the cold floors.

"Last room on the right." Her voice held a silent warning as I skidded to a stop outside the door, not caring in my fit of rage what lay in wait.

I welcomed the fight. Dared them to challenge me. My wolf snarled for the taste of purist blood. I kicked in the metal door, bending it in two, and shoved it the rest of the way open.

Weak moonlight spilled from the single window that overlooked the patient bed. White tubes and tape connected to her shaved head. All her hair was gone. She looked so pale. Worried eyes filled with tears as she stared at me.

I howled in fury, claws extending. "What did they do to you?"

A hornet sting pricked into my neck and I swatted at it almost absentmindedly as I took a step toward the bed. My vision swam and I staggered, shutting my eyes as the blinding bright lights flicked on in the room.

Poison.

"Alpha, we're loaded up," Jimenez growled through the pack link.

"Go." I barked out the order, sinking to my knees. The world spun and I clawed at my own throat, listening to my little sister scream.

21
† Kera †

"Someone needs to tell me what the fuck is going on." I paced the length of my office, carrying the cold pit of dread in my stomach. Three of my fastest runners had made the trek to Anubis and back. Not a single one of them was able to get in contact with Alpha Jareth.

"It's unclear." My grandmother Lisa had come from her lone cabin in the woods and was sitting with her head in her hands at my desk. "I saw him fall. Heard the screams of the children. But I don't have anything familiar to pinpoint a location with."

The knot in my gut twisted harder. Sweat slicked my palms as I clenched them into fists. I felt like I was going to be sick.

"Try the tea leaves or something." I shouldn't have growled at her, but it was midmorning and I hadn't slept at all last night.

Because I *knew* something was wrong. The ache of it settled in my bones. If this was some kind of premonition for the future, I had to warn Jareth and the rest of the packs. But it didn't feel like something that was coming. It felt…

I clenched my teeth to stop from crying out.

It felt like it already happened.

My fated mate was lost to me.

No. He isn't, my wolf snarled.

It would be my luck, I thought bitterly. I had a chance at happiness and I let it slip away. I didn't fight hard enough to keep him here. He left.

I wasn't enough.

The sneers of my father came as whispers of the past, reminding me of my faults. I didn't deserve a future with someone I loved. This was always meant to happen and I'd been foolish for believing differently.

"Skoll is heading out now." Coral mind-linked me before she threw open the doors to the office.

"You can go with him." I gave her permission, seeing the worried look in her eyes.

"And leave you alone to terrorize the pack?" She snorted as she motioned to the three runners standing at attention against the wall. "Fat chance."

Gods, I forgot they were still standing there. I hung my head, needing to ask them again, "You're positive there was no other attacks?"

My gut could be wrong. There still might be time to give them warning.

"There was nothing, Alpha. The Beta Griffon says he will be in touch as soon as Alpha Jareth gets back from wherever he has gone."

"You're dismissed." I kept my voice even, trying not to let the panic leak through.

He went to save his sister.

He wouldn't be crazy enough to go on his own.

But I didn't really know him. He might be crazy enough to do just that. Why else would he not be answering and not let me know where he was?

A dark thought entered my mind. Maybe he didn't want to talk to me again. I'd imagined our growing connection. He was too much of a coward to reject me outright. And here I was, acting like a lunatic.

He needs us. My wolf growled to silence those thoughts. She was amped up and pacing, ready to fight some unknown threat.

We don't know that for sure.

I know.

I swallowed down my self-pity, looking to Coral for some words of wisdom. "What if I'm wrong?"

"Don't doubt yourself." Her big brown eyes narrowed. "Your Alpha instinct is strong, but the connection to your fated mate is stronger. If you feel that something isn't right, I believe you."

I straightened my shoulders, bolstered by her confidence, and my wolf gave a growl of approval.

"And Skoll is actually driving so he'll be there this afternoon." Coral stood beside me and I leaned against her, drawing strength from my friend.

"It'll be okay." My grandmother reached for my hand. "I see a future beyond this one. I just don't know how to get to that point."

There was something hidden behind her bluish gray eyes, the same color she passed down to me, which spoke of a hard truth. But I didn't question it when she said things would work out. She always knew when they would.

I had to trust in the people around me.

Which meant, I had to wait.

*

We ran the perimeter around the territory in wolf form, checking the guard posts where I had shifters positioned to give us warning of incoming attacks from the purist city. My beast was drawn to the southern lines and I had to keep coaxing her back.

Everything was quiet. An abnormally warm fall day with brown leaves drifting lazily from the trees. Coral was silent as she ran beside me, giving a solid presence to counteract the anxious energy that was tearing me apart.

I couldn't bring myself to eat.

Things were getting worse.

And my wolf fought the change harder than she'd ever done when we came back to the training grounds to work. I had to leave without talking to the pack. They deserved a better Alpha than me.

I was so lost in my own damn head that I couldn't do much else besides sit numb on the porch of our cabin and stare at the road.

"It's going to be okay." Coral's optimism was like putting salve over a gushing wound, well-intentioned but pointless. Until I knew what happened and had a plan to act, I wasn't much more than a mindless beast. I was an Alpha. I needed to be in control. Sitting here waiting was killing me.

The sun dipped low on the horizon and the stars came out to dot the night sky as Sage and

Maddock took up stationary positions beside us on the porch. I needed to snap out of this. Do something. Fight something. Tear something apart.

The rumble of the truck engine brought the sweet relief I was aching for. Answers. I'd never been happier to see that thick skulled alpha wolf in my life.

Skoll stepped from the truck and Coral rushed to his side. He embraced her gently, inhaling her scent, before his pained expression glanced up to me. And, suddenly, I didn't want to know anymore.

*

I stared at the folded piece of paper on the table, numb and dejected from myself. A spectator standing on the outside and watching the events play out. It was only my wolf that kept me grounded, whining for me to come back like she'd done so many times when I was a child. This numbness. The fear. Watching hope slip through your fingers.

It's funny how those things can't be outgrown.

"I wrestled this information from Beta Griffon." Skoll was talking and I tried to focus on his words. "He didn't want to give you this letter. Jareth said it was only to be sent if he didn't return and Griffon swears he is coming back."

"How many pups did they recover?" Maddock asked. The sound of his deep voice was an anchor to reality.

"It must have been at least a hundred." Skoll tucked Coral under his arm. "They were bringing wet nurses in from all over Anubis."

"I can't believe the purists really had all those pups. If they weren't taken from out here, were they bred in there?" There were tears in Coral's eyes.

Sage sat at the table, staring at the glass of whiskey she rolled between her palms. "I can believe it."

She raised the glass to her lips, flicking her gaze up to me. Something snapped and I blinked as I slammed back into my body.

"Why didn't he alert the other packs? Why didn't his Beta go with him?" I clawed for more information, needing control so I didn't sink again.

Skoll's expression softened. "You have to understand the way Anubis works. In a pack that large, the council is needed to help manage it. The same council has been there since his father's time and they've seen him grow up. Jareth has always been a genius. But the council resists change and he's used to fighting them every step of the way to make the pack better for his people. They would have broken him if he didn't rebel. Throughout the years, he's learned that if he wants something done, he has to do it himself. And now he doesn't trust people to help."

I lowered my face, nodding as I looked back to the paper on the table. There was a time when I felt the same. I watched the people of this pack refuse to stand up to my father and abandon me. If things were going to change, I had to be the one to step up to do it. But unlike Jareth, I had a support system now. I'd learned to trust my circle. I understood his need to save Ophelia, especially if she was the only one close to him in the lonely position as an Alpha.

I braced myself to read the words in the letter.

His handwriting was awful. I had to squint to make out some of the lines, rereading it again as a lump formed in my throat. It burned to swallow past it and I blinked back the moisture in my eyes.

If it helps you to forgive me, I want you to know that I didn't think you'd ever see this. But I hope you of all people understand why I had to go. I made a promise to my shifters, to my parents. Alphas protect. It's what we do.
I regret that we didn't get enough time together.
My parents were fated mates and they were happy. I wish you could have met them. My mother always believed that souls lived on. If that's true, I promise to find you in the next life and I'll try not to make as many mistakes then.
I could never have rejected you.
Be happy. Find love. Live for us.
I wasn't good enough for you anyway, princess.
-J

"I'm not a princess." I smiled bitterly, folding the letter as my wolf howled in pain. The room was quiet. My family was waiting for my response.

I looked up to see their eyes on me. "He's not dead."

"Griffon doesn't think so either." Skoll sat heavily on the chair. "Jareth is smart. I don't think…"

"You don't have to think anything," I snapped. "I know he isn't dead."

Skoll nodded, keeping his beast in check, as Coral put her hands on his shoulders to calm him.

Her gaze met mine, full of determination. "What do we do? Should we wait like Griffon was ordered to?"

I huffed out a humorless laugh. "Jareth isn't my Alpha. I don't take orders from him."

Like this stupid letter. *Be happy, huh?*

No.

He didn't get to escape and try again in some other life. This was our life. I wanted it. I wanted him.

"He told me he'd send word if he needed help. I'm considering this message an SOS."

"You can't fight a war against the purists in their city." Maddock shook his head. "He made the decision to go alone knowing the consequences."

"He did what he could with what he had." I slammed my fist against the table, forcing my uncle to look at me. "If Coral or Sage were taken, do you think I wouldn't have done the same thing?"

Maddock was growling. Skoll started growling.

Yeah, that touched a nerve.

I growled back at the two of them, daring one of the men to challenge me.

Coral waved her hands in the air, trying to calm everyone down. "Now isn't the time to make rash decisions and obviously none of us want a war."

"There won't be one." I tucked the letter in my pocket. "I'm going alone to get my mate."

"Stop it." Coral stomped her foot on the floor. "How many times have we been through this? You're not alone. We're your family. If you go somewhere, so do we."

I squeezed my eyes shut to stop the tears that tried to well up again as my wolf let out a pathetic whine. "Please don't make me choose between your safety and my future happiness. I'm an Alpha. I can take care of myself."

The instant quiet in the room was startling. I opened my eyes, expecting to argue further, but no one was looking at me. Skoll pulled Coral onto his lap and hugged her close. Sage touched Maddock's arm, silencing his beast.

"What?" I asked, feeling my chest deflate. It was easier when everyone was yelling. I could command the room with Alpha power. Make my position known and heard. But when they went silent, I needed to hear them speak.

Because they were my family.

It wasn't easy to know how to be in a real one, learning this late in life, but I was still trying, damn it.

Sage took another sip from her whiskey. The amber liquid reflected the flame from the lantern the same way it did in her big brown eyes. "You may be the Alpha, but you don't make my decisions for me either. Sit down."

"What's that supposed to mean?" I sat back onto my chair. Sage never talked to me like this. To

Coral she did, but she'd never once raised her voice to me. I glanced at my Beta. She looked away.

Growling, I refocused on Sage.

I couldn't command her like she was a wolf. Witches marched to their own beat. But she had to know I couldn't risk anything happening to them.

It would kill me.

"You need us." Sage rubbed Maddock's arm again when he started growling. "Even if you could somehow find the source Jareth was in contact with and get through the fence, you wouldn't know your way around the city."

She's right.

"The pack needs you here to take care of them," I argued, knowing it was a weak point and I was about to lose this fight.

"Then we'll be quick." Sage winked.

Maddock snarled as he pushed back his chair. Skoll clung to Coral tighter. Control was slipping from my grasp and I realized I was on the men's side. Fat lot of good that would do me now. Coral and Sage always got their way.

"This is too dangerous," I tried again.

The sisters shared another look. One of the silent ones that went beyond communicating with a pack link. And I knew whatever they were thinking, we wouldn't like.

"This is my future. My mate. I won't risk you getting hurt for me." My voice was losing its power.

"As much as I want to see you happy, this is bigger than you." Coral leaned into Skoll, soothing his beast, but riling mine even more. "If they're experimenting on pups and breeding them there, we have to do something. The people deserve to know what the government is up to. I couldn't live with myself if I didn't fight back."

Curse the Gods. Why was Coral always right?

"We can't win a war alone," Maddock said. His tone was also losing its bite. "And even knowing what we do now, it'll take a long time to get all the other packs to agree."

"If they ever do," Skoll added bitterly.

I put my head in my hands. We didn't have another choice. This wasn't what I'd signed up for when I took control of my pack, but I refused to turn a blind eye now that I'd seen the truth of the world.

"Are you sure this is what you want to do?" I asked, raising my face to look at each one of them as they nodded. Their minds were already made up. Even Skoll and Maddock begrudgingly accepted this had to happen. All they were waiting for was me. They wanted to make sure I was okay, because I wasn't alone. Not like Jareth.

I had a family.

He is our family too. My wolf howled a battle cry and I felt the call of it in my bones.

I was going to save my mate and change our world in the process. "Have the pack meet me on the training grounds at first light."

"Do you already have a plan?" Coral smiled encouragingly. I'd leave it to her to handle the humans while I figured out a way to keep everyone safe.

"Not a damn clue yet." I stood from the table, wishing I had more words to explain how much I cared about everyone in this room. "But whatever we end up doing, we'll be working together. Any one who wants to join us, will make their own decision to come too."

*

I gave into my wolf's urge to run, needing to burn off this anxious energy and have the time to work through the logistics of what we needed to do. My original idea was to storm the gates and throw Jareth and Ophelia over my shoulder, killing anyone who got in my way.

But Coral was working on a *less violent* plan.

I guess if I didn't want to start a war, we'd have to try things her way.

"Kera, wait." My uncle Maddock's wolf trotted up next to me and my beast slowed her pace.

"If you're here to convince me to get Sage to change her mind, you're barking up the wrong tree." I huffed. It wasn't like I actually wanted Sage or Coral to put themselves in danger, but I wasn't as thick headed as my uncle. I knew better than to try and control those women.

"Like you'd be able to stop her." Maddock chuckled. Maybe he wasn't as dense as I thought.

"What are you doing out here then?"

His wolf exhaled a heavy breath, fog misting from his snout. *"I'm worried about you."*

"Don't be." My wolf continued to trot alongside his, but I assumed the conversation was done. He was never one for words–normally, he didn't even like mine–but he was full of surprises tonight.

"Your father wasn't the greatest Alpha."

"That's putting it nicely." My wolf snorted.

"Hear me out," Maddock said. *"I wasn't the greatest uncle either. We should have done more for you."*

My wolf whined, not liking this conversation.

I felt the same.

It was in the past. Besides, Maddock had always been rough around the edges, but he was my hero when I was too young to fight back and then he was the one who taught me to fight. Everyone else had walked away. But not him.

Ghostly tears threatened to fall, but I still refused to cry even if I couldn't physically do so.

"Old age is making you soft," I teased, needing normalcy now more than ever.

"Maybe." His wolf didn't seem pleased with the joke as he turned to glare at me over his shoulder. *"But I'm not on my deathbed yet so there's still time to tell you how proud I am of you."*

I urged my wolf faster, trying to outrun the uncomfortable praise. In true Maddock form, he wasn't going to let me win this race. The crisp night air ruffled through both our fur coats as our wolves ran. Sleeping critters woke and scattered. Decayed leaf matter crunched under our paws.

My wolf was breathless by the time I choked out a *"thank you."*

I swear on all the Gods that his wolf smiled. *"Don't thank me yet. We still have to keep the girls safe and save your... mate."*

Maddock's wolf growled and I looked up. Without me realizing, my wolf had run to the southernmost border of our territory. No man's land surrounded the hundreds of empty miles and barren landscape with the road that led to the purist city.

I stared at the distance through her eyes, wishing I could see even a speck of light.

"Do you love him?" Maddock asked gently.

My wolf and I both nodded.

"I'm not sure he deserves you, but I'll do whatever it takes to make up for the life you suffered. Just know that if he hurts you, I'll kill him." Maddock's wolf put a paw on my head before sprinting back to the cabin.

Jareth needs us. My wolf paced the border, walking back and forth where our land ended.

We're going to help him.

What if it's too late?

Hush now. I swallowed back my own fear. *You know we can't think like that.*

My wolf stood panting as the bright autumn moon shone down on us. Her howl was painful, the mourning wail of a brokenhearted lover, sending a promise across the unknown distance that we would be there soon.

22
† Jareth †

Blue-gray eyes that held the strength of a raging storm swam through the darkness. They were gone in a whisp of fiery red hair. Long bare legs running through the night forest, urging my beast to give chase. I couldn't move. Couldn't rise to the challenge. Though Gods knew I wanted to.

Kera.

I tried to blink, hoping to drag my mind out of the cloudy fog. My body was too heavy. Every muscle weighed twice the amount it normally did. My wolf was slow and sluggish. He let out a soft groan before burying back down in my mind again.

Poison.

I'd been drugged.

My throat was scratchy and my eyelids filled with grit. I wasn't burning through whatever chemical they injected me with fast enough. It kept pulling me under, like a wave crashing back onto the shore and drawing grains of sand into my mouth.

We need to get up. I drew from the weak strength of my wolf, fighting against the foreign invasion to my body. There was a bed underneath me. A thin mattress and chemical smelling sheets.

Everything in the air here was toxic.

I forced my eyes open. Bright light blinded me and I winced, shutting them again. My pulse skyrocketed when I tried to cover my face, finding my hands bound. Muscles straining, I pulled at the ties. Blood rushed through my veins faster and the cursed chemicals started to filter out through the sweat on my skin as I fought against the restraints on my legs and arms. My wolf woke with a snarl, lending me more strength.

"The patient is awake, Doctor Bradley." A woman's voice was followed by the click of heeled shoes somewhere near the foot of the bed.

I stilled, leaning into my senses. Two human bodies were in the room. The woman behind me wasn't fully human though. Her diluted blood held the remnants of a pack I couldn't place. The man smelled of baked clay and some kind of putrid sweet-smelling soap. Also, toxic.

Dr. Bradley I presumed.

"Perfect." Dr. Bradley leaned over me, emitting a strong whiff of decay buried beneath the toxicity. "Twelve hours for this round. Make a note on the charts for me, Moira."

Twelve hours? I tried to swallow past my tongue which felt like a swollen cactus.

"My sister," I croaked out the words.

"Should I ready another syringe?" Moira's heels clicked to the other side of the bed. It was driving me crazy not being able to scent her pack. Then again, if she was like most of the mixed generation shifters in the Fringes, she might not know she had wolf blood either.

"Hang on." Dr. Bradley's face came into my field of vision as I continued to blink. His skin was too taut. Paper thin as if it'd been stretched and smoothed despite his age. Dyed blond hair leaked more chemicals onto his forehead. A straight nose and cold eyes stared down at me.

"What did it say?" he asked.

It? My wolf growled.

My upper lip curled. "Where is my sister?"

I could feel the poison leaching out of me now and tested the binds at my wrists carefully, trying not to attract any notice.

"Ah, Ophelia. She's a lovely patient. So cooperative." Dr. Bradley smiled with straight white teeth. Gods, even his breath was toxic. "How about you? Are you going to behave for us too?"

"No." I smirked.

The ties on my wrists snapped and my claws extended as I slashed at his face.

A damn hornet needle pierced my neck again, sending burning hot liquid into my veins. My back arched against the thin mattress, muscles spasming with pain, as drips of purist blood fell onto my chest.

"Doctor!" Moira screamed as the room and bright lights started swimming again.

"I'm alright." He waved her off. His voice was underwater, fading. "This is one of their alpha wolves. Get security in here with silver chains instead of these flimsy straps."

Shit.

I fought against the second wave of drowning with darkness tunneling my vision, reaching out through our link.

254

"O…"

"Stop fighting, you idiot," Ophelia growled. *"I'll never get to see you if they think you're a threat."*

There was some word there, some response that I knew I needed to make. But it was hard to cling to the sarcastic banter stuck inside my head as my thoughts muddied.

Fight… Even my wolf sounded weak, being pulled to oblivion.

Sleep won.

I slipped into a drug-infused dream of a beautiful she-wolf with hair the color of a desert sunset.

23
† Kera †

Our numbers were growing larger by the day. I looked over the shifters gathered on the training grounds in the twilight gray hour right before the dawn. Math was never my best subject, and I hadn't gotten much sleep, but I could have sworn we didn't have this many shifters yesterday.

After my run last night, I'd come back to the cabin to find Coral and Sage elbows deep in a plan to cause the *least* amount of bloodshed in the purist city.

It was so crazy it might just work.

But I refused to let my guard down and think it would be easy. Change is wrought through blood and pain. I was willing to fight for it. I was ready to protect Sage and Coral. And I was going to save my mate, even if that required me to spill some blood.

Purist blood though.

I twisted my hands behind my back, nervous about this part of the plan. The other Alphas were so adamant about not getting involved and risking the lives of their shifters. Staring at my pack, no matter how gruesome and rugged they looked, gave me pause. These were the people I vowed to protect. I didn't want to ask them to risk their lives for me.

"You've got this." Coral gave me a thumbs up as I marched to the front of the pack.

I resisted the urge to roll my eyes.

Motivational speeches were not my thing. Even if I was certain I could protect them all, I wouldn't give them false hope. I didn't know what we were walking into anyway. We could plan and scheme all we wanted, but these were real lives on the line if anything went wrong.

The more I looked at them–thought of their families–the more I realized I shouldn't do this.

"You're their Alpha. They'll follow you." Coral still had the bright smile on her face as she mind-linked me, sensing my hesitation.

"That's why I'm worried." I swallowed down the knot in my throat, raising my chin to the crowd.

These weren't the most loyal of shifters. Many of them had abandoned their packs, drawn by the novelty of the infamous Cerberus graveyard or looking for a place to start over. Although I didn't turn anyone away, I hadn't done enough to earn their loyalty yet. A few Alpha challenges and busted noses didn't make me a leader they'd want to follow into battle. I reminded myself of this as I took a steadying breath.

"Thank you for coming." I drew on Alpha strength to project my voice across the crowd. "Gossip spreads fast here so I'm sure you know my fated mate is Alpha Jareth of the Anubis pack."

I smiled as whistles rang out, not bothered by their crudeness. They may not all be Cerberus born, but these were my people. We were cut from the same rough fabric of the earth.

"What I don't think you've heard yet is that Anubis territory was attacked by the purist city. They stole a handful of pups and slaughtered their parents. Luna Ophelia went voluntarily with them to help protect the children."

Low and dangerous growls came from some of the elderly shifters. It was those I looked to, ignoring the confusion on some of the younger faces. The veterans had seen this before and knew I spoke the truth.

"After the other pack Alphas denied the request for aid from Anubis, Alpha Jareth took it upon himself to save his sister, Ophelia, and the stolen babies." I kept my voice even, not letting emotion sway my tone. If my people joined me in this fight, it wouldn't be from sympathy or because I was putting on a show. I stuck to the basic facts.

"Jareth was successful in saving the pups, but not his sister. The two of them remain trapped within the purist city walls. I plan to go save them." Silence greeted me as I took another breath. Crickets chirped in the distance. It was as I thought. They didn't care about my love story and I didn't blame them.

Sage cleared her throat and I glanced over my shoulder to meet her gaze, sighing before I turned back to the crowd. "I also want to make sure nothing like this happens again. I don't expect any of you to join me and I will only take willing volunteers, but I won't be able to sit here as your Alpha knowing the purists are committing atrocities against shifters and their own people just outside our territory while I did nothing to stop them."

The growls of approval bolstered my wolf, but a pang of fear shot through my heart. Wolves loved a good fight. But this wasn't some rumble without repercussions. They had to understand the seriousness of it.

"The humans aren't the only species that take control by using something the people don't have. Money, resources, strength… Power comes in many forms. In this case, it's knowledge. Their leaders keep the purists in the dark and blind. I may not be the oldest or wisest or richest Alpha, but I will always fight for the truth. I'm telling you the truth now when I say that I might not be able to protect you if you choose to come with me. We are trying a different way…" I paused to glance at Coral and she gave me an encouraging nod.

"We're going to give the humans a taste of freedom by letting them know the truth. And I am going to save my mate. If we cripple a corrupt government in the process, so be it. At the very least it will teach the sheep a lesson not to fuck with wolves again."

I gave a final nod, ending the speech, and fully expected the quiet contemplation that hung in the air. It was a lot to take in. I'd basically shocked the foundation of their whole world and suggested something that hadn't been done before. I'd be worried if they didn't hesitate.

Coral would stay behind to relay information to any of the stragglers that decided to join us after the crowd fell apart.

"Dismissed." I turned to leave, needing to get the runners sent to other Alphas and the rest of my affairs in order before I set out for the purist city.

Clapping started from somewhere in the back of the crowd. A single noise like an ill-timed cough. I took a step away as another shifter clapped.

And then another.

Like the light of a spark, more hands joined in and the noise spread like wildfire. Hundreds of hands were clapping and feet began to stomp on the earth.

Howls rang out around the crowd, raising the hair on my skin and feeding my beast with their bloodlust. Sage and Coral's eyes widened as they turned to me.

Ah shit. I didn't think this would happen.

Well, it did. Own it.

I turned my face to the sky as the power of my pack chorused through my veins, sucking in a deep breath and letting out a ferocious howl that rattled the trees around us.

Their voices joined me in the battle cry of Cerberus. And I felt like a complete asshole for it.

*

"That was so badass." Coral came rushing into my office just as I sealed the letter to be delivered to my grandfather Alpha Nolan.

"Was it?" I shuffled through the drawer, looking for another blank page. Someone had taken some of my paper.

"You don't have to be so humble all the time." Coral sat on the edge of my desk and pushed over the stack of paper that was hiding in plain sight.

"This isn't a game." I growled, grabbing a page and addressing it to Alpha Uki. "Wolves like to fight. I gave them an opportunity. Of course, they would take it. But shifters might die."

And those deaths would be my fault. I'd carry the weight of their souls on my shoulders. Their families would curse me over the ashes.

I'd deserve it too.

"Kera, stop." Coral growled, bringing me out of my spiraling thoughts. "You didn't hear them after you left. This isn't some macho wolf fighting thing. Every single one of them swore allegiance and wants to protect you."

I'm supposed to protect them. I rubbed my forehead to ease the building headache.

"Your Beta is correct." The door opened and a female shifter with a baby strapped to her chest came marching into the office next to Skoll with her mate trailing behind. "Just when I think you couldn't surprise me more, the young Alpha gets an entire pack ready for battle without asking them to come."

"Sarina." I cracked a smile, putting the pen down on the letter I was drafting for Uki. "I was just going to send word to your Alpha about this turn of events."

261

"No need. Skoll sent a message last night and Uki sent me to see what all the fuss is about. I enjoyed your speech this morning." Sarina handed the baby to Coral.

Godmother duties took precedence over Beta responsibilities so I didn't bother to stop Coral from dancing down the hall with the pup.

"Word travels fast I guess." I was talking to Skoll, but his attention was on Coral. A wishful smile turned the corners of his lips.

Sarina took a seat across from me and propped one foot on my desk. "Don't shoot the messenger. He knew I'd want to be here if Jareth was causing trouble again."

"More like he's the one in trouble." Our mating bond wasn't complete so I shouldn't have felt the urgency as strongly as I did. But somehow, I knew we were wasting too much time.

Let's go now.

As soon as we get this handled.

My wolf had never been this impatient.

"Yeah. Skoll told us that too." Sarina cast a look at the big brute and I did the same, waiting for him to explain what his angle was by getting the other packs involved.

"I know we don't always see eye to eye." He was still looking at Coral as he spoke. "But I worry about their plan."

"Save your breath." I shook my head. "Like I told Maddock, I have no intention of stopping Coral and Sage. This may not be the plan I would have chosen, but it's better than starting an all-out war. And I support my friends."

Skoll chuckled. "I couldn't stop her if I wanted to, but that's not what I'm saying. We needed more support so I sent out word."

"I'm assuming that's what you're doing here." I looked to Sarina.

"Me and a few hunters." She winked. "I may be retired, but I figured they'd want to see this. What I didn't expect was for you to start a volunteer force. Now all the boys took it upon themselves to spread the word to the other packs."

"Volunteer force? Remember, I didn't even ask anyone to come." I huffed out a short laugh to hide the fact that I was mentally freaking out.

No. No. No. I can't be responsible for more deaths.

Maybe Jareth had the right idea. Sneaking out in the middle of the night seemed like the better option now.

"It's revolutionary." Sarina was practically glowing with excitement. "Shifters making their own decisions and not ruled by an Alpha's command. This is the stuff Jareth and Skoll used to talk about when we were young."

Skoll had the decency to look embarrassed. "We were all dumb kids once."

Their familiar banter had me glancing at Coral. It was easy to forget that Jareth grew up with friends from the other packs since he made such a big deal of not relying on anyone else. I couldn't imagine what it would be like to have alliances with shifters my age. But it didn't matter now. The past couldn't be changed. All I could do was try to carve out a better future for my family. And I wasn't too proud to admit that I was scared of letting them down.

With a resigned sigh, I nodded. "Thank you for coming. We'll take all the help we can get."

"Good." Skoll took the opposite chair from Sarina. I got the feeling he expected more of a fight. "And Beta Calder is on his way with some of Fenrir's best warriors now."

"Alpha Nolan is sending aid?" My jaw about hit the table and I placed the sealed letter to my grandfather on top of the unfinished one to Uki.

Waste of paper, apparently.

"In a way." Skoll shrugged. "He couldn't be one-upped by his granddaughter and deny his shifters their choice. Calder wouldn't want to miss this fight and I'd feel better having trained warriors for backup. They'll all answer to you, of course."

That makes me feel a whole lot better.

What did I tell you? Own this shit.

I shook off my wolf's misplaced confidence, keeping a level head as I ran through a million questions. "Why does he want to help me?"

"Don't start acting like Jareth now." Sarina rolled her eyes. "The stubborn bastard always thought he was alone in this world."

Isn't he though?

I tried not to look a gift horse in the mouth, but I understood why Jareth felt that way. No one had stepped up to help him when he requested it. Then

264

again, these weren't Alpha shifters standing in my office. They were used to taking orders from their pack leaders. Maybe they needed someone to take charge before they joined the fight.

Skoll seemed to read the confusion on my face. "He didn't ask me for help because he wanted me here with you. He wouldn't have dragged Sarina into this either since she has a child. And he didn't tell you the truth because he wouldn't have wanted you to get hurt."

"Oh," was all I could manage, feeling that burning sensation behind my eyes again. Jareth and I weren't so different after all. We may be alone in having to make the decisions for the good of our pack, but we took on that burden because we wanted to protect those we cared about.

I think I was really falling in love with him.

Which sucked, because he wasn't here.

I'd save him though.

I swore to the Gods I would. Then I'd kick his ass for putting me in this position. And hold him close so he never felt alone again.

"Alright, I got my baby snuggles in." Coral handed off the pup to its mother and gave me a bright smile. "Are you ready to change the world now, Alpha?"

24
† Jareth †

The darkness was becoming familiar and the fever dreams were almost tangible. If I let myself get lost in them, it was like I could feel her.

Kera.

But my body was getting used to the chemicals they injected me with and I was burning through them faster. Each time I jerked awake with new aches and pains that I didn't want to think about.

At least they hadn't castrated me.

I woke again, taking stock of my surroundings. The room was still empty. I was still at the mercy of their bindings and injections. Never in my life had I felt this weak and alone.

But there was no time to dwell in self-pity. I had to find a way to outsmart these purist scum and get my sister out of here.

Keeping my heartrate steady and my breathing even, I flexed just enough to test the holds on my limbs. The bite of silver burned into my flesh. My wolf whined in pain as he buried himself down deep. I remained as silent as possible, riding the wave of agony. How these humans had silver or knew its effects on shifters was a mystery. It wasn't a resource we used anymore in the natural world.

They were experimenting on the pups.

Anger rolled through me again and I clenched my teeth, breathing slowly through my nose. It was difficult to fight against my basic nature urging me to protect and seek revenge while I was trapped.

Those pups had it worse, I reminded myself. And it wasn't just my own shifter babes in cages. There were others. Probably born here. Condemned to a life behind bars and subjected to whatever this evil was.

Once I got out of here, I was burning the research facility to the ground.

"You're up." Ophelia's voice came to me as a whisper. Which made no sense. It wasn't like they could hear us communicating. *"Don't fight them this time, please. It's easier when they trust you."*

"Already figured that out." I grunted as I moved my feet. The metal pinched down like burning, biting teeth. Scorpion stings. A minor inconvenience. Nothing I couldn't handle.

I continued to lie to myself as I breathed through the pain. *"Why are you whispering?"*

"I don't know." Ophelia sighed. *"It may be safe now to talk since I'm not hooked up to the machines."*

"Machines?" I thought back to when I saw her strapped to the table with the wires and tape attached to her head. *"Your hair."*

I started growling, remembering how short it was shaved. How long ago was that night? Hours? Days? My heart started to race and I willed it to slow down as the machine started beeping in the room.

"It'll grow back." Gods, she sounded so positive. My sister and I were polar opposites. How did Kera ever think we were mates?

Waking thoughts of Kera made my beast whine and I quickly changed the subject so as not to upset him further. *"What are they doing to you?"*

I probably didn't want the answer to that.

At least my wolf got angry instead of sad.

"I think they're trying to study telepathic communication," Ophelia explained. *"You'd probably understand it better than I could."*

Not at all. It wasn't something you could replicate. You either had a connection with your pack or you didn't. But maybe I could take advantage of the human's ignorance. I filed the information away for later.

"What about the pups?" I asked. *"What else are they studying?"* Thoughts of superhuman soldiers with spliced DNA had my wolf growling.

"That I don't know." I could picture Ophelia chewing her bottom lip, nervous about what she was going to say. *"I did get the purists to let me read and sing to the pups every day for an hour before you rescued them."*

I couldn't hold back the groan that escaped from both me and my beast.

"I didn't ask you to come here," Ophelia cried.

"Did you really think I wouldn't?" I yelled.

"I wasn't thinking!"

I didn't point out that was obvious.

She was worked up enough already.

"It's fine. I'll get you out." Just as soon as I found a way to break these damn chains.

"I know this is hard for you, but maybe stop the Alpha bullshit for a while so we can get on their good side." She was well and truly pissed now.

"I can't make any promises," I grumbled.

"Shut up. They're coming," she barked at me. *"I'm serious. Behave."*

Every muscle of my body tensed, needing to protect her from whatever or whoever was coming. Behaving wasn't in my nature. I was born to fight.

You're smarter than this. I forced myself to focus on our connection through the pack link. She didn't seem frightened or in danger. It was almost as if she was... laughing? Of course she was laughing.

That was my sister. She'd be the one pouring tea for the Gods of the underworld.

Knowing she was okay for now, I leaned on my other senses to get a better read on the building. We were still in the research facility which made escape easier. I still had the layout memorized.

There was movement and soft chatter, voices so low it was hard to make out what they were saying, on the floor below me. Based on the silence of the floor above, I theorized I was on level five. Pings of electronic devices and machines whirring was a background soundtrack to the facility. Some kind of ventilation systems forced recycled air through the room. Coupled with the chemical smell of cleaners, it all felt toxic.

Poison. My wolf snarled. **Everything is bad.**

I would kill for a cigarette to flush the putrid taste of this place out of my mouth.

The machine to my right beeped again and footsteps sounded down the hall. I risked a quick peek through one cracked eyelid. With shifter vision, I scanned the darkened room I hadn't been moved from. I was alone with wires strapped to my chest and connected to the machines.

The lock to the door clicked open and I shut my eyes as the lights turned on. I steadied my breathing again as a cart on wheels was rolled into the room accompanied by the smell of plastic and diluted shifter blood.

The woman who'd been here earlier was back.

Moana or Molly or something. I could memorize almost anything, but I really sucked at names.

She hummed softly as her heels clicked across the floor to where the screen on the machine was. "Our patient is awake."

So much for the element of surprise.

The machines must have been monitoring my vital signs. I vaguely recalled reading something once about human medical treatment. Since the game was up, I let my eyes flutter open lazily and got a good look at the woman.

I supposed she could be considered pretty. She had voluptuous curves hidden under a lab coat and long legs that dipped into high heels. Her sleek black hair was pinned up in a bun on her head and dark glasses perched on the bridge of a delicate nose.

She was no Kera, but I forced a pleasant smile anyway. "Good morning, gorgeous."

No. My wolf grumbled his disapproval at my attempt at flirting and the low growl I used to silence him made my chest vibrate. Her pupils dilated behind the glasses upon hearing the sound and I knew this was the angle to play.

"If you wanted to get me alone, you didn't have to tie me up." I winked, ignoring my wolf's disgust.

"I… Um…" The woman swallowed. "Doctor Bradley!"

"No need to call for him." I chuckled. "I prefer waking up to you. What's your name, beautiful?" My wolf gagged and I licked my lips, trying my hardest to appear relaxed while tied to this damn cot with silver chains. Her gaze tracked the movement of my mouth.

A hint of color flushed her pale skin. "I don't think that's appropriate."

"There's nothing appropriate about me." I shrugged with one shoulder the best I could.

Stop. This is embarrassing. My wolf put his paws over his face.

The woman sucked down another breath.

I focused directly on her eyes, drawing on my Alpha power to command her even though the shifter blood she carried was buried beneath the smell of clay. "Why don't you come sit with me and answer a few questions?"

The fabric of her pencil skirt brushed the edge of the cot and slid across my fingers as she took

271

a step closer. I choked down the nausea, thinking of how far I might have to take this.

"Moira," she said. Her lips stayed parted as she reached out to touch my arm.

"Moira." I tried not to spit out her name, cringing at the feel of sandpaper brushing against my skin. My wolf started growling a warning to back off, but all she heard was the rumble in my chest.

Her eyes widened further in response as she leaned down to whisper in my ear. "You're playing a dangerous game."

"Nurse Sanchey." Dr. Bradley coughed from the open doorway. His scent hit me like a ton of bricks.

Moira let out a squeak as she jumped a foot back. I smiled at her as my wolf shook off the feeling of being touched by a woman who wasn't Kera.

"Have you forgotten your training?" Dr. Bradley scolded, marching into the room with a presence as decrepit as the dried clay he smelled of. "Jareth Anubis is an Alpha wolf. They're the most dangerous and lethal kind."

That did nothing to ease the heavy scent of her arousal. I could still smell it clear across the room.

"I'm sorry, Doctor," Moira muttered, never taking her eyes off me.

"I'm glad we're all introduced." I gave her a subtle wink. "Now if we were all on equal footing, things would be much more pleasant."

Moira giggled.

Dr. Bradley scowled.

I wiggled my toes and fingers, trying to appear non-threatening even though I could snap the doctor's neck like a twig.

"You're in better spirits today." Dr. Bradley studied me with that scowl still etched on his face. "I assume you are trying to get on our good side so you can plot your escape."

It wasn't a big stretch to figure that out, so I didn't give him any undue credit in the intelligence department. I gave a partial, one shoulder shrug again, trying not to wince as the silver dug into my skin. "You've got me figured out."

"I thought so. You beasts are so simple to read." He moved to the cart and readied another syringe.

My wolf started growling as I faked a yawn. "If good behavior doesn't earn me any extra incentives, what reason do I have to play nice?"

That earned half a smile from the crusty old man. "Oh, you'll cooperate with all our tests if you want your sister to remain alive."

My wolf fought the control of the silver as he snarled and forced himself forward. The growling intensified in my chest as my beast shone through my eyes. "You will not touch her."

"That depends solely on you." Dr. Bradley didn't look the least bit fazed as he pushed out the air bubbles of the liquid in the syringe. "And since you cost me my latest batch of test subjects, it's time to earn your keep."

I struggled against the silver chains, seeing red. Screw playing nice. I was going to rip this asshole's head off and eat it.

"Nurse Sanchey," Dr. Bradley barked as Moira jumped to attention. "Ready the patient for transport. We'll be working in the cage."

Another one of their needles pierced my neck. The chemical intrusion burned through my veins as my body convulsed. The darkness tried to drag me back. I fought against it, screaming. My voice was thick with my wolf and Alpha power, but our demands remained unanswered as we slipped back under again, wondering how the hell they were going to fit me in one of the cages.

25
† Kera †

"You're trusting me to lead the pack." Lennox laughed, running his fingers through his greased hair as he looked me over like I'd grown two heads.

"No, you dumbass." I glared at him. "These wolves would eat you alive. I'm trusting you to keep an eye on things. Your inn is the only building in the center of town that has a two-story window. If anything happens or if you don't hear from me soon, take these letters and the shifters staying behind to Fenrir lands. Alpha Nolan will protect you."

I wasn't above calling in a favor for this.

"Is anyone staying?" Lennox looked over my shoulder. I didn't need to turn around. Hundreds of bloodthirsty wolves were breathing down my neck.

"A few of the women and children." I smiled, trying to maintain an air of confidence.

This wasn't a potential slaughter we were walking into. The shifters made their own decisions to come. They wanted to follow me.

No pressure or anything.

"I can take care of a few lonely women." Lennox winked.

I growled as I pushed the letters into his hands. "Seriously, man. You need to find your fated mate before your cocky mouth gets you killed."

*

Dusk came earlier than I expected as if the Gods were giving us cover to travel down this path. The energy was a deathly undercurrent in the quiet evening. Hundreds of wolves urged me forward, their singular purpose bolstering my drive as I took the lead. The only real sound was the humming motor of Sage's ridiculous little car.

I could sense Maddock's worry through the pack link as he rode in human form with Sage. It mirrored my own. I was worried for our witch, but with this much protection, she was safe.

Until we got to our destination.

That was another part of the plan I didn't like.

But I couldn't focus on that now. We were taking things one step at a time. The wolves ran behind me through Cerberus territory toward the vast emptiness between our land and the purist city.

My wolf's heart beat harder for both of us as we crossed the border with Skoll and Coral at our side. She clenched down on her teeth, holding in the battle cry, as I sent a wave of Alpha power through the pack to comfort the beasts who came after us.

We made good time under the cover of night. Silent and deadly, my pack moved as one under my command until we got close enough to the purist city that we could scent the wrongness of the place in the distance. My wolf ground to a halt as Sage's car rolled to a stop on the broken road.

I turned to speak with my pack through the link. *"Spread out. No fires. No noise."*

Silence and stealth were the objective here. I sent scouts out in either direction and spread the wolves into groups, watching the sky as we set up a perimeter and waiting for something to fly over us like the machines the purists used in Junction City.

We had volleys moved out earlier in the day, but I didn't want to use them and give away our position yet.

The wolves hunkered down to wait for my command. Even the air was quiet. The predators made no sound as they climbed the rocky outcroppings of boulders that served as coverage and lookout points.

Once everything was in position, I returned to our command setup. My wolf's paws padded softly across the eroded asphalt to where Sage parked her car behind the rocks a little off the road.

My wolf made short work of the boulders, leaping up them silently as we made it to the top. I kept my senses trained on my shifters, listening for any warning, as I took in the dome like structure in the distance with a cloud of neon lights surrounding it in a smoggy haze.

He's in there.

My heart beat harder in anticipation. Being this close should have soothed my beast, but she pulled back her lips and snarled, anxious for a fight. Each minute that ticked by was the racing of a clock.

We both knew we were running out of time.

I forced the shift and jumped down from the rocks, catching the long shirt Coral tossed to me and

277

pulling it over my head. I squatted down next to Sarina and Coral as they kneeled over a map spread on the ground.

"Beta Calder is almost here," Skoll informed me.

I nodded, turning my attention to Sage. "How long do we think this will take?"

"I'll go as fast as I can." Sage grasped Maddock's hand. My uncle was paler than I'd ever seen him. Standing under the moon light added to the white glow of his skin.

His jaw was clenched as he brushed a hair away from his mate's head. "I'll be the first one through."

I wasn't going to stop him or worry about his role in the fight. The bond would be a beacon, making it easier for him to find and protect her. His place was at Sage's side.

"We'll be right behind you." Coral's smile was grim. Skoll nodded as he tucked her under his arm.

"And you know where to go." I turned to Sarina.

"We'll be here, just inside the fence line." She leaned back so the hunters and Amarok shifters behind her could look at the location on the map. Without being able to communicate with them through the pack link, it was better to keep them at a distance for backup in case this plan went to shit.

I prayed it didn't come to that.

*

A handful of wolves slunk through the night like ghosts, approaching so silently they were almost upon us when I turned to growl.

"Easy, Alpha." Skoll touched my shoulder. "Beta Calder is here."

The wolves shifted quickly, baring their necks to show me respect as Calder embraced Skoll like a long-lost son. My wolf was on edge and pacing, snarling as we scented the new group. Fenrir's salty smell was prevalent, but so was the dusty desert scent of Anubis shifters from the two men who stood in the back. My fangs extended as I looked them over, wondering what the hell they were doing here.

"This is Shelby and Neil," Beta Calder said. "We ran into them near our southern borders when I was setting up camps for our warriors to wait. They were with Jareth on the mission in the purist city and followed orders to remove the pups."

My vision narrowed, emotions warring. If they abandoned my mate, I'd kill them. "Why was Jareth left behind?"

"We didn't know there were so many pups," the shifter called Shelby explained. "Alpha Jareth commanded us to get them all to safety while he left to find our Luna."

"And why is your pack not fighting to save your Alpha?" I snapped, needing a release for this pent-up aggression. It wasn't their fault. Rationally, I knew that. If Jareth used an Alpha command, they had no choice but to obey.

279

And the look of shame on their faces twisted the knife deeper into my heart.

"Beta Griffon is going against the council and has shifters lined up at the Anubis borders awaiting your command." The younger one, Neil, stepped forward and held out a box. "There is still a shifter within the purist city. Foster refused to leave until Alpha Jareth gave him the word. If you find him, he wants to help. As do we. Just tell us what to do."

Gods, why is this happening?

They need you to lead.

I nodded, dismissing them to go with Beta Calder. They could set up a perimeter around the purist city as another line of defense. Those were Jareth's wolves. I wouldn't risk them getting hurt too.

"It's a radio," Coral said when she caught me staring blankly at the box in my hand. "But there is no signal out here. We'll have to get closer to the fence."

She was right. We weren't close enough.

"Ready the troops." I raised my chin, steeling myself for the chaos to come.

Coral and Sage took off while a black wolf with silver streaks and charms in her fur came trotting to my side. I reached down to pet my grandmother, saying my goodbye.

"You're not going to die today." She nudged my palm and gave me a knowing look, before heading back to Cerberus land as we agreed.

I turned my face to the moon, wondering if I should have asked her about tomorrow.

But it was too late to turn back now.

26
† Jareth †

"Test subject A032M. Lycanthrope alpha male. Early twenties. Optimal health with no visible deformities."

A robotic sounding voice tugged me from the darkness, reminding me where I was as the last of the Gods awful chemicals burned their way through my system. I didn't normally care what I put in my body. Shifters healed fast and didn't get diseases. But after this, I was going to go through some sort of detox.

As soon as I smoked a cigarette.

Groaning, I rolled my head, expecting the resistance from the chains and the thin cot mattress behind my back. My skull struck something hard instead. I inhaled the bitter chemical smell of someplace new. My eyes shot open.

Oh yeah. They said something about a cage.

Steel bars surrounded me. Outside the bars were metal walls and floors. An enclosure in the corner was surrounded by some sort of thick plastic and served as a viewing area.

And there the bastard was. Dr. Bradley in the clay treated flesh. His ugly face was watching me from behind the clear plastic along with a few other men. I didn't need to scent them to know they were human. Their cold and calculating eyes were devoid of magic, studying me like some sort of spare part.

We're going to kill them all. My beast growled.

Soon. I nodded, climbing shakily to my feet as I reached out to my sister. *"Ophelia, are you okay?"*

I rubbed my wrists and tested the strength of my ankles. The burns where the silver bit into my skin were already healing.

"I'm fine." She was still close enough to communicate. *"Where did they move you to?"*

I looked around the inside of the bars. There was a cot too small to fit my entire body on and a sleek metal toilet with some kind of sink basin on top that had a faucet. They were crazy if they thought I'd drink that water. I had enough of their chemical poisons for one lifetime thank you very much.

"It looks like some kind of observation room and I'm in a cage." I closed my eyes, remembering the layout of the research facility.

"You're in the basement." Ophelia gasped.

My lips curled as I snarled, turning to look at the humans behind the plastic window. *"Did they put you in here too?"*

"Well, no. But I'm not an asshole." My sister sighed.

"You know what, I'm getting sick of…."

A loud buzzing cut off my train of thought. I clapped my hands over my ears as my wolf began to howl.

"Increasing frequency to 35,000 hertz," the robotic voice droned throughout the room.

Loud. Screechy. Stop!

The whistle pitch continued to rise, beating against my eardrums. My wolf whined as I dropped to the floor and put my head between my knees.

"40,000 hertz."

The robotic voice was a welcome reprieve that lasted no longer than a second. The whistle went higher, so loud I couldn't hear myself think. Rushing liquid sloshed around my brain as the screech intensified.

"Turn it off!" I commanded, screaming to be heard over the sound as I slammed my head back against the bars.

"45,000 hertz."

I lost all sense of time and place as the pitch reached a new height. My wolf panicked, forcing the shift so he could get us to safety. I scratched at the floor with my claws to keep them away from my ears.

"Fascinating."

The whistle stopped abruptly. I looked up, panting, with vibrations still ringing in my eardrums to see Dr. Bradley standing outside the bars, oblivious to the sound. I climbed to my feet. My wolf buried himself back down, hiding from the pain. I wiped my nose. Hot blood smeared across my hand.

Dr. Bradley smiled.

I lunged for the bars, intending to rip his throat out.

But the doctor stepped out of reach. "Save your strength. We have a few more tests to run tonight."

284

"I want to see my sister." I could barely hear myself growl over the ringing in my ears.

"We know." Dr. Bradley gave me his back as he walked to the enclosed viewing area. "Consider it your incentive to be a good dog for us."

*

Laughing through the pain, I sat back against the cool metal bars as the burning blisters on my arms began to pop and heal. They'd doused me with fire and snuffed out the flames with some chemical smoke from a hose. I assumed I passed their healing test if that's what you called being roasted alive.

I was very much alive.

The pain let me know.

I only hoped they'd get cockier and want to test my physical strength too. Hand to hand combat with any one of these *doctors* would help to soothe the itch. I was going to kill them all, slowly.

Just as soon as I got out of this cage.

"Forty-five minutes to full skin elasticity and cell regrowth," the robotic voice explained.

Seemed longer.

I wasn't sure where the voice was emitting from, but I raised a middle finger in the general direction of the sound waves from my position sitting naked on the floor.

"That's all for tonight," Bradley spoke into the intercom as the rest of the doctors filed out of the viewing room.

The lights to the basement dimmed and the cage was shrouded in darkness. Anger burned red hot within my skin, clawing to break free.

This was sick.

Dehumanizing.

I wouldn't even treat an animal this way.

That's all I was to them. An animal. An oddity to be poked and prodded and studied. They tested my abilities as if I wasn't natural, when I was more natural than the air they breathed.

We are an Alpha shifter.

I was stronger than this.

The door to the viewing room shut and I jumped to my feet to start testing the bars of the cage for weakness. I didn't expect to find anything, but it soothed my beast to be doing something proactive with my hands while my thoughts ran rampant.

This was only the beginning. The tests were too simple. They'd studied my hearing range and skin regeneration capabilities. There'd be more tests the longer I stayed here and I wasn't planning to stick around to see what else they had in store.

We'll kill them all. Destroy this city.

Of course we will.

I took a step back from the bars, surveying the walls outside the cage in the dim light and looking for patterns in the ceiling tiles. There had to be a maintenance hatch somewhere. I'd seen the layout of the early blueprints. The tunnel ended in the basement.

There. The shadow of a ridge marked the tile on the back corner of the room. It was in the wrong spot to be the maintenance hatch though. Possibly, some kind of air vent. I studied the way it slightly differed from the other tiles. In the low light, I could almost make out a grate.

Whatever it was, it could be an escape.

Too bad it was on the outside of the cage.

Growling in frustration, I walked to the toilet and turned on the faucet for the sink basin.

Could I flood the room? My wolf and I both cocked our head to the side.

That wasn't the best idea.

But we were crossing them off the list.

I climbed on top of the toilet, using it as a stool to test the top bars of the cage.

"What are you doing?" Ophelia's unexpected voice in my head caused me to slip and almost lose my footing.

"Trying to escape and save you." I steadied my stance and grabbed the bars above with my fists. My muscles strained as I pulled, trying to tear them apart.

The purists must have paid for the good stuff.

I wondered where they were mining iron from.

"You know they have cameras watching you." Ophelia sounded bored.

"I knew that." I huffed as I jumped to the floor, looking around the room for the camera lenses.

"No, you didn't." She sighed. *"You don't have a plan."*

I sat on the metal cot and put my face in my hands. She was one of the only people I didn't have to always be an Alpha with. It helped that she'd known me since before I stepped up into the role.

"I had a plan, but seeing all those pups in the cages…" My thoughts trailed off. I couldn't go there again. Not when I needed to be clearheaded and override my animalistic instinct to get us out of here.

"I had a feeling they were taking the pups for a reason," Ophelia said. *"It's why I forced them to take me too."*

"I know." I looked down at my hands. All my life, I'd been tinkering with something, fixing broken parts, or fighting to lead a pack of thousands of shifters. And now these hands were useless.

Powerless.

"Do you think Griffon and the other Alphas will come?" Leave it to my sister to always think the best of people.

"No." I hated myself for ruining her dream. *"I ordered him not to."*

Which meant by now my Beta would have given Kera her letter. I lowered my face, picturing her soft smile and the storm clouds brewing in her eyes that held the power and steadfast nature of the earth. The way her strong body responded to mine. The essence of her redwood scent. A lifetime of things I wanted to learn, to explore, to teach…

"Maybe it's for the best." Ophelia sighed, resigning to her fate. *"I don't want anyone to get hurt."*

"No." I growled as I jumped to my feet. I refused to die like this. It wasn't our time. Not yet. *"We're getting out of here."*

Movement outside the door to the basement holding area had my wolf snarling and baring his teeth. I crouched low in a defensive stance, ready to fight.

"What's happening?" Ophelia asked.

"Someone is coming."

The door opened and a cart came rolling into the room. I was momentarily blinded as half the lights in the basement flicked on.

"It's probably food. Who is bringing it?" Somehow my sister had become the expert on this place.

I stood, stalking forward to the front of the cage, and keeping the female in my sights. Her heels clicked across the metal floor.

"It's that nurse Moxie or Megan or whatever."

"Moira." Was it possible to hear someone roll their eyes? *"I think we can trust her."*

"We can't trust any of these humans." I plastered on a fake smile as Moira neared the cage. She picked up a tray off the cart and carried it to the slot near the floor. Whatever it was looked like vomit.

We're not eating that.

Moira returned my smile.

"Jareth, I love you, but you're going to have to trust in people eventually if we want to get out of this mess," my little sister scolded me. *"Trust me now when I say to get your head out of your ass. Also, eat. It's not poison."*

289

27
† Sage †

It was like she didn't trust me.

I tried not to hold it against her. This was a lot for anyone to deal with. And I wasn't about to comment on her age.

Nope. I wasn't going there again.

Kera and Coral had proved their worth more times than I could count. The girls were natural born leaders. Coral shined in diplomatic roles like I always knew she would and sweet Kera was an amazing Alpha who led with a quiet sort of strength.

I was so dang proud of…

"Are you okay?" Kera glanced down at me.

I inhaled deeply, filling my lungs a final time with the non-toxic fresh air. "Why wouldn't I be?"

"Because you're crying." She deadpanned.

"Am I?" I asked just as Coral and Maddock said, "She's fine."

I touched Kera's arm and focused on soothing her worries. "I was just thinking about how proud I am of you."

"Sage," Kera growled my name as a warning, plucking my fingers from her arm. "Now is not the time for my wolf to get belly rubs."

"Oops. Sorry." I bit down on my lip to hide my embarrassed smile. It was like someone had turned up the notch on my magic these past few months. Although feeling the earth's energy running through my veins and commanding it with my touch was awesome, it could be a bit much sometimes.

"Are we ready?" I backed away from the group, turning to my trusty Kia who was still chugging along out here in the wild.

"We're ready when you are." Kera made a point to look into my eyes. I'd learned that shifters didn't like to meet an Alpha's direct stare, but it never bothered me. There was something so old in her gaze. A wisdom well beyond her years. She'd seen too much already. I refused to look away and leave her alone.

Kera deserved her happily ever after more than anyone I'd ever met. The damn purists were going to pay for getting in the way of that.

No one messes with my family.

"Angry Sage is scary." Coral nudged Skoll's side, trying to lighten the mood.

"Grrr…" I did my best to growl. It was a running joke. One that didn't get many laughs. It's not my fault that I lived with a bunch of wolves that growled all day when I couldn't. And those wolves just stared at me now.

"Right." I took another deep breath as Coral gave me a small smile. She knew better than the rest of them what the risks were in coming back here. But my little sister wasn't a kid anymore and I had to trust that she'd be able to handle herself.

As much as I wanted to live in our fairy tale bubble forever, what the purists were doing was wrong. We owed it to the shifters who'd given us a safe haven to fight for them too. And we wouldn't be our father's daughters if we didn't at least try to help.

I nodded at Coral and she returned the gesture. We'd already said all we needed to say. Things would work out.

We've got this.

The masculine scent of aged scotch wrapped around me as Maddock pulled me to his chest. I breathed deeply, letting it calm my soul in a way the lavender oils never could.

"It's not too late to turn around." The words rumbled deep in his chest as he spoke softly, just for me. His wolf was an anxious ball of protective energy. I could feel him pacing and growling inside my mate.

"Yes, it is." I placed my hand over his heart, feeling it beat in tune with mine. "I'll be waiting for you."

Maddock took my hand and moved it to his lips to press a kiss against my palm. "Nothing will stop me from finding you again."

*

Remember when you said you were never coming back?

I drummed my fingers against the steering wheel as my little car jostled along the weather beaten and corroded road. We didn't belong in that awful city–me or the car–we belonged in the real world.

Ethica was a rot festering beneath the surface. I thought we were free of it, but it kept coming back. I couldn't wait to be rid of it. Again.

Think of the babies, I reminded myself, taking another deep breath in as I checked my rearview mirror. The wolf's eyes reflected the red glow of my brake lights. Maddock's massive beast was a terrifying sight to anyone who didn't know him, but he wasn't the mutant monster I was taught to believe.

I smiled at him, knowing he could sense it even if he couldn't see it, and pressed on the gas.

The fence line was marked with warning signs bent and facing the other direction. The forcefield hadn't touched me the first time I'd crossed it, but I could sense it now that I knew what magic felt like. It was like a division between what was natural, sealing the tainted air on the other side. We'd always been taught it was keeping the infection out, but in truth, the infection was within.

Maddock howled as he came to a stop, blocked by the human deterrent. Tears filled my eyes and I blinked them away as I focused on the road ahead. Those jerks were going to pay for this.

*

"ID card, miss," the gate guard said. His LED flashlight swept over the car. I'd forgotten how bright those things were; forgotten how suffocating it was to be back in the fake climate with Ethica's city walls looming on either side of the guard tower.

I took my time digging through my purse, searching for the card that would brand me as a traitor and alert the authorities of my return. "I know it's in here somewhere."

There were no cars behind me this late at night and the guard failed to hide his boredom. If I could stall long enough, maybe he'd lean his arm on the open window.

He yawned, leaning back. "You need to get one of those Burberry 5000 series bags. I got one for my wife last year. Everything is organized in the pockets."

"Are those the ones the McQueen Dynasty rolled out?" I had no clue what I was talking about. The name was something I'd heard once. But the guard smiled, seeming more relaxed. It wasn't like people in the Fringes knew about designer fashion.

"I'm not sure the name, but the wife says it's all the rage." He maintained a professional distance from my vehicle and open window.

I nodded, grabbing the identification card I didn't want him to see. *Maybe I can touch his hand.*

"Hey, I have a random question. What's up with the fence at the border? It was doing something weird and my distant cousin, who I was bringing cast off donations to, said she saw some sparks." I waved my wallet in the air, giggling in the way that made men think I didn't have a brain cell in my head. "Got it."

"Was that tonight?" His thumb brushed over the radio on his belt as he glanced over his shoulder.

"Yeah, but you guys can push a button or something to fix it, right?" I took a really long time wiggling the card out of the plastic sheath in my wallet.

"We can fix it here." He smiled to placate me. Can't have precious citizens concerned. I held out the card, gripping most of it with my hand for a little bit of accidental skin contact, and watched in slow motion as he used two fingers to pinch the corner.

"Oops," I cried, dropping the card to the ground by his feet. I inhaled deeply, drawing on the well of my magic despite the oppression of the looming city. It was a part of me now and they couldn't take it again.

"I've got it." He dropped to one knee.

"No, let me." I flung open the car door, slamming it straight into his head. The guard fell back to the pavement.

I gasped as I jumped outside. "Oh, science. I'm so sorry."

"Is fine," the guard mumbled, dazed as he tried to sit up.

"Here, let me help." I grabbed his hand and sucked in a deep breath as I accessed the power thrumming through my veins. It responded with a soft caress. A hello from a dear friend.

"You want to hurry up and check the fence. Do you know what would be awesome? If you could show me what you do. This job doesn't pay well. You don't get enough appreciation. I can give that to you." I dug deep, drawing on what I hoped were his desires.

He blinked, smiling shyly.

I had him.

"Sure. I can show you around. Move your vehicle to the lot over there and we'll head upstairs."

I wasted no time parking the car and tucking the useless ID back in my purse. I'd been practicing enough with my magic to know it would last for a few hours before it wore off. But the longer Maddock waited, the more anxious he would get.

I didn't want to deal with a grumpy wolf.

The guard droned on and on about the latest security measures. He took the steps two at a time, happy to have an audience to talk to.

"Barry, watch the gate for a minute." He poked his head into the security office.

Another guard–Barry–fumbled with his coffee cup as he jumped to attention. He leaned over to click off the Tetris game playing on the computer screen.

"No problem, Gus." Barry's eyes widened as Gus stepped back to let him pass and he caught sight of me. "What's going on?"

"Graveyard shift is boring, isn't it?" I laughed as I patted Barry's forearm. "You want to change things up occasionally."

Barry relaxed as my magic washed over him. "I sure do. You two have fun. Don't get into any trouble."

I chuckled, following Gus up the stairs.

There was about to be a whole lot of trouble.

296

"These systems control the backup generators for the fence," Gus said, scratching the back of his head as he looked over the day's readings from the monitors. "They aren't reporting any discrepancies. It's common to have a few glitches, but today has been a good one. A few days ago, there was a major outage and the IT guys have upped their game since then."

"Crazy. Maybe my cousin was seeing things. She isn't the most reliable witness." I lowered my voice in a conspiratorial tone, "There's a reason she lives in the Fringes."

The guard laughed. A good-natured response to the "haves and have nots" our world was built on.

Funny how it was all a lie.

Yeah, it wasn't that funny.

"We monitor this hourly along with checking the borders and patrolling the wall, plus the gate duty," Gus continued to explain.

I looked around the office full of computer screens, thinking of how to keep us on the important topic. "I don't know why I thought there'd be some giant red switch that turned the fence on and off."

"That would be too easy, wouldn't it? Everything is digitized and you need a password to access it." His chest puffed with pride. "Only a few of us have that kind of clearance."

"What's your password? Is it something cool?" I managed another flirtatious giggle as I brushed my fingers across his back.

"My wife's name. SallyMae37." His ruddy cheeks reddened further.

I'm not sure he really wanted to tell me that.

Desires are funny. They come and go. And if you act too quickly, it may be one you didn't intend to see through.

"It's okay." I smiled gently as I patted his hand and yawned. "Graveyard shift is the worst. It's messing with your circadian rhythm and making you more tired than normal. Why don't you take a little nap?"

His body slumped to the floor and I stepped over it. The sound of his snores filled the room as I clicked through the computer screens.

Tech-friendly I was not, but he'd left the maintenance program open. It took a few seconds of toggling between pages before I found the emergency overrides.

"Thank you, Sally Mae," I said as I entered Gus's password. She'd earned that designer bag.

Monitors on the camera feeds flashed with warnings of a system shutdown. The howl of fury vibrated through our bond, teasing the deep reaches of my soul.

I brushed my fingers along the claiming mark imprinted on my neck and skipped back down the stairs. It was time to put Barry to sleep too before my mate got here and decided he was a threat.

298

Least amount of bloodshed.

That was our plan.

Though I was really hoping to have a violent word or two with dear old Dr. Bradley if I got the chance.

One minute the static was there, its electric pulse keeping the wolves at bay, and in the next breath it was gone.

"I knew she could do it." Coral howled, pumping her fist in the air. I gave a look to silence her and she nodded, returning to the radio.

Maddock's wolf was a streak of fur as he crossed the dividing line. I stepped over the useless barrier with the wolves of Cerberus following behind. The unease of not being able to directly communicate with Sage had me on edge, but I never should have doubted the crafty witch. Still, I'd feel better once we reached her side and I could see for myself that she was okay.

"What is he saying?" I edged closer to Coral, directing the shifters to spread out like we planned. The voice on the radio and my Beta had worked out some kind of code already.

"He's going to meet you at the Black Water Hole." Coral let the radio go silent as she looked around the gathered shifters. "Should we change up the plan to go with you instead?"

"It'll be fine," I reassured her. "Skoll can mark the scent of the building and the path on your way to get Sage."

Greg's scraggly gray wolf, still scarred with one eye missing like his human form, formed a half circle of protection along with Ashton and a few of his buddies at my back.

"We'll meet you at the gate." Coral grabbed me, ignoring protocol as she wrapped me in her arms.

"Stay safe." I embraced her quickly, turning to the wolves that remained as Skoll and Coral shifted before racing toward the purist city.

I needed to get them all inside and in position before the fence came back online. "Move out with your teams," I directed Sarina to take the hunters and Amarok shifters. "Beta Calder's people will meet you at the western border. See if you can connect with Anubis to the south. But don't let anyone step further than I tell them too."

The muscular black female wolf growled in acknowledgement, rounding up her shifters and taking off in the night.

I turned my face to the sky, sending a prayer request for protection from the Gods, and wishing there was more I could do to prevent the purists from taking flight with their machines. We'd have to move swiftly so as not to frighten them off like chickens in a hen coop.

I looped my travel pack around Greg's thick, furry neck. He and his group of ragtag shifters had somehow worked their way through the ranks and appointed themselves as my body guards. Might as well make them useful since they did once challenge me for my Alpha position.

My fangs and claws extended as I shifted, falling to the ground on four paws with a silent thud. *"Stay behind me,"* I signaled to the Cerberus shifters.

Quiet and deadly, my pack moved through the foul-smelling clay-baked and plastic burnt air as I followed the scent trail of Coral and Skoll.

"What are you seeing?" I asked my Beta, sensing her presence moving a few hundred yards ahead.

We came to the outskirts of the Fringes. Babies cried and couples shouted behind closed doors. Mildew and petrified garbage lined the streets.

"Sage and Maddock are at the gate. She took care of the guards."

My wolf's eyebrows shot up, wondering what our Luna witch had done.

"They're asleep," Coral said.

That was more in line with what I was expecting. I knew Maddock and Skoll's worries, feeling them as my own, and if there was a violent situation to handle then we would take care of it for them. The girls were the brains of this operation.

I would be the muscle.

And changing the plan to meet with this *source* and the Anubis shifter left behind was making my protective instincts go haywire.

Greg and Ashton growled behind me, sensing my distress. I shook the thoughts away and focused on the mission. If I started to doubt, they would too. It was imperative to keep my head on straight.

"Where are you?" Coral asked.

My wolf lowered her snout, sniffing around the circle of marked scent Skoll left behind. We backed into the alley of some broken buildings. Cracked and blacked out windows shone with flickering lightbulbs. Shouts behind the walls. The stench of unwashed bodies and blood. A neon sign flashed above the door across the street. Black Water Hole with the vowels burnt out.

"Made it to the bar." I shifted, digging into my travel pack on Greg's side for a shirt.

"Do you want us to meet you there?" Coral's anxiety riled my beast.

"No." I hurried to pull on some clothes. *"Don't lose our foothold at the gate. I'll be there as soon as I'm done."*

I turned back to the alley, using the pack link to send the second wave of shifters in human form to spread out in the shadows around the darkened streets and await my call.

Greg and Ashton's group still refused to leave my side. I could command them to go, but one look around the rundown sad excuse for a main strip and I figured a little extra protection wouldn't hurt.

Coral explained the Fringes was where the nightlife thrived and forbidden parties raged until dawn. Supposedly, the crowd was rough.

"Stay," I commanded the wolves, stopping them from following me as I chuckled.

I was curious to see how the purists' *rough* compared to the gnarly beasts watching my back.

*

"What are you drinking, sweetheart?" The female bartender had a mass of sweaty brown curls piled high on her head and a handful of rings pierced in her face. I was in awe of her pain tolerance.

The bar was dark with strobing red lights. A beat thumped from somewhere but I couldn't see any musicians playing the awful tune. Half dressed women danced around the customers, most of which were human men in various stages of unbuttoned suits. The scent of arousal was heavy in the air. I really didn't want to drink anything in here.

"Whatever it is, I'm buying." A bulbous man with whiskers protruding from his face like a feral cat took the empty stool next to me.

I growled at him without meaning to, sending him scurrying away, as I put one of Sage's small diamond gemstones on the counter. "Can I have a beer?"

The bartender snatched it quickly, pocketing it faster than a shifter normally moved, and smiled as she poured beer from a spout into a dirty glass. "Are you looking for a good time tonight?"

The music thumped louder.

She licked a ring on her bottom lip.

"You could say that." I dragged the glass across the chipped plastic counter. "I'm meeting a friend."

"What kind of friend?" Gods, she was nosey. And I wasn't just saying that because of all the pieces of metal in her nose.

"A private friend." I slid over another gemstone, wondering what the hell purists saw in these things as she greedily snatched it up.

"Let me know if you need a room." She winked before working her way back down the bar.

I glanced over my shoulder as the front door opened with more drunks piling in. This source and shifter needed to hurry. I wanted into the city before the sun rose so I could make my way down south in the cover of darkness.

And this place had my skin crawling. Lewd eyes and gestures followed the woman dancing on the pole. The way she moved her hips was mesmerizing. Her body turning the awful music into a work of art. The dim red light caught the sequins on her bodice.

There was no way she could hide a weapon in that tiny skirt.

I turned my gaze to the foam of the beer and pushed out with my other senses, too strung out to actually take a drink in this fine establishment. A hint of shifter blood here and there had my nostrils flaring, but when I glanced up at fully human faces, I returned my attention to the beer.

Greg's rough voice came over the pack link from his position in the alley, *"We've got someone coming."*

"Finally." I pushed off the stool and spun to face the door. The shifter who smelled of Anubis came in first. Behind him was a human runt with a diluted wolf scent who scanned the room with wide

eyes and tucked himself deeper into his black hooded sweatshirt.

I tried not to growl, cursing Jareth under my breath.

"No kids allowed in here," the bartender spoke behind me. I slid over another jewel which she grabbed. "The first room on the right is open upstairs."

*

"What are you doing here?" I stayed standing as Foster and the pimple-faced kid took a seat on the sofa in the rented room. The music continued to thump below us in the bar. I don't know what I was expecting from the cryptic messages of the *source*. I'd almost assumed it was a trap and I'd get a chance to exterminate some purists. Now I was sneaking information from the playground.

"I got in contact with Beta Griffon and he told me you were coming." Foster bared his neck in respect as I growled. "I'm here to help get my Alpha and Luna out."

"Not you." I grit my teeth and looked to the kid. "Who are you and what do you want?"

"You can call me Ethan." He puffed up his chest, acting like it was some kind of code, but I couldn't scent the lie. "I've been working with Jareth for years and I'm here to help."

Since you were in diapers? I kept my expression neutral despite having serious doubts about my fated mate's sanity. "How can you help?"

"I know where he is." That was a really good freaking start, but I didn't let the hope show on my face. Coral and Sage assumed he was being held at the research facility. Which was why I needed to leave fast to get clear across the human city by dawn.

"The research facility?" I asked, hoping for verification.

Ethan's face fell for a moment as his pride took a hit. "Yes, but..." He lowered his voice and looked over his shoulder, "I hear you are planning something big. I can hack into whatever systems you may need."

"Right." I blew out a breath. The kid was what? Twelve? I looked to Foster, wondering if this was some kind of joke.

The shifter sat there, stone-faced. "Alpha Jareth trusted him. If Ethan says he can do something, he will. We're here to fight with you."

This was exactly what I didn't want. More people trying to play hero. I already had an entire pack to look out for plus the shifters we'd picked up along the way. I didn't want this kid's blood on my hands. Especially not if Jareth trusted him.

"Our Alpha shouldn't be alone." Foster's words made me hesitate. He wasn't alone. Not with me here. But I wasn't cocky enough to pretend we didn't need the help.

"The source says he can hack into systems. I'm assuming that means something to you." I mind linked Coral.

"No freaking way," Coral cried. *"Can he override the emergency broadcast intercoms?"*

The kid fidgeted nervously as I stared at him, trying to understand what Coral wanted. "Can you do something with a broadcast system?"

"Child's play." Ethan smirked.

"He says yes."

Coral's scream almost busted the inside of my eardrums as it echoed through my head.

I sighed as I ran my hands over my face. "Alright. Let's go. You two stay with me."

"Now?" The kid jumped to his feet, grabbing his backpack.

"Yes, now." I was already racing down the stairs with Foster right on my heels.

Jareth, you crazy asshole. Let's hope I can trust your judgment on this.

29
† Jareth †

I eyed the tray of what I assumed was food skeptically, wondering how long it'd been since I ate something solid. The dinner with Kera was the last meal I could remember tasting.

Kera.

Gods, what was she thinking now?

Probably that you're an idiot. My wolf growled, still amped up from the tests and not liking that Nurse Moira lingered outside the cage.

Maybe I was an idiot. But what was I supposed to do? Let my sister rot in the purist city while I settled down with my fated mate and had a whole brood of pups. It's not like I could fish all day and grow fat living a fairy tale anyway.

Without meaning to, I pictured Kera's muscular stomach swollen with our children. Her storm-colored eyes looking at me with adoration. A deep, yearning ache made me jump to my feet and approach the tray of food.

I needed to eat to keep my strength up.

People were depending on me.

"I assure you it's not poison." Moira glanced over her shoulder as if she shouldn't be speaking to me. I agreed.

"It smells like poison." I sniffed a meat shaped patty that had no animal in it.

"That's soy. It has lots of protein." Moira watched me like a scientist would, but there was a hunger in her eyes. Hopefully it wasn't for my meat because I wasn't making the mistake of trying to get on her good side again. But Ophelia thought she could be trusted. I decided to test it out.

"What exactly do you people plan to do with me?" I bit into the soy patty that tasted like poison and swallowed it anyway.

"We're running tests." Moira pushed a bottle of some green liquid through the slot. "It's a rarity to have an alpha wolf to study."

"I figured as much." I twisted the cap off the bottle, sniffing the contents. Some kind of vegetable compound flavored by the plastic container.

My favorite. How'd they know?

I plugged my nose as I chugged down the liquid and wiped the remainder from my lips. "Do you run tests on every shifter you come across?"

"We don't get many full blooded mutants from the wild lands in here, but we study everything. The science behind mutation is fascinating." She left out the part about breeding shifters which I was almost one hundred percent sure they were doing. "Slide your tray back through the slot when you're done."

I lapped the rest of the juices from the soy patty with my tongue.

"It isn't science. It's magic," I explained as I put the tray where she wanted it. "But I am curious, do they test everyone with shifter blood?"

310

I stared at her pointedly, noting the color that flushed her face and listening to her heart beat faster. My theory was right. She knew she had shifter DNA buried deep inside that human body. I waited for her to lie.

"Some people know how to survive in here." She picked up the tray and returned it to the cart. It was half a truth, but I'd take it.

Maybe Ophelia was right after all.

"I don't know what they've told you, but the outside isn't all that bad. You should come visit Anubis lands someday." I sat back on the cot and laced my hands behind my head.

A flash of hope lit up her eyes.

"Your sister mentioned it was an interesting place." Moira pushed the cart hard, making the wheels squeak and covering the sound of her soft voice so the cameras wouldn't pick it up. "Try not to die in the next round of tests. I'm curious to see if you're as strong as she says."

Well, that was ominous.

I watched the diluted shifter woman leave and let out a heavy sigh. The food settled strangely in my stomach. Hopefully it wasn't another test.

I closed my eyes, seeking out Ophelia through our link. She was sleeping somewhere above me on the higher floors. I pulled back on the pack link so as not to wake her and rubbed my chest bone as I stared at the darkened cage.

There was a steady hum in my chest where the mate bond pulled, reminding me of what I could

311

lose if I didn't get out of here. At least the worst of the moon sickness had passed. If I'd claimed Kera, maybe I'd be able to reach out to her over this vast distance. Probably not. But it was a romantic thought.

We need to escape. My wolf continued to snarl and pace.

I plan to.

Ophelia found a way to earn their trust and that seemed like my best bet too. It would take much more than these tests to kill me. I'd participate for a while longer until the perfect opportunity arose. They would slip up. I was sure of it.

All I had to do was wait.

How long can Kera wait?

The pain came again, deeper this time, as I thought of Kera waiting and lonely. I'd asked her to paint me something. Hopefully that would keep her busy. And she was an Alpha. She had a pack to lead. As long as she was safe at home, I could take my time.

When I got out of here, I was doing things differently. I'd woo her harder. Buy her more flowers. Take her to see some art. I'd be the mate nature intended me to be and show her what it meant to be my princess. She'd fight it. I knew that. But it was going to be fun.

I let thoughts of the future drift through my mind, soothing my beast, and drifted off to sleep as I dreamed of the red-haired tempest waiting for me.

30
† Kera †

Adrenaline pumped through my veins, keeping me on high alert as we raced through the Fringes with Ethan riding on Foster's back. The Cerberus wolves coming on this wave of the offense flanked us on either side. We moved like shadows, too fast for the stumbling and intoxicated humans to notice, as I followed Coral and Skoll's scent to the gate guard tower.

"Finally." Coral embraced me. "Is this him?"

"You're up." I nodded to Ethan, shoving him forward as I pulled my shirt back on. "I don't understand half of what he's saying."

Ethan fumbled with his backpack zipper and pulled out a box. It lit up with a button as he balanced it on the hood of Sage's car. Maddock and Skoll crowded him, making the kid's hands shake.

"Give him some room." Coral elbowed the males back as she moved to take their place.

Ethan coughed to clear his throat. "As I was saying earlier, the guard change is in an hour. If you want to keep this gate open, you'll have to deal with the incoming shift."

"Not a problem." I growled, directing some of Cerberus wolves to start sniffing out defensive positions. That was the plan anyway. I didn't want too many wolves inside the city. If things went wrong, they could trap us inside. It was better to surround the purists and have leverage if we weren't going to attack. Least amount of bloodshed.

I was starting to doubt this plan.

"Or there is a better way." Ethan's fingers flew fast as he punched more of the little buttons. "Jareth went through the service entrance down south which pops out right at the research facility."

I leaned closer, intrigued, as images of different areas came like moving pictures on the screen. If that was true, I could move our positions closer to the wall with a less guarded entrance. It would save us precious time instead of running through the populated city.

But that would mean…

I looked to Coral and she seemed to read my mind.

"The plan hasn't changed. You go get Jareth. We can handle this." Coral grabbed my hand as Sage stepped beside her.

"No." I shook my head. I hadn't liked when they planned to go their own way, but this new version was worse. I wouldn't know where to find them, wouldn't be able to protect them.

"The faster we get this done, the faster we can get out of here." Sage moved to touch my arm and thought better of it as she fisted her hand, not wanting to infuse me with her magic.

"I won't have eyes on you." My heart was thumping too hard in my chest. Panic threatened to make my decision an emotional one when I needed to keep a clear head.

"I can help with that." Ethan dug out another piece of equipment from his backpack and grinned like a kid in a candy store. "Tracking devices."

Whatever he pulled out seemed to give Sage and Coral confidence. Not me.

"We'll be alright." Coral sensed my hesitation. "This is our job. Your job is to save your mate."

"My job is to protect all of you." I growled as my wolf started to whine.

We're wasting time.

"No, it's not." Sage's eyes filled with tears. I felt her struggle as she caved, raising on her toes to wrap her arms around my shoulders. "If we need help, we'll let you know. But you need to do what you do best. You're strong enough to save him. Trust that we will be okay."

I looked to Maddock and Skoll, half of my heart breaking as I realized the truth in the witch's words. I was useless when it came to their technology and purist stuff, but I had no issues storming a building to save the ones I loved.

"I guess we don't need two vehicles anymore." I blinked back the burning sensation behind my eyes, turning to address the wolves waiting for my command. *"Spread the word that we're heading south. Get in touch with Sarina and Calder, let them know to move reinforcements there."*

"Mia's already on her way." Coral dried her eyes, giving me a brave smile. "We'll be fine. Go get your man."

"Where is this service entrance?" I turned to Ethan who was attaching something to Sage's car.

He pulled out yet another device from his pocket. "Um… I can drop a pin to the location and you can follow it from there."

Both my wolf and I cocked our heads to the side, not understanding.

Foster growled in frustration as he grabbed Ethan by the back of his hooded sweatshirt. "No worries, Alpha Kera. He's coming with us."

31
† Coral †

"Where have you been?" Mia cried, letting go of the wheel and crushing me in a giant hug as I slid onto the passenger seat. "I thought you were dead."

Her voice sounded different. Older somehow. Even her scent had changed. Or it might have been my nose that changed, but that was beside the point.

When I'd used Sage's phone to call, because my own phone was destroyed thanks to my wolf's tantrum–my wolf rolled her eyes at the memory–I wasn't sure what to expect. So much happened in the last few months. I wouldn't blame her for writing me off. But she answered the call and didn't hesitate to show up. It felt like we were kids again. Mia would never let me down.

I knew that I could trust her.

"I'm so sorry I couldn't tell you everything before I left." I leaned back against the seat and wiggled my eyebrows. "But I'm going to rock your world now."

"Start with explaining the hunk in the back seat." Mia bit her bottom lip as she glanced in the rearview mirror.

I clamped down on my wolf's snarl.

Mia is our friend. Besides, Skoll isn't going anywhere.

My wolf snickered, sending me an image of him tied to the bed. Hmm... That was something we could try out. Later.

Mia pressed on the gas and Skoll's heavy hand landed on my shoulder. His anxiety pulsed through our bond. It was too late to warn him that Mia was a terrible driver. Not Jareth fast, but easily distracted bad. To prove my point, she jerked the wheel to avoid hitting the curb.

A warning rumble vibrated in Skoll's chest.

Mia's eyes widened. "Is he growling?"

"Right." I exhaled, getting ready to catch her up to speed. "Before I start, switch to autopilot. You're not going to be able to focus on the road."

*

"Curse science. You're serious." Mia's hands were over her mouth as she breathed through a panic attack. The vehicle drove itself through the business district with Sage's car following behind.

"Yep." I retracted my fangs and nodded. Skoll's grip tightened on my shoulder. He didn't like this plan all that much, but he was going to have to trust me. I knew how the citizens of Ethica thought.

They lived for the scandal.

No one would pass up the opportunity to be entertained. And finding out the government was lying to everyone was the juiciest thing I could give them. It would be breaking news. We were going to change the world. Give them the truth and bring the corrupt government down.

Well, we were going to try at least.

My mother had spied for the packs before I was born, but the more I thought about it, the more I realized espionage wasn't my style. If I was going to challenge the system, then they would damn well remember my name for the history books.

Screw hiding. We were stepping into the light.

"I know it's a lot to ask, but does your cousin still work for Panem Pop?"

"You want to announce it on the radio?" Mia turned fully in her seat, ignoring the car altogether.

Skoll growled again and his fingers dug deeper into my skin. "The road."

"The cars drive themselves." I patted his hand as I gave her a little wink. "I want to break into the media network facility."

Mia blinked like an owl. A real owl. I'd seen so many of those now and they were more beautiful than the nature documentaries I'd grown up seeing. The whole world was such a pretty place, nothing at all like we'd been taught.

But the lines of disbelief etched on her face made me realize that the ingrained brainwashing went deep. This was the moment of truth. Where I asked my friend to go against everything she knew and break the rules. We'd done petty stuff as kids, but this was asking for a lot.

Sage and I talked about this. How most of the people we knew wouldn't believe. She was ready to knock Mia out and help her forget this conversation if we had to. Don't get me wrong, I'd feel like a jerk if it came to that, but we'd come too far to turn back now.

"Please." I gave her my best smile, remembering all the times she'd been my ride-or-die growing up. We should have gone to the university together. I wanted to be her bridesmaid when she finally married Jake. Things were different now. The bridge between us lengthened and changed, but I still had hope that the bond we shared was strong enough to cross those boundaries.

"Welp." Mia popped the *p* as she put her hands back on the wheel. "We're going to have to go faster than autopilot if we are going to make it to the media department before the government assholes get there."

32
† Skoll †

Lights blurred and whipped around the car like some magic induced nightmare. Tall buildings rose on either side of the road, massive and crammed together. It was as if this whole purist city was bearing down on us and threatening to swallow us whole. And this metal box was moving so fast.

I was going to be sick.

Don't like this.

Me either. I buried my face in Coral's hair for a moment, breathing in her scent. The female human not actually driving the vehicle wasn't as repulsive as I assumed she'd be. It had something to do with her love of my mate. I could tolerate her. But everything else reeked of the humans and my blood was boiling, making me ready to snap.

I did my best to hold onto my beast and ignore the bile rising up the back of my throat. It was hard to keep my thoughts from Coral, but I forced myself to hold back now.

This was a really stupid plan.

I didn't give a shit if the humans learned the truth. It was better if they stayed in their plastic bubble and left the packs alone.

But they didn't stay in their disgusting city. They'd attacked another shifter community. A small town, like the place I was born in, and they took the pups from their parents.

My wolf paced inside me. Ants crawled and rippled through my skin. Flashes of memories. The black boots. Their plastic shields. My mother and sister's screams. Blood spraying the walls. My breath came too short, not wanting to inhale the toxic air, and I leaned closer to Coral again.

She was the only thing grounding here in this unnatural place. They wanted less bloodshed. I wanted to burn it all to the ground. But I was trying to go against my nature to be there for my mate.

I risked a glance behind my shoulder through the back window, still holding to the back of Coral's seat. Maddock sat as the passenger in Sage's car, looking as grim as I felt. He should. This was all his fault. *"Trust our girls,"* he always said.

We should have kept her in the cave.

My cheeks filled with toxic air as I blew out a heavy breath. *Anything for Coral.*

I swallowed down the bitter taste on the back of my tongue. Living in Cerberus had turned me soft. Or maybe my mate had done that. Jareth was getting his ass kicked as soon as Kera got him out.

Red and blue lights flashed brighter than the others. A siren sound blared through the night. My fangs extended as my heart thumped harder in my chest and worry came from Coral through our bond.

"What is that?" I growled, wrapping my arm around her shoulders to keep her safe from the new threat.

"There's a police unit coming up." She chewed her bottom lip. "Can we outrun them?"

The tires seemed to seize on the asphalt, bringing the vehicle to a screeching stop.

Mia moaned as she put her head against the steering wheel. "Automatic lockout. They got us in the digital net."

Coral cursed under her breath.

My wolf was already pushing through my skin, ready to fight. "What are the police?"

"A type of enforcer for the humans, but they aren't as deadly as you or Maddock." She pulled down the visor and looked in the mirror. Her eyes met Sage's in the car behind us as the witch pulled over to the side of the road. "But that doesn't mean this won't suck."

33
† Kera †

"Talk to me." I ground my teeth as I paced along the outside of the wall where Ethan begged us to stop. Something happened to the girls. I knew it before his buzzer on one of the devices went off. And now I was ready to scale this damn wall to get them out of there.

"The police still have them pinned on the road in front of the media center." Ethan turned the screen on his box to me as if I could understand what the blinking dots were.

"Coral. Maddock. Skoll." I tried the links again.

Screw this. I wasn't waiting anymore.

The wall was at least forty feet high made of slick metal corroded with age. I pressed against it, checking for footholds or grips. This was my fault. I never should have left them alone.

It was their plan. My wolf growled, urging me to get ahold of myself and continue on our path.

The shifters who'd run with us down south were mulling about and pawing at the ground. My distress was making them anxious. I fisted my hands in my hair and took a steadying breath.

"Coral, damnit. Talk to me."

"We're fine. It was a little hiccup with the cops, but Sage worked her magic."

The breath left my lungs in a solid exhale. *"Don't scare me like that again."*

"We'll try not to, Alpha." Coral's thoughts were rushed as if she was running and focusing on something else. *"Give us a few minutes to set up the broadcast and then tell your boy to do his thing. We're using a video feed if Mia can figure out how to set it up."*

"How much longer to the service entrance?" My claws extended as I looked to Ethan.

"About five miles." His shoulders relaxed at whatever he saw on the screen.

"Let's go. They still need a few minutes to set things up before you can help." I nodded to the shifters waiting, letting my wolf finish taking over my skin.

"Five miles is…"

Foster's wolf cut Ethan off with a growl and the kid hurried to scramble onto his back.

*

There was a junkyard outside of the service entrance full of garbage that created its own neon green haze in the dark. The stench was overpowering, but I still picked up the faint traces of *him*.

Catching the trail upped my wolf's desire to hunt and she paced rabidly in my mind. That earthy scent of sagebrush and pepper didn't belong in this unnatural place.

"You sent him this way." It wasn't a question.

Ethan nodded. "The idiots haven't figured it out either. They upped security and put more guns in at the research facility, but did nothing to block the literal hole in the wall."

The talk of added weaponry at the place they were holding Jareth made me nervous. I'd seen the chaos those guns could cause. The wolves around me paced through the junkyard, sneezing and huffing as they waited for my command.

"How much longer?" I asked Coral.

"Just a second. We're connecting now."

"I've got them." Ethan's fingers flew over the buttons on his laptop.

"I'll be right back." I inched closer to the service entrance, giving them time to work their technological stuff out.

As I walked, I reached through the pack link to sense how all my shifters were fairing. Their combined bloodlust was muted, waiting for me to direct them to kill. But we hadn't needed them yet and I hoped we never did. If I had my choice, none of them would step foot past these walls. They'd all be safely home in their beds. Maybe I could slip through alone and get Jareth out before they noticed.

"I know what you're thinking and it's not going to work." Greg's scarred old wolf nudged my thigh. The rest of the wolves I thought I'd left in the junkyard flanked me on either side as I edged closer to the tunnel that went through the wall.

"Fine." I growled. "But it's your hide if things go south."

"You know you could have killed me after I challenged for Alpha." Greg chuckled as his wolf brushed his

scraggly coat under my hand. *"But you didn't and I figured out real quick that a woman strong enough to put me on my ass was one worth dying for."*

"It seems like you have a death wish." A small smile turned my lips.

"Maybe." Greg gave me a wolfy grin. *"Or maybe I want a life well lived."*

"They're on in 5, 4, 3…"

I took off at a trot with the wolves following me, rushing to Ethan's side.

A *video* moving picture of Coral lit up the screen. Her beaming smile was captivating, like always, and Sage held her sister's hand in solidarity.

"Citizens of Ethica," Coral began. "Your government is lying to you."

A stillness settled over the junkyard. I backed away from Ethan, leaving him to furiously click on multiple devices, and went to check the service entrance again.

A human passed on the other side. Probably a guard running a perimeter sweep. I pressed my back against the wall, counting his steps until he moved further away. A few minutes ticked by without another human scent filtering down the tunnel. That was good news. What would be even better is if the miracle kid had a schedule of their rotations.

"It's done. The broadcast should be on every major channel now." Ethan blinked slowly, powering down his device.

"Thank you." I nodded.

His pimpled cheeks flushed. "No big deal."

"We'll meet you at the research center." Coral mind linked me. I looked back to the gathered wolves who were edging closer to my side.

"Last chance." I winked, praying they would heed the warning and stay back with the hundreds of other wolves strategically placed around the Fringes where they were safer.

The soft and deadly growls echoed around the junkyard as the first rays of the morning sun crested the sky in the distant east.

My fangs extended as I turned back to the wall, ready to lead the forward team through.

*

"How much longer until the next guard change?" I asked as we crept along the tunnel. Sludge and grime were tacky against the bottom of my bare feet. Foster's wolf lifted one paw after another awkwardly to keep from sticking to the residue left from the garbage waste as Ethan clung to his back.

"They won't have anyone else out here until nightfall. Trash doesn't get moved through the city in the light of day," Ethan whispered, adjusting to the deathly quiet we carried.

We weren't the only things silent.

I strained my ears, listening for commotion on the other side of the wall. There was nothing. The sun was rising and yet no one was moving. I could sense them though. Hundreds of thousands of clay bodies crammed inside the city. You'd think it'd be

328

louder, but it was a collectively held breath that raised the hairs on the back of my neck. The sense of unease grew stronger the closer we got to the exit.

"This is as far as I go." Ethan climbed down from Foster's back. "I don't have the right identification cards and it's a death sentence if I'm caught inside. See that building over there? That's the research facility. I can stay here and give you some coverage by shutting down their security system."

He's in there. My wolf howled.

The mate bond thrummed stronger now. A tether to the ominous building surrounded by high fence and barb wire, still cast in shadows despite the slowly rising sun. *I'm almost there.*

But my sense of dread increased with a sound in the distance. I sank deeper into the darkness of the tunnel to listen. The crash of something. Breaking glass. There was a subtle shift in the air.

"Curse science." A loud beeping came from one of Ethan's devices and the wolves surrounding us growled as he hurried to shut it off.

A growing murmur vibrated in the distant city to our left and I peeked out past the exit of the tunnel to see. Like the whip of an eastern storm wind catching the leaves of the trees, energy sparked in the atmosphere.

Shouting started. My hackles raised. Greg and his team growled as they moved closer to my side.

Engines rumbled and car doors slammed. We slid deeper into the tunnel.

"What's happening?" I asked Ethan.

His face glowed in the darkness, lit up by his screens. "I didn't know. I didn't think…"

"Spit it out." I resisted the urge to wring his neck, leaning into my pack links to check on Coral and Maddock and Skoll. Their anxious emotions were a punch to my gut.

I grabbed my stomach, holding back my wolf. *"Where are you?"*

The silence on their end had my fangs and claws extending.

"It's um… They are…" Ethan continued to sputter his nonsense as he focused on his electronics.

"Tell me!" I grabbed him by his sweatshirt.

"They weren't supposed to actually care," he squeaked with his feet dangling above the ground.

"What?" My brow creased in confusion.

"It's some kind of roadblock. They're starting a riot." Coral's panicked voice came to me. *"Don't worry about us. Get Jareth. We're going to find another way out."*

I set Ethan down on his feet, shaking my head as I backed away from him. "Did you do something to betray us?"

"What? No," Ethan cried. "It's them. The people. We didn't think they would care this much."

I rushed to the exit, blood pounding in my ears. Something was wrong. Coral and Sage were not okay. I was an idiot for letting them go alone. An Alpha doesn't abandon their pack.

You couldn't have stopped them. My wolf was riled up and barking, as torn and confused as I was. We looked to the research facility and back toward the city. My heart was being ripped in half as the sounds coming from the distance grew louder. Boots stomping. Screams on the streets.

A single gunshot rang out.

"Do you know where Sage's car is?" I was already running, dragging Ethan onto Foster's back as he raced beside me.

"I do, but I can't go in there," Ethan clung to the wolf's neck.

"I'll keep you safe." I growled as I shifted into my beast and she took off, sprinting away from the research facility. *I'll keep all of them safe....*

34
† Jareth †

"Is it time already?" I rubbed the sleep from my eyes as the fluorescent lights flicked on. Without windows, it was difficult to tell the time of day but it had only been a few hours since they'd left me alone. From the scents of the human doctors filtering into the viewing room, freshly showered and coffee drifting from little white cups, I assumed it must be morning.

I laid on the cot a moment longer, forcing my body to relax. Today I wouldn't fight. I was under no illusion they'd trust me this soon, but I had to start somewhere if I wanted out of this cage.

"Test subject A032M. Vital signs normal. No visual or internal lingering affects from previous testing," the robotic voice trickled over the speaker as the machines in the viewing room whirred to life.

I glanced down at my bare chest, remembering the pain of the scalding burns from last night as my wolf let out a little whine. You'd think the humans would be a little more *humane* in their scientific approach, but apparently not.

Moira opened the heavy metal door, pushing another cart and wearing a different set of heels that tapped along the floor.

"Do I get breakfast before we start the activities today?" I swung my feet off the cot. I could

332

do this, be agreeable, right up to the moment I tore them all apart.

Moira's pinched expression made me worry as she cast a glance to the viewing room. The doctors inside huddled around Bradley, checking their phones.

"Patient is alert and responsive." Her tone was icy and clipped like the robotic voice. It was only her eyes that gave away any emotion. Pleading. Trapped. Trying to convey some sort of apology as she slid the tray into the slot with another soy patty on it.

Shit.

Something bad was about to happen.

I swallowed hard, looking between her and the viewing room.

Dr. Bradley's cold eyes met mine. "Change of plans today. We're prioritizing experimental methods of expulsion."

Expulsion as in removal?

Removing us from this cage? My wolf shook himself awake.

"Where are we going?" I controlled my rapidly rising heartrate, staring at Bradley with a slight smirk as if I was bored.

I didn't expect him to answer me directly. I'd seen enough low-level wolves on power trips to know they took a sick sense of pleasure in toying with their prey. I was wrong.

Hate dripped from his tongue as he sneered. "It seems your time is up, mutant. Enjoy your final meal."

Like hell would I enjoy this food. I pushed the tray back toward the slot. My wolf pressed forward, baring his teeth at the audacity of this human.

Threats weren't something an Alpha could take easily. I clenched down on my teeth, trying to keep my aggression in check and not fly at the bars in a fit of rage.

"This is it? What a waste of a good specimen. Do you at least have the decency to tell me why?" I was stalling, trying to think my way out of this. Something had changed. After all the trouble, killing me now didn't make any sense.

Dr. Bradley–the dick–didn't respond. Hushed whispers broke out in the viewing room and the waft of fear grew stronger. I leaned into my wolf's hearing, picking up the undercurrent of fear as a familiar voice echoed on their devices.

It sounded eerily similar to the trouble maker.

"Eat fast." Moira used their distraction to talk to me as she slid the tray back into the cage. "I added a dose of synthetic antioxidants. It's all I could do."

Antioxidants?

The clack of her heels hurried away and the door to the viewing room opened as the doctors left.

Eat it. My wolf growled, deciding to trust the female nurse. I hurried to shove the soy patty into my mouth, pacing as I tried to think.

Antioxidants were for health.

They rid the body of toxins.

But shifters didn't need them.

I racked my brain, running through old medical textbooks I'd flipped through once before I moved onto more important things.

Mechanics. Engineering.

Pages of books swirled in my head, thousands of words I'd read and memorized.

The doors clicked shut, locking me alone in the basement. In the cage.

We need to get out.

We need to think.

A panel on the wall slid open. The slow hiss of gas was pushed into the room. I took a breath and tasted something bitter. A passage from a book I once read came in perfect clarity.

Work hazards in the field.

Pain blossomed in my chest as a tickle wormed its way down my throat.

Heavy metal toxication.

Fire spread through my lungs as I began to cough. Tears burned my eyes and I shut them tight.

Toxic air. Silver particles.

I was fucked.

I dropped to my knees, trying to hold my breath as I clawed at my throat. *"Ophelia!"*

"Are you okay? There's something happening outside." The urgency in her tone reached through the white hot pain shooting through my skull as the air forced it's way up my nose.

Let me out. My wolf shot forward. I gasped and started coughing, struggling to hold him back. The natural instinct to protect overrode rational thought. His senses were too animalistic. He'd fight too hard and fall too quickly. My wolf couldn't protect us here.

"You know I love you." I curled into a naked ball on the floor, stripped of dignity and not able to call on my wolf as I tried to conserve our energy. The air around me soaked into my pores, stinging as sweat beaded on my skin.

"What are they doing to you?" Ophelia was screaming. I had the random thought that I wanted to hear her laugh. Just one last time.

My lungs were burning, begging for fresh air that didn't exist in this cage. *"When you get out, send some painting instructors to Cerberus for Kera."*

I focused on the pain, holding it inside as if I could delay the inevitable. My mind was spinning. Facts and numbers and memories blurred as my chest started to shake. My wolf howled his fury.

"Jareth! Fight it! Don't give up." My little sister was crying. Darkness danced on the edge of my vision. There was a flash of red hair. A beautiful girl running through the trees.

I didn't normally pray to the Gods, but I tried my hardest now. *Please take care of them for me.*

I thought I had more time. The Alpha's curse? There's never enough time.

No matter how much I tried to think it through, to command my body, to lean into my wolf's brute strength, I was nothing more than an animal in a cage. Nature always wins in the end.

I gasped, sucking in the toxic air.

35
† Kera †

Fire licked up the side of an overturned vehicle. Black plumes of smoke billowed into the air. The distant human screams of a mob were muted by the sound of boots marching in formation.

"Coral! Maddock! Skoll! Talk to me!" I felt like I was on repeat now, calling for them every few seconds. My wolf leapt over the concrete barriers lining the city streets as she followed the link to our pack members. When I got close enough to sense them without needing the tracking device, I turned to Foster and barked at him to get Ethan back to the tunnel where it was safe.

I wasn't running blind. I was following my intuition. Their fearful and primal emotions were a homing beacon that helped my Alpha instincts pinpoint where they were.

It was Coral's presence that drew me first. Our link was stronger because she was my Beta. But she was more than that.

She was my best friend.

A siren screeched up ahead, down the next major street. It was loud enough to make the wolves racing along side me flinch. They slowed, growling, and pawed at the ground.

Fuck that noise.

338

My wolf slid on the asphalt, careening onto the busy street where crowds of people were being pushed back by men in black boots carrying guns.

My claws scraped the metal frame of a vehicle parked in the middle of the street serving as some kind of roadblock as I scampered to the top.

The stench of fear hit me at once. Sickeningly sweet. Prey was being herded back behind closed doors. Humans screamed. The uniformed men marched in a line with shields over their faces.

In the midst of the chaos, in the middle of the street, facing down the hoard of booted men was a massive gray wolf with glowing green eyes.

Skoll.

Coral stood in human form by her mate's side.

A shiver ran through my wolf, sensing his horror through the pack link. His beast had taken over and bloodlust clouded his mind.

He leapt for a man in black, tearing at the armor with his teeth. A spray of blood arched in the air as he shook the body like a ragdoll.

"Kill the mutant!" The uniformed men started shouting, guns pointing in Skoll's direction.

Oh hell no. If anyone was killing that thick-skulled shifter, it was me.

My wolf jumped from the top of the vehicle and dove straight for the sea of men. She landed on the back of a guard, knocking him down. Our jaws crunched on the bone of his shoulder. Screams rang out mixing with the sound of gunshots. Bullets flew wildly in the air. My beast latched down again, cracking his clavicle and neck, as his life force drained onto the street.

We released him and leapt to the next closest guard. The plastic uniform tore easily under our fangs. Erratic jerks came from his body as he tried to swat her away. My wolf clamped down on his arm, breaking it with a snap of crushed bone. His free arm released our fur and fumbled blindly around for the useless weapon on the ground. She snapped down onto his neck before he touched the machine.

The growls of my pack sounded through the chaos. Humans cried out as they ran from the vicious wolves. The line of guards marching through the street scattered into every direction.

I leapt over the fresh kill and lunged for another. His plastic face shield cracked as it hit the pavement. Our jaws snapped on the back of his exposed neck, vertebrae shattering as we ripped out his spinal column.

Panting heavy, I turned in a circle with the taste of blood filling our mouth and looking for our next kill. The firing had stopped, but the screams and growls still echoed. Blood ran down the street, staining it red.

Skoll's wolf looked up to me from across the pavement. His green eyes were glowing with pain. Bodies of the fallen guards lay at his thick paws. Coral's white fur was matted with gore as she panted, pressing her wolf's body against her mate.

"What happened?" I continued to circle, checking on Greg and his team that had followed me

into the fray. They were tangled up with their own kills and chasing down the rest of the guards. *"Why didn't you answer me?"*

"Um, we were kind of busy." Coral's wolf whined at Skoll's side, sending him comfort through their mate bond. He'd laid six to waste in the time it took me to kill three.

He was never going to let me live this down.

I backed up slowly, taking stock of the situation and making sure none of my wolves were injured. *So much for the least amount of bloodshed.*

Then again, it could have been worse.

"Where are Sage and Maddock?"

"Coming." My uncle grumbled through the pack link. The toy car came speeding down the road, swerving around the barriers set in place. His brown wolf sat solemnly in the driver seat with blood coating his snout as the tires bumped over the bodies on the ground and Sage came to a stop.

"Seriously." Coral shifted to scream at her sister. Her naked body was dripping with blood and her hands stayed buried in Skoll's fur as she stomped her foot on the ground. "I told you to leave the freaking car!"

*

It was chaos in the streets. Purists rushed up and down moving sidewalks. Glass shattered in storefronts as metal pipes smashed against them. But they weren't fighting against the men in black boots, not with their arms full of stuff and shoving against each other instead. The guards were so caught up with trying to force people back into their homes that they barely paid any attention to the wolves running down the highway.

"I thought you said they were peaceful people." I growled at Coral as we ran, still trying to make sense of what I was seeing.

"Obviously, I was wrong," Coral screamed. *"Are you really going to call me out on that now?"*

No. I wasn't. Maybe after I got us all out of here. My wolf's legs pumped harder, racing south.

The sleepy quiet of the morning was replaced with a frantic energy as humans reacted like squawking birds with no clear direction. Armored vehicles rolled down the streets toward the city center. More stomping boots formed lines with plastic shields, pushing humans back. Fires breaking out and smoke canisters shot by big guns turned the air foggy and made the sun blaze a blood shade red.

I howled for my wolves, urging them faster as Sage's car sped behind us through the mayhem of the city streets.

We broke free from the cluster of the high-rise buildings. The open parking lots and garbage station lay ahead. Wolves were already pouring through the service entrance. Some were Cerberus, but different coats were scattered among them.

Anubis, Fenrir, Amarock… All moving as one with the thrill of the hunt thrumming through their growls as they raced toward the research facility.

I forced my wolf to focus her attention on the distance. Time slowed as I took the scene in. The armored vehicles and guards we'd seen in the streets were here too. Lining up in a defensive position outside the facility's fence. The wolves were heading straight to their guns.

I was too far away.

"No!" I screamed, forcing my wolf to run faster as protective instinct drove me to act.

It was too late.

The purists opened fire on the mass of advancing wolves. They ran straight into the gunshots. Furry bodies contorted as they were blown apart.

Alpha power swirled in my veins as I howled, sending out a command so loud it shook the ground.

"Fall back!"

Cerberus shifters froze on my order and quickly spun around. The others were confused. Anarchy making them restless with no clear Alpha's directions to follow. I partially shifted, letting my monster form take over with my jaws and claws extended, sucking in a deep breath to project my voice, "I said, fall back now!"

Wolves whined as they turned and sprinted to me. I raced to the service entrance. I slid in hard, landing next to Foster and Ethan who were struggling with some shifters to disable a metal door coming down to block us out.

I rushed to help them, slamming a shoulder under the panel as Ethan worked on some wires.

"Who gave the order to attack?" My words were still coming out as beastly growls from my half-shifted form and Ethan ducked behind Foster, clearly done with the events of the day.

Foster's eyes were red-rimmed as he put the kid back in front of the wires. "It might have been my fault. Luna Ophelia was able to connect with me now that we're so close and I let the pack know that we can't get in touch with Alpha Jareth. She thinks something happened. No one can reach him."

No.

Not like this.

My heart skipped a beat. And then another.

I looked over the carnage in the distance. The wolves were still racing back to my side, leaving their fallen brothers on the ground. Their eyes were crazed. Panic and bloodshed driving their animalistic instincts. I failed to protect them all.

What if we were too late?

Was the blood spilled worth it?

Coral and Sage had their hands on my shoulders. Their soft voices broke through the war drums pounding in my ears. My wolf howled her grief as they tried to wrap me in love. It wasn't a whine. It was a battle cry.

Shifters gathered around me, baring their necks in respect as they lowered to their bellies.

"Reach into your heart. See if you can still feel him," Sage spoke softly into my ear.

I did.

I searched and hacked my way blindly through the overwhelming emotions, gripping for the weak tendrils of our mate bond. Maybe I'd been searching my whole life for it, because the moment I caught it, I vowed to never let it go. It was a dull spark. A flicker of hope. It was all I needed. A chance.

"Now would be a good time to shut down those security systems," I barked at Ethan, giving into my beast as I marched into the crowd of shifters waiting for my orders. "Flank them. Move teams around the back on my command. We don't fight like humans in a line. We attack like wolves."

*

I led the first wave to the gates, sending teams of Cerberus shifters guiding groups of the other packs around the sides of the fence. The souls of hundreds of wolves leaving their positions in the Fringes called to me, begging to be unleashed at my command.

We were on the humans in a skilled flash of jaws and teeth, overwhelming them from all directions, rendering their weapons and defensive line useless. Somewhere in the back of my mind, I knew time was of the essence and we risked the purists deploying their flying machines. I could only hope the towering buildings would slow them down.

Shifters were scaling the fences behind me, climbing over the fallen clay bodies left in our wake.

My wolf was the first through the doors of the facility.

"Search all the floors. Kill anyone who resists." The order I gave to the Cerberus shifters was monotone, coming from some distant place that didn't sound like me. The building was dark and humans started screaming as my wolves rushed inside.

He's not up there. My wolf followed her gut, taking us below the earth. To the depths buried beneath the hunk of metal and concrete above.

Her claws slipped on the steps going down, down, down. The staircases spiraled, making us dizzy. Our lungs were burning. Adrenaline still coursing through our veins. The taste of blood in her mouth fueling the need to kill. Fear and rage pulsed through the links to my pack as they continued their battle overhead.

Without their power, without their weapons, this fight was ours to win.

But what was the cost?

My wolf ran faster, trying to drive out my human thoughts of failure and death. We couldn't have come this far for nothing.

"They've cleared the floors above," Coral said. *"What are your orders now?"*

"Grab Ophelia and get her out of here," I barked. My wolf was still running, slipping down the steps, following her heart away from the fight.

The darkness was swallowing us as we continued down the stairwell. Sage clung to

Maddock's back behind me. Coral and Skoll's wolves brought up the rear.

I had no clue what we were running to.

They could have been following me into hell.

We reached the bottom landing and pushed open the door with the smooth metal bar. A concrete hallway stood before us, lit by dim emergency exit lights. The air this far down was stifling. The walls were closing in. My wolf's heart was racing.

I pushed harder, lending her more of my human senses so she could find the way to her mate.

A commotion up ahead had her ears twitching and she snarled as she bared her teeth.

"Dr. Bradley?" Sage gasped. Her voice echoed down the empty hall. A crusty old man in a white lab coat came stumbling out of an office, carrying a stack of paper files. His eyes widened in recognition as he looked at Sage. The witch slid down from my uncle's back.

The doctor turned and fled.

"Don't worry." Coral growled. *"He's mine."*

She sprinted down the hall in a flash of blood-stained white fur with Skoll's wolf running protectively beside her.

My wolf sniffed the empty office the doctor came from, sneezing at the dust and decay.

Heels clicked on the hallway floor.

My beast spun with teeth bared as Maddock's wolf placed Sage behind him.

It took me a minute to recognize Ophelia in a paper-thin blue gown with her black hair shaved close to her head. She clung to a human woman who smelled faintly of diluted wolf blood.

"Kera." Ophelia had no problem recognizing me. Her skinny arms flung around my wolf's neck, sobs racking her body as she cried. "I can't feel him anymore."

My wolf shook her head, backing away. She could feel him. These dramatics made her angry. I leaned into her aggression, putting a numb distance between myself and the situation as I tentatively reached for the bond.

We turned and followed the pull of the thread down the hall. I clung to the frail filament in my chest, afraid to let it slip from my grasp. Heels clicked along beside us. My wolf stopped, whining as her claws scratched against the metal door.

The woman who smelled like diluted wolf pulled out a set of keys. "Hopefully the power being turned off helped." Her hands were shaking. Tears ran down her cheeks. My wolf snarled, not liking the emotions coming from this newcomer.

I forced the shift before my wolf decided to tear her apart and grabbed the keys from her hand, shoving them into the lock.

Crystal dust whooshed in the air, pushed back by the draft of opening the door. Silver particles drifted to the floor. They cut into my bare feet, stinging and slicing the skin, as I stepped into the vast room.

In the middle was a cage.

Ophelia's scream echoed in the dark space.

I growled, rage making me blind as I ignored the burning skin of the soles of my feet and raced to the bars. I fought with the keys, shoving multiple pieces of metal into the lock until I got the right one.

He lay there, motionless, with his face turned to the ceiling. His tanned skin was a sickly grayish green pallor. Dark lashes closed over his sunken cheekbones. His chest and stomach were caved in.

"Jareth!" Ophelia was still screaming, rushing into the cage to drop beside her brother. "You can't leave me. You promised you'd…"

I tuned out her cries, staring at the body of my mate. Numbness crept in. My pulse pounded in my ears as the rest of the world fell away and my heart tried to rip itself from my chest.

Not like this. The words beat around my head.

The Alpha of Anubis.

Reduced to an ashen lump.

The spark of his life, of his power, dimmed.

Alone and abandoned in a cage.

Howls of victory sounded throughout the building on the floors above us. My pack tried to reach me to share the triumph. I stood there, distancing myself as everything I was fighting for slipped away. He was gone.

My mate was…

"No." I growled; voice thick with my beast. Power pulsed over my skin. It wasn't going to happen like this. Not in my story.

I refused to let it end this way.

"He's not dead." I shoved my way into the cage, rushing to Jareth's side. Their pity, their despair, wrapped around me.

I brushed it away with another growl.

Alphas don't die like this.

"Get up, you asshole!" I screamed, yanking his body from Ophelia's grasp. Tears burned my eyes and I let them fall, cutting paths through the silver dust on my cheeks. I lifted his arms over my shoulders and tried to pull him up.

My mate. My beast was howling. Her soul and mine were bleeding out as we kept trying to fight.

He was alive.

He had to be.

"Kera, he's gone." Maddock rested his hand on the top of my head.

"Not yet." I pounded my fist against my chest, screaming as spit flew from my mouth. "I still feel him. He's in here. I have to move him."

Tears ran down my uncle's cheeks as he nodded, moving to lift Jareth's legs. "I'll help."

My mind was shattering like glass. My beast feral as she growled. We didn't want anyone to touch him. She snapped, extending her fangs through my mouth. My uncle ignored my outrage.

Our muscles strained under Jareth's weight.

He was still alive. I knew it. I knew it like I knew how to breathe.

"Please wake up," I begged, choking on the sound of my words. My wolf was whining, crying pitiful sounds, and they were coming from me.

Maddock helped me carry his body out of the cage and away from the toxic silver coating every surface in this Gods forsaken room.

I slipped on the blood coating my feet, going down in the hall as I cradled Jareth's head against my chest. We growled, crying as everyone rushed to help us. I couldn't breathe anymore.

"Get up. Please. Jareth. I need you." The words were pouring out as fast as my tears. "I want you. I want us. Please don't leave me alone."

Sage was kneeling at my side, giving space to my protective beast as she tried to lift Jareth's arm.

Her gasp of shock echoed loudly in the hall.

My tear-soaked eyes shot up, looking at the witch.

"He's still alive," she said.

Hope blossomed, spreading through my chest like early spring branches reaching for the sun.

"I know!" I cried. "Help him, please."

There was a flurry of activity. Sage and Maddock rolled him over. Ophelia prayed to the Gods as she grabbed his hand. I kept his head in my lap, fighting to control my beast, as my tears fell onto his ghostly face.

Sage pressed her palms against his bare chest. Magic hummed through the air.

"I can't." She pulled her hands away, covering her mouth as she cried. "He's too far gone. I can't force his body to work harder. It's already done all that it can."

"Maybe I can hook him up to an IV and flush his system," the human woman who smelled like wolf was talking. Their voices were distant, underwater, as my wolf continued to growl.

Mine. My mate.

Ours.

I blinked, giving my beastly nature full control. We could fix this.

Our fangs extended.

"What is she doing?" The woman shrieked.

I lowered my mouth to his neck, chomping down on the tender flesh. The taste of his blood was wrong. Too metallic. We drank anyway, feeling the weak pulse dribble down our throat. I clamped down harder, willing with everything I was for the mate bond to snap into place.

Ophelia stepped back and let go of her brother's hand, allowing me the space I needed with my mate. She turned to console the panicked woman. "The Alpha is giving him her strength."

36
† Jareth †

Somewhere in the darkness, beneath the cloud of consciousness, I floated in a sea of black watching my wolf trying to break free. It was a struggle to understand what he was fighting against. He was more beast than sentient, acting on some primitive instinct.

I focused on his wants, leaning into my human senses to figure it out. Ophelia was out there somewhere, crying. There was a respectful murmur of mourning voices. The steady pulse of earthly power surrounded my physical body.

Great.

Somehow, I'd broken the barrier of reincarnation and was waking up at my own damn funeral. I hoped they didn't decide to burn me.

Once was enough for one lifetime.

Mate. My wolf started clawing at my mind with a frantic urgency. The one word, broken and raw, defied the rules of physics and magic, bringing me back.

I inhaled sharply, filling my lungs with that first painful breath. And then it was everywhere.

Pain.

White hot and raking its razor-sharp knives into every nerve ending. I choked on it. Gasping for relief, I coughed up slices of metal that tore my throat to shreds. My body wrenched itself in half, trying to force out every foreign particle that had seeped into my being. The pain was vaguely familiar.

I'd gone down like this.

I was still alive.

My eyes shot open. Burst capillaries scoured my vision, making it blurry as I looked up into what could only be a dream.

Fiery red hair fell around my face like a protective curtain. Tear filled storm blue eyes looked at me with such intensity that I knew I'd died and gone to heaven. She was a lighthouse, drawing me through the dark depths.

"Kera." My voice was a hoarse whisper.

Let me out. My wolf clawed at my mind, ignoring our own pain, because the suffering on her face was worse.

"Don't talk yet." She smiled through the tears that dripped onto her chin as she swept her hair to the side, exposing her slender neck.

Claim my mate.

Not like this.

I tried to push myself up, but the pain intensified, pressing me back down.

"I can't," I choked out the words, needing her to understand.

"I'm not going to tell anyone." She snapped her fangs.

I wanted this. I'd made my decision that day she challenged me on the training grounds. But not like this. Not laying here on my back. Her frustrated growl made me smile despite the pain.

"You deserve—"

"You can make it up to me later." She grabbed my chin and forced my teeth to her neck. "Complete the bond so I can heal you and let's get out of here before the wolves burn this place to the ground."

Hell yes. My wolf took over, not giving me time to think. My fangs extended and pierced her porcelain flesh. The power of her blood was potent. A punch to my chest that kickstarted my heart. My muscles seized from the force of it as I buried my teeth against bone, branding and claiming my mate.

The bond slammed into me, awakening parts of my body and fusing them with hers. Binding us for eternity. Seeking solace and strength for the parts of me that were lacking. Forcing that which was broken to mend as it filled with her essence.

The feeling was unlike anything I'd ever experienced. Too magical to explain. I couldn't form thoughts if I tried to. Our souls merged as I fell into the depths of the storm that was Kera and discovering she was the anchor in it all.

A new wave of pain washed over me as I coughed out the burning coals in my lungs. My skin crawled with scorpion stings. I released my jaw from its hold on her neck as my muscles spasmed.

I clung to Kera's hand in mine. Her light merging with my darkness. Our power crashed against each other, fighting for control, as the bond snapped into place. Still, I held to her hand like a life raft in a turbulent sea. Pain made me weak. My bones were shaking. Silver bled from my eyes as my lungs fully expanded.

With a righteous growl, I tore through the pain as my body came back from the brink of death. Breathing heavy through the worst of it, I crawled shakily to my knees and clung to Kera.

"Mate." My wolf took control of my voice as I stared into her beautiful eyes.

"Yeah, asshole. You're my mate." She grinned. "Now let's get the hell out of here."

*

Sweat coated my skin and my legs were still shaking as I stared at the Gods awful stairs. "Has anyone got in touch with Ethan?"

"Foster is out there with your *source,*" my sister teased.

That was a relief. "Can you tell him to turn the power back on? An elevator would be nice."

A few minutes later, I was hobbling down the hall while I leaned onto Kera's shoulders.

We crammed into the box together, watching the doors slide closed with a beep. Music played as we rode up to the ground floor like some bad sort of joke.

"Where is Skoll?" I put more weight on Kera's shoulders than I cared to admit.

"He and Coral will meet us outside the city limits. They took a friend of yours out for interrogation." Kera nudged me playfully in the ribs.

Gods, that hurt.

The elevator dinged. It opened to the lobby of the government research facility with the building's front glass doors blown to diamonds all over the ground. My wolf was alert, scanning the empty entrance room for a threat, but I barely had the strength to lend him my senses.

My body was healing, but not fast enough.

Ophelia slipped under my other arm and helped keep me steady as we made our way outside.

Stop. My wolf growled, smelling the smoke– the bloodshed–and the lingering remains of the fight.

I was in no condition to protect my mate and sister.

"Wait." I tried to hold them back. If we could hole up for a few hours so I could lick my wounds…

"Stop it." Ophelia sighed.

I tensed, realizing she was right.

"Sorry," I mumbled. *This is fine.*

We were alive. I'd been given a second chance. And if that required me to lean on someone, so be it.

I focused on my pack links instead, trying to distract myself from the pain. There were a few Anubis wolves' scents mingling with the shifters that I could sense were gathered outside.

"Foster?" I reached out to him.

"Alpha!" His relief made tears burn behind my eyes. *"We're holding strong at the service exit with your smart kid."*

I nodded, holding to Kera as we stepped carefully over the broken glass. My body continued to knit itself together, forcing silver out through my sweat.

"Do you have enough strength to shift?" Kera's face was impassive, but I heard the concern of her voice in my head. The rightness of it shocked me. Our bond was complete. A channel of communication between only us that no one else could touch.

"Careful, princess. Someone might think you care." I smirked.

"Almost back to your old self." Kera rolled her eyes. *"Also, I'm not a princess."*

We stepped outside, into the light. Smoke and dust lingered in the air. Wolves patrolled the parking lot. A mixture of different packs.

My brow furrowed, wondering where they'd all come from and what drew them together here.

The howling started.

Primal cheers of triumph and respect sounded throughout the distance. It sure as hell wasn't for me. I looked to Kera from the corner of my eye, seeing her chin held high, and touched on the foreign emotions drifting through our mate bond.

Discomfort, humble confusion, pain at the loss, and a small bit of pride that she would never admit to herself.

The wolves continued to howl for her.

An Alpha. Their hero.

And she couldn't see what all the fuss was about.

I didn't know what I'd done in a past life to earn the woman standing by my side. My mate. She was going to move mountains one day and I thanked the Gods that I was still around to watch her do it.

"Is it still alright if I come with you?" Nurse Moira stepped forward, asking Ophelia. My sister looked to Kera instead of me.

Kera chuckled, glancing down at the woman's feet. "You might want to lose those heels so you can keep up. We don't do damsels in distress out there."

*

The destruction didn't end once we'd left the city. Smoking machines lay grounded throughout the Fringes from where they fell from the sky. People were already tearing them apart in their own form of rebellion.

"What the…" Kera's voice was in my head. I didn't have an answer for that. We left them to their own devices as Kera led the wolves outside the fence.

My healing was kicking in rapidly now, bolstered by Kera's strength, and my wolf stayed dutifully at her side as we trotted out into the barren landscape. But it wasn't empty anymore.

Tents and equipment stretched out in either direction, surrounding the horizon as far as we could see. Kera's wolf turned to look at me. My wolf nudged her forward with his snout. She glanced over the herd of wolves following, making sure the injured cleared the fence, and then took off at a sprint.

My wolf howled as he hurried to keep up.

Alpha Nolan of Fenrir pack met us at the first outpost. His team of advisors surrounded him. The brute of a beast melted with an adoring smile as Kera shifted into her human form. I grabbed a shirt from a nearby shifter, handing it to Kera as she approached her grandfather.

Her confusion mirrored my own as she quickly pulled the clothes over her blood stained and dirt-streaked body.

"My apologies for taking so long." Nolan embraced her in a bear hug. He motioned to the tents in the distance waving the Amarock symbol on their flags. "Uki wanted to be here sooner, but I had to borrow some equipment from Anubis pack."

"You shot down their flying machines?" Kera blinked, looking back to the purist city where smoke still billowed in plumes.

"I wasn't going to let my granddaughter have all the fun." Nolan shrugged as he clasped my hand. "How are you doing, son?"

"Better." That was an understatement. I wrapped my arm around Kera's shoulders, hoping to give her some of my strength. Her embarrassment was strong, making my wolf whine with his need to protect her. "Thanks to Kera."

Seeing my mate blush was the highlight of my year. I was glad to be alive.

"That's my girl." Nolan's eyes glistened with moisture and he coughed to clear the emotion from his throat. "Alpha Kera, we helped set up the

Cerberus command center for you. Let us know what your orders are after you get settled in."

"What is happening?" Kera blinked, shaking her grandfather's hand as she leaned against my side.

I smiled as I kissed the top of her head and held her close, not wanting to ever let her go again. *"It looks like you're commanding an army, princess."*

Two days later

The camps set up were filled to the brim with more shifters arriving every day. The other Alphas had dug their heels in and word was even Alpha Oscar of Cadejo pack was on his way.

The bastard couldn't let us show him up.

I didn't get more than a few moments alone with Kera over the past two days. Only some stolen whispers and soft kisses in passing as she organized the show of force, daring the purists to retaliate.

Seeing the other packs defer to Kera and trusting her judgment filled me with a quiet pride.

My mate was a badass.

I left a teary-eyed Griffon in charge of the Anubis camps down south. He'd done well in my absence, moving our heavy artillery around to the other packs to target the purist drones and shooting them down like ducks over a pond.

"You know what to do?" I checked over the tires on the armored vehicle.

"Of course, Alpha. But remember that you don't get to keep her all to yourself." Ophelia kissed my cheek, excited to be included in the surprise I was setting up. We had to start now if I had any hope of finishing soon. I tucked her and her skirts into the car, looking over Anubis forces gathered at the border a final time, before giving into my wolf's desires.

He was anxious to get back to his mate.

Can't say that I blamed him.

*

Skoll stared out over the horizon at the human city in the distance with that bitter look of disdain, guarding the tent behind him.

"You didn't spill enough of their blood yet?" I asked.

"Nope." He spit on the dirt. "But Coral says it was more than enough."

It was a little odd how easy it'd become to listen to a second opinion on basically everything.

But when I caught the scent of Kera and saw her fiery red hair whipping around her head in the wind as she marched up the hill, I realized it wasn't all that bad. She looked like a Viking warrior princess from the ancient history books. My heart skipped a beat when she smiled.

"Are they ready?" Kera asked Skoll, slipping her hand into mine. Her sheer relief of seeing me again pulsed through our bond, making my wolf puff out his chest in happiness. This was everything.

Skoll nodded, moving to open the tent flap. "But I still think we should kill him."

Dr. Bradley sat in the dirt with his hands tied behind his back, looking worse for the wear under Sage and Coral's watchful glares.

"This is everything?" Coral asked, scanning through the pages of the written manifesto that documented the purists' crimes against shifters.

"He filled in most of the information gaps that I didn't have access to," Moira said.

"Traitor," Bradley mumbled under his breath.

"If I were you, I'd be really careful about the words you use when speaking about your hosts." The witch growled. "It's only because you knew our father and helped us when we were young that we aren't killing you now. But I can't say the same for the rest of the packs if we leak this information."

Dr. Bradley nodded, struck silent as he waited for his fate to be decided.

"Are we ready to send this clay pot back yet?" Kera sighed.

"I think we have everything." Coral put the pages in a locked briefcase. "Make no mistake, *Doctor* Bradley. Your one job is to convince the government not to retaliate. If they so much as send a drone outside the city, every pack in the region and world will know you've been using shifter magic to create anti-aging serums. That you capture and breed innocent little wolves for your beauty treatments, you sick fuck..."

Skoll caught Coral as she lunged for the man.

I would have loved to see her get a hit in.

It might have been less of a blow had they been creating an elite army or studying magic for actual scientific purposes. But this was all so... disgusting.

"Come on." Sage grabbed the old man's arm, lifting him to his feet before her sister tore him apart.

"You're going to tell everyone anyway, aren't you?" I chuckled, watching Maddock shove the doctor into Sage's awesome car. The solar power technology was fascinating.

I needed to make time to study it.

"Damn straight." Kera rested her head on my shoulder as we looked over the sprawling encampment of shifters. "I don't do secrets and dishonesty. But they'll agree to my terms first. I'm not starting a war. And a few people are staying behind, like Coral's friend Mia, to keep tabs on the government and make sure they don't pull this shit again."

Ethan too. I tried to get him out of there, but he was excited to stay in this *new era* that he swore was coming. I think he just didn't want to get too far away from reliable wi-fi, but it was his choice.

"Well, what do you want to do now, princess?" I laced her hand through mine, feeling the power of our bond pulse between us. The anchor that brought me back to earth. My mate.

You finally did something smart.

"I'm not a princess." Kera bit back her smile, looking to me with stormy, love-filled eyes. "And now? I want to go home."

37
† Kera †

Three months later.

"Alpha, you're going to want to see this." Coral smiled as she leaned against the doorway to my office.

I growled and dropped my forehead onto the desk. "If it's another one of those liberated human caravans coming to check out the wild, send them straight to Cadejo lands. We have enough tourists here already."

"It could be worse." Coral laughed. "We're lucky most of the purists didn't even care that the government was lying to them."

She was right. Like always.

But for the life of me, I couldn't understand why someone would actually prefer to live a lie and ignore the truth sitting just outside their fence.

"What is it then?" I lifted my head, brushing off the receipt that had gotten stuck to my cheek.

Paperwork sucked.

It was better than leading an army though. I was really glad that mess had been settled.

"I'll race you there." Coral stripped and shifted, leaving me to catch up.

I think it's him. My wolf started prancing, begging to be set free. Her giddiness when it came to our mate always made me smile. True, our life wasn't a traditional one. But we'd been on a few dates when we made the time. He'd even arranged this private painting night complete with snacks for me last month. The asshole was better at painting than me, but I was learning.

One day I'd show him up.

Main Street was teeming with life. The market was overflowing with vendors and shoppers. The normal line was gathered outside the Witch's Tavern.

I caught sight of Lennox ushering a newly pregnant Moira into Cerberus Inn. Who'd have thought we'd find his fated mate and bring her home? Lennox didn't spare a look in my direction.

Good for him.

"Hurry up, Alpha." Coral's white wolf was at the edge of town and pawing at the ground.

"Take it easy on the commands, Beta," I teased.

"Never. Now let's see if you can keep up."

*

We ran carefree, nipping at each other's heel pads, through the expanse of forest that was etched in the map of my heart. I always said these lands were mine, but they weren't. Not really. This was the place I protected and grew to take care of so many shifters that didn't have a home.

Now that spring was coming again, the graveyard of Cerberus never felt so alive. Even the ghost of my father who made his presence known on the dark days would be proud of what we'd accomplished.

Maybe not. But in my fantasies, he did.

Up ahead, at the edge of our southern borders, was a new sound. My wolf's ears twitched as she took it in. Hammers swung and shifters called out to each other. Not Cerberus shifters. *His.*

My wolf slowed to a trot as we looked at Coral suspiciously. *"What's going on?"*

"Go see." She nudged me with her snout.

My wolf took a few cautious steps out of the cover of the trees. The mate bond in my chest that always thrummed a soft song grew taut, pulling me closer as I took in the foreign structure on Anubis lands right outside Cerberus borders.

How the hell did I not notice this before?

But more importantly, what was my crazy mate up to now?

He's here! My wolf did a little dance in the wildflowers. Jareth stood on the ledge of a window high up in a stone tower waving like a lunatic.

My heart skipped a beat.

I looked for Coral, but she was already running away.

"Have fun." Her fluffy white tail swished in the air as she disappeared back into the woods.

My wolf howled to her mate and he howled back as I stared at the building. Stone columns and archways led into the courtyard gardens. Two towers made up the sides of the storybook mansion. And all of it was surrounded by…

Is that a freaking moat and drawbridge?

"What is this?" I laughed, turning in a circle under the high arched ceilings in the hallway trimmed with exposed lumber beams. Jareth planted a kiss on my cheek and draped a silk robe over my shoulders.

"I built my princess a castle." He shrugged like it was no big deal. This was a really big deal.

"It's too much." My voice echoed off the stone walls. I stared in disbelief at the hardwood floors, grand staircase, and stained-glass windows lined with burgundy velvet drapes.

"Or is it not enough?" Jareth winked.

Gods, he was a smug asshole.

I couldn't wipe the smile from my face as he grabbed my hand, leading me from room to room.

*

We stood outside the master bedroom with the king sized four poster bed covered in a downy white blanket. Pillows were stacked onto the full seating area near the bay sized windows. I was already looking around at the soft items, thinking of building a nest. And my heat wasn't coming for at least another month. Oh, I had it bad.

"We can't live here," I whispered, too afraid to speak loudly and ruin this little dream.

"No, we can't. But we can escape here when we want to be alone." Jareth put his nose in the crook of my neck and inhaled my scent.

Like always, my heart fluttered as I breathed him in too. The anticipation was making me nervous. My thighs clenched together with the rush of slick.

We'd been dancing around this moment for months. Each teasing kiss and stolen moment were making this tantalizing need so much stronger. This wasn't the way mate bonds typically worked, but nothing about our story was normal.

"I'm ready." I breathed out the words, unable to stop the desire coiling in my lower belly.

Jareth pulled back. His dark blue eyes searched mine as a smile curved his perfect lips. "We can wait. I haven't shown you everything yet."

I fidgeted with the silk robe, twisting my hands behind my back. He was offering me an out, again, and giving me more time. But I was tired of hiding this vulnerable part of myself. I wanted this. More than wanted it. I needed to connect deeper with my mate. Finally.

"I'm ready." I spoke more forcefully this time. He was the only one I trusted to see this part of me and not break it. I knew him inside and out. His demons came to play with mine.

"If this is because I built you a castle…" His voice trailed off as he whistled.

I growled and punched his shoulder. "Jerk."

The breath left my lungs as my feet were swept out from under me. I tensed, ready to fight while Jareth cradled me in his strong arms.

He growled back a warning. "As much as I will enjoy wrestling you into submission one day, princess, now is not the time for that."

"Not a princess." I sighed, resisting the urge to pout. My breath was coming quicker now, wrapped up in his scent. My wolf howled her approval. My stomach was tying itself in knots.

"You're my princess." Jareth smiled, placing me gently on the soft bed. His eyes smoldered as he looked me over. Appreciation and restraint pulsed through our bond. "Do you trust me, Alpha?"

"Yes," I said. It was the truth. I trusted him more than anyone to expose myself like this. Maybe it helped that he was my mate, but even if he wasn't, with him I'd be willing to take this next step.

"I'm going to take care of you." His breath danced along my cheek as he pressed a kiss below my ear.

"I know." I smiled.

Silk slid across my shoulders as Jareth untied and pushed down the robe. My hair fell forward to cover my breasts. He chuckled, tucking it behind my back.

"Beautiful," he whispered, reverently, as he gently laid me down again.

I shut my eyes. My heart was beating so fast. My knees knocked together as he grabbed one of my ankles, kissing a sensitive spot I never knew I had there. I'd been naked more often than not in my life, but never on display like this. So raw and bare.

My core was throbbing, already wet, as Jareth moved to hover above me. "Open your eyes."

I wanted to fight his demand, just because I could, but I gave in. This once.

He balanced with his hands on either side of my face, holding himself up on the bed. His eyes were watching me with the deep intensity that made me want to lose myself within them.

"Don't fight me this time. There'll be more opportunities later to challenge what you can do."

It took me a moment to nod.

"Gods, you're perfect," Jareth moaned, dipping his head down before I could check out more of his sculpted abs and chest.

His lips trailed along my neck and lingered on his mark. He traced it gently with his teeth, sending goosebumps pebbling my skin, and dragged his mouth lower.

Hot breath blew against one of my breasts. A little nip of teeth before he sucked my nipple into his mouth. I gasped as he pulled away, leaving the hardened bud wet and exposed to the cold air. He moved to my other breast and I reached out through our bond, needing to feel what he was feeling. The tightly wound coil that was his desire washed over me. I bit back a moan as he continued an assault of kisses down my stomach.

He splayed his fingers over my sex and I stilled. No one had ever touched me there.

That's because you are mine." His deep voice filled my head as he explored the bond through his end. Growling, he pressed his mouth to my clit. Vibrations rocked my spine.

I grabbed his hair, needing something to hold onto as he licked between my folds and came back to circle my clit. Stars danced along the sides of my vision as he feasted, bringing me close to an edge I'd only ever gone to myself.

"You taste so sweet." He pulled back.

I groaned at the absence of his heat, frustrated that he left me wanting. He smirked in response. I growled, reaching to touch myself.

"Patience, Alpha." He pushed my hand away. "It's coming." He pressed a finger inside me, stretching out the sides.

And then he added another.

"Your body moves for me." He seemed pretty damn pleased with himself.

"I think that's how it's supposed to—" My response was cut short as he curved a finger, dragging it along a spot that made me cry out in need. "What was that?"

"My new favorite place to touch," he teased, leaning forward and pressing his lips to mine. I tasted myself on his tongue, panting into the kiss as he worked his magic fingers faster against that spot and used his thumb to draw lazy circles around my clit.

My claws dug into his back as he brought me higher. So close to that cliff. My body turned to liquid fire in his hands and the tension inside me tightened.

He pulled away before I could release it.

I wanted to kill this beast.

"Jareth!" I screamed, kicking my legs against the bed as I dragged my claws down his muscular arms. I didn't care if I drew blood. This was torture. It wasn't fair.

"I said I'd take care of you." He nipped my neck gently with his teeth. "We have to work on the trust part."

Frustrated, I sighed and nodded as I laid my head back against the pillow. My core was on fire and clenching. Every part of my body wanted him closer. The absence of his mouth–his hands–left me too damn empty.

I looked down, gasping a little as his massive cock lined up against my entrance.

That was not going to fit.

"It's going to fit." He chuckled, dragging it along my center and spitting on his hand as he pumped the base. His cock was throbbing and wet, glistening. I couldn't tear my eyes away from it.

Couldn't stop my racing heart or panicked breaths either.

"This might hurt a little, but then I'm going to make it feel good for you. Do you trust me?"

I nodded, so deliriously gone and ready that I couldn't formulate real words. Jareth kissed me again, sweet and passionate, as he pressed in slowly. There was a sharp pinch and a feeling of tightness as he filled me to the brim. His hand slipped down between us, rubbing my clit as my body adjusted to his size and my legs relaxed.

"Good girl," he whispered.

374

His praise made me stiffen a bit, but my wolf preened in it, needing to hear words that I never thought were important before.

"Are you ready for more, princess?" Jareth smiled against my lips, pulling back a bit and rubbing my clit faster as my walls fluttered around his cock.

"Not a princess." I moved in response, slamming my hips against his as my ankles locked around his back.

Jareth's growl was feral and possessive as he met my demands.

The pain eased, taking with it all sense of reason. My control was lost and I clung to him as he pushed in deeper, carrying me higher.

Our souls merged with each urgent thrust. The cliff I'd only ever come to by myself took me by surprise. It was a mountain now. A peak higher than I ever realized. I reached through our bond, seeing that he stood there with me. It was too much.

I couldn't hang on.

The need stretched from my toes to the top of my head as my body clenched, listening to Jareth growling my name. His warmth filled me from the inside as my soul exploded outward in a rush of sensation and release.

I didn't fall off the edge this time.

I flew.

And I wasn't alone.

Jareth's breaths were soft, sleepy and sedated, as he curled around me on the bed. I lifted his arm gently from my chest and slipped out of the cocoon of warmth, still riding the high of our love making and too wound up to sleep.

I padded barefoot down the unfamiliar halls and committed them to memory. My crazy mate had really built me a castle like this was some sort of fairy tale. It was the most messed up one I'd ever heard of, but hey, at least I got my happy ending.

I sure hoped it was the end.

I didn't want to bring him back to life again.

Down the hall, past an empty room with a crib that he better not be planning to fill with pups anytime soon, and up a set of wood stairs, I pushed open a heavy oak door.

Moonlight shone through the large windows in the tower that looked out over Cerberus forests to the north and Anubis desert lands to the south.

In the center of the room was a stool and easel set up with a brand new canvas. A sheet was draped protectively over it. I ran my fingers along the glass jars of paint on the table and touched the tips of the new brushes as I smiled to myself.

He really thought I could make something of my silly little hobby.

"You found your surprise." Jareth leaned against the doorframe. His unruly black hair was mussed from sleep and the moon made shadows of the ridges of the muscles on his bare chest.

"Are you planning to lock me in a tower?" I smiled over my shoulder, moving closer to the windows that overlooked our land.

"I'm not dumb enough to try." He smirked, closing the distance between us with a shifter's speed and wrapping his strong arms around my waist.

I felt him pull at our bond, diving into my thoughts, and I opened myself up to him.

"It's okay to be happy." His lips found the mating mark on my neck.

"I know." I nodded.

"I wish I could have found you sooner." His teeth moved to my earlobe and he took a gentle bite. Shivers danced along my skin.

"Do you think this will last?" I inhaled his scent before turning my face to the moon.

Jareth laced his fingers through mine, resting his hands on my belly. His touch and warmth made my wolf feel safer than she'd ever been.

"I don't know what the future holds."

"Not even a conspiracy theory?" I teased.

"No." He growled, pulling my body flush against his. Our souls intertwined, merging into each other. His darkness playing with mine as he held me like he'd never let go. "But I do know that fate brought us together for a reason. You, princess, are my destiny."

Epilogue
† Maddock †

Almost one year later…

Up ahead. Need to move fast. There. The bend in the river.

I listened to my wolf's panic attack as snow crunched under his heavy paws. He'd been at this all morning and I was sick of it. The border was fine. Between Skoll and some of the other young alpha wolves' markings, I was hardly needed for this job anymore.

As if that wasn't enough, that weird Alpha Jareth had rigged up some flying mechanical bird type things that flew circles around the empty land between us and the purist territory. The world was changing with this new wave of Alphas leading the packs.

Which was fine by me. I had more time to fish and spend with Sage. My beautiful mate. Who I should be home with right now.

Just a minute, my wolf barked as he raced to the river. **They get lazy here. The water washes the markings away. We have to protect.**

Protect what? I huffed out a laugh.

This was the border between Cerberus and Fenrir pack. Even if they weren't Kera's family, none of these surrounding Alphas would do anything to hurt our niece.

378

They still treated her with the respect she was due. Kera was born for her role as Alpha. I shouldn't have held her back for as long as I did. If Apollo could see her now from his place in hell, I knew the bastard would be proud.

My wolf lifted his leg and a hot stream hit the clearly marked border, melting the snow. Ice chunks broke and crashed down the rushing river toward that hydro-electric whatever it was Jareth gifted Kera for Cerberus pack.

Are you satisfied yet? I sighed, anxious to get back to my mate. My wolf nodded as he sniffed his handiwork. He turned with a proud chuff and started trotting east through the woods.

We should bring her another rabbit.

The icebox is full of rabbits. I groaned. *She says she never wants to eat another rabbit again.*

Oh yeah. My wolf's eyes tracked over the game trails through the trees. His pride was wounded a bit, but the arrogant beast didn't stay down for long. **I'll get another deer.**

We have enough meat, I reassured him again.

And I'd had enough of this. We'd been gone all morning, sent away by the girls so my wolf could run off his anxious energy. Even my mother told us to leave. But I was done with my wolf.

I wanted Sage. The warmth of my cabin. It was too damn cold out here.

My wolf whined. **But she needs–**

Her mate, I cut him off.

379

She needs me. His fur bristled as his chest puffed up. Snow kicked into a flurry as he picked up speed, racing through the woods back to where we belonged.

*

He slowed to a trot as we neared the cabin, nervously sniffing the air. Something was amiss. I reached out through our bond, feeling for Sage. She wasn't close. Wasn't in our cabin. My wolf growled, worry making him spin in a circle as he pawed the ground. His heart thudded harder in our chest.

"Coral! Kera!" I called through the pack link. *"Where is she?"*

Skoll came walking around the corner holding my wood splitting axe, pausing when he saw my anxious beast. "Sage is at the restaurant. Coral and Kera are with her."

Damn them. I growled, narrowing my wolf's eyes at Skoll. *"You better sharpen that when you're done."*

"Good luck." Skoll gave me a salute.

My wolf took off at a sprint while I cursed the Gods for making stubborn women. Sending me to blow off steam had been a ruse. She promised to take it easy. I leaned into the bond, sensing the frustration, but I couldn't tell if it was hers or mine.

My beast dodged the crowds of vendors setting up for the market, ignoring the cries of congratulations directed our way.

As he nosed open the back door of the tavern into the kitchen, our eyes softened. Sage waddled around like a fluffy duck, doing inventory while Kera and Coral took boxes from her.

"Don't start." Sage spun on me, holding up a finger in warning as I shifted. Her swollen stomach stretched out between the two of us, making it hard to pull her close from the front.

I reached out tentatively, hoping not to get bitten, as I tucked a sweaty piece of brown hair behind her ear. "You're supposed to be on bedrest."

She melted into my touch for a moment and I breathed in her scent to calm my beast. It was sweeter now. More brown sugar than cinnamon, caused by the pregnancy hormones from my pup.

Or pups.

From the size of her belly, we weren't sure.

"I know." Sage huffed as she pulled away and stomped her swollen foot on the floor. "But I need to make sure everything is taken care of and I can't do that from our bed."

"Sage…" I growled, knowing it was pointless.

"We tried." Both Coral and Kera shrugged.

Sage rolled her eyes. "I'm almost done. Get that box of potatoes out from the pantry so I can make sure none are rotten."

I hurried to do as she commanded, stopping with the box in my hands as a new scent filled the air.

Like candied apples but more bitter.

A gush of fluid splashed on the ground.

"And now we are going home," Coral cried.

"Why?" Sage froze, looking at us instead of the liquid running down her legs.

It's time! My wolf started yipping, running in circles inside my head as I put down the box. "The potatoes can wait."

I ignored her grumbling protests as I gathered my sweet and stubborn mate into my arms.

*

"Screw what I said about doing this naturally!" Sage screamed. "Take me back to Ethica. I want science. An epidural."

"It'll be okay." Lisa was laughing.

Neither my wolf or I thought this was funny. **Need to protect. Need to kill something.**

"There's nothing for him to kill." Sage grabbed my shirt and growled in my face.

I nodded, turning to my mother. "Can you do something for the pain?"

My heart was in my throat as Sage writhed on the bed and held a death grip on my hand. I ached to take this away from her, doing what I could to ease the burden through our bond. But every time I got too close, she shoved me away. I'd never felt so powerless watching my mate shoulder this pain alone.

"That's it. Breathe through it." Lisa rubbed some sort of tincture under Sage's nose. It smelled like shit, but Sage took a deep relaxing breath.

Thank the Gods!

I pressed a kiss to her sweaty forehead, soaking in the sweet smile she gazed up at me with.

The charms in my mother's hair jingled as she positioned herself between my mate's legs. "Now you're ready, mama. On the next contraction, it's time to push."

*

The moment my mother put that little girl into my hands, the entire world came to a standstill.

Soft daylight filtered through the bedroom window, giving her fuzzy brown hair an angelic glow. Cloudy big brown eyes, just like her mother's, blinked as she stared up at me. I choked a little, tears misting my vision as tiny fingers grasped hard around my thumb.

She's strong. My little hunter.

My wolf cried with a protective fierceness. I sniffed the babe, sensing her wolf just below the surface, ready to come out at any time.

"Alright. Let's push again."

I glanced up with wide eyes as Sage screamed. Another slippery babe moved into my mother's waiting hands.

"Come cut the cord for your second girl." Lisa laughed, motioning to me with the knife.

Two girls! My wolf howled in triumph.

I stumbled forward, trying to cradle my precious first born in the crook of one arm and worried senseless I would drop her as I reached for the knife.

"Hurry." Sage grunted.

The agony in her tone pushed me to action.

Two!

Oh Gods.

My mother wrapped my other daughter in a blanket and carefully handed her over to me. It was a balancing act to get the second girl comfortably seated as I cradled her sister in my other arm.

She was a mirror image of the first. I stared in amazement at what our love had created. The pups I never thought I'd have.

"They look like you," I whispered, turning to my mate and hoping she could feel my glowing pride through the bond. She was the strongest woman I'd ever met.

"After all this work, they better." Sage shot me a death glare.

Then she cried out as another contraction contorted her face in agony.

My heart stopped beating.

The worst was over. She shouldn't be in pain.

Something is wrong. My wolf was frantic.

I kneeled beside the bed, leaning my face closer to Sage to kiss her because my hands were too full to caress her instead. "What's wrong, beautiful?"

She closed her eyes, sucking in a deep breath, and pushed with the last of her strength.

"And that makes three." Lisa spoke some kind of incantation over the baby's head.

What?

I staggered to my feet, swaying a little as I looked down to my arms and the girls bundled up in them.

"Another healthy girl and we are done." My mother leaned back and shouted. The sounds of Coral and Kera and their mates cheering came from outside the bedroom.

Three? My wolf gulped.

"Three?" I asked, looking around the room for a place to set one down. Two arms. Two hands. Three babies.

"Cerberus triplets." Sage sighed, resting her head back against the pillow as she took the last pup onto her breast. "Fate is screwing with us."

It'll be okay, I told my wolf as the two girls in my arms started to cry.

There was an odd silence in my head.

Where'd you go? I bounced my girls, trying to calm them and failing miserably.

"Is something wrong with your wolf?" Sage arched an eyebrow as she nursed our third little girl.

I gave her a sheepish smile and shrugged. "I think he fainted."

"Alpha Kera says we can do whatever we want," Alex murmured as she swung her skinny legs off the tree branch.

"First of all, that was Aunt Coral." Trish lined up her slingshot with the acorn as she zeroed in on the squirrel. "And she was saying we could be anything we want. Not do. Stupid."

"Can you two stop fighting for once?" Meg planted her hands on her bony hips and growled as she looked up at her sisters hiding in the tree. "It's time to go."

The girls groaned, grabbing hands as they jumped down and landed on their feet. Trish spun at the last moment, letting her slingshot release.

"Nice." Meg snorted as she watched the acorn meet its mark. "Mom is going to love squirrel."

"It's not for Mom." Trish picked up her kill.

"It better not be. She'll yell at me if you bring home squirrel." Maddock chuckled as his massive brown wolf stalked into the clearing.

"Daddy!" All three girls shouted, rushing over to clamber on top of his back. There was a tangle of brown hair and gangly limbs, wrestling with the beast of a father who nipped them with soft teeth.

After they'd gotten most of their giggles out, Maddock's wolf stood and shook off his fur.

"Let's get going." He nudged them one by one as they shifted into their identical goldish-brown wolves.

"Now what are the rules of hunting?" Maddock stalked slowly beside his daughters, watching for dangers and keeping them close.

"Only kill what we eat," Meg's wolf offered, looking at Trish from the corner of her eye.

"The squirrel is for Grandma." Trish growled. *"She needs the tail for a potion."*

"Gross." Alex scrunched up her snout.

"Another rule?" Maddock chuckled, knowing this one would take a long time to learn.

"Oh. We have to be quiet." Alex picked up her paws dramatically, making more noise as she put them back down. She was still growing into them.

"Anything else?" Maddock gave his daughter a proud nudge with his shoulder.

The girls stopped and looked at him. Six big brown eyes blinking as they tried to remember.

A rustle in the bushes caught their attention. Alpha Kera came prancing onto the path with her mate, Alpha Jareth, at her side.

"Kera!" The girls squealed as they bounded over. *"Dad is teaching us the rules of hunting again."*

Kera gave a wolfy smile, brushing against Jareth as she pawed at the girls' heads. She let them play for a minute before lowering her snout so she was down on their level.

"Don't forget the most important rule." She gave her uncle a subtle wink, remembering all the time

they'd spent in these woods together when she was small. *"Never let the boys show you up."*

*

Dear Reader,

What did you think?!? Are you happy with the way this series turned out? I hope I did the characters justice. This was such a fun group of people…er… shifters, humans, and some amazing witches. It's always bitter sweet when I have to say goodbye to characters I've been working with for a while.

Sage, Coral, Kera, and their mates will have a special place in my heart. While our girls' stories may be over, I did something a little extra for you. If you're not ready to be done with the *Fated Destinies* series yet, I wrote a short story about Coral's mom, Melinda, and her time in to Ethica called *"Worst Spy Ever."*

You can get a free copy of this story if you sign up for my paranormal romance mailing list at:
www.heatherkcarson.com
You can also join my reader group on Facebook to get the inside scoop on new projects and yell at me to write faster here:
www.facebook.com/groups/heathercarsonreaders

And finally, you can find me on Tiktok/Instagram/and Facebook @heathercarsonauthor if you want to continue to be a part of my publishing journey.
Thanks for reading and for taking a chance on my books! I'll keep writing them for you if you let me.

-Heather

More Works by Heather K. Carson

A low-ranking female wolf shifter. A powerful and possessive Alpha. Their fates collide and sparks fly on the popular dating show, *Mating Season,* where Alphas and Lunas come to meet their matches…

Check out *Luna Trials,* book one of *Mating Season,* by Heather K. Carson @
https://www.amazon.com/dp/B0CY6GQ5MV

Made in the USA
Middletown, DE
19 October 2024

62926766R00234